Romania, present day

HUNGARY

MOLDOVA

UKRAINE

SERBIA

BULGARIA

Black Sea

Bistrita
Dumitra/Dreptu

TRANSYLVANIA

Brasov
CASTEL BRAN

Bucharest

Danube River

BULGARIA

Black Sea

MOUNTAINS

© 2013 Meighan Cavanaugh

Stoker's Manuscript

Stoker's Manuscript

ROYCE PROUTY

G. P. Putnam's Sons
New York

PUTNAM

G. P. PUTNAM'S SONS
Publishers Since 1838
Published by the Penguin Group
Penguin Group (USA) Inc., 375 Hudson Street,
New York, New York 10014, USA

USA · Canada · UK · Ireland · Australia
New Zealand · India · South Africa · China

Penguin Books Ltd, Registered Offices: 80 Strand, London WC2R 0RL, England
For more information about the Penguin Group visit penguin.com

Library of Congress Cataloging-in-Publication Data

Prouty, Royce.
Stoker's manuscript / Royce Prouty.
p.   cm
ISBN 978-0-399-15855-1 (hardback)
1. Booksellers and bookselling—Fiction.   2. Vampires—Fiction.
3. Stoker, Bram, 1847–1912. Dracula—Fiction.   4. Romania—Fiction.   I. Title.
PS3616.R687S76   2013   2013001636
813'.6—dc23

Printed in the United States of America
1   3   5   7   9   10   8   6   4   2

Book design by Meighan Cavanaugh

This is a work of fiction. Names, characters, places, and incidents either are the product of
the author's imagination or are used fictitiously, and any resemblance to actual persons,
living or dead, businesses, companies, events, or locales is entirely coincidental.

To my wife, Marilyn.

I am my Beloved's and my Beloved is Mine.

ACKNOWLEDGMENTS

No project such as this is created in a vacuum. Accordingly, I wish to place a spotlight on those who helped bring this from concept to hardcover, and beyond. First, I wish to thank my wife, Marilyn, for her wisdom and patience, forever keeping me on this side of the reality bridge. None of this would have happened, but for you.

To Ed Stackler of Stackler Editorial Agency, for his creative and technical genius, I can never repay you for all you have done. Yours is a unique talent. To Scott Miller, my agent at Trident Literary Group, thank you for taking a chance on an unknown. You are the best at what you do. To editors Rachel Kahan and Meaghan Wagner, and all the incredibly talented staff at G. P. Putnam's Sons, thank you for all you have done, and continue to do.

To my sister, Christine, who helped during this story's conceptual period, your knowledge of the mythical characters and genre was invaluable, and rather than just cheerlead you opted to help with constructive comments. For that, along with being so supportive, I will always be grateful.

As with any endeavor that spans much time and exacts great effort, there are those who lend encouraging words, prop up when down, give praise when none is warranted, and generally keep the interest of others above their own. In triumph, they celebrate with you, and in defeat they point toward the next triumph. By name these selfless souls are Bob, Taylor, Jack, David, Michael, Clifton, Dr. John, Sheila, Armando, and my stepchildren, Jason, Laurie, and Lisa.

To God, thank you for my gifts and your high expectations. I can only hope that my work is worthy to be on your bookshelf.

Stoker's
Manuscript

Lost in the night, somewhere, there is
all that once was and no more is,
what got lost, what was uprooted,
from living time to time that's muted.
In Hades is—all that is passed.
From Acheron, the river vast,
all memories to us return.
In Hades is—all that is passed
the Aprils and loves we yearn.

—Lucian Blaga
Romanian poet

To Whoever Finds This,

How to describe insanity in a modern world? Is there a line that, once crossed, spells no return? Or is it a continuum of wander toward an alluring place you were warned of but not shown? I have resolved to think of it as being led by temptation beyond the precincts of known science, far enough that you no longer hold the confidence to discern fact from fancy. Upon return, you bring back all the iniquities you picked up and hope no one asks you of your travels.

In this briefest account I shall attempt to describe events I endured, and continue to endure, en route to a fortune most can only dream of, a fortune measured not just in books of account but also in the slowing of the passage of time itself. Before you turn me out as addled, ask yourself the following: What if you could cheat death? What if you could recognize its approach, sidestep, and continue without concern? Would you do it?

Most of us would pause to ponder if it was a trick question. Once established as legitimate inquiry, an assenting answer would follow. After you read and shelve this volume, however, if your answer remains affirmative, then I pity you for foolishly heeding little and repeating my own missteps.

Before beginning my tale, I must beg forgiveness, for I scribe these events postnate, and some descriptions might lack the clarity or chronology of the original. Of one thing I can be certain: It all started with a particular phone call that arrived in the ordinary course of business as I tried to claw out a living, much as you do.

I lived in a place where the weather holds a grudge against humans. Winter in Chicago is winter defined, a corpse's white shroud covering all in the grim hopes of warmer days, breeding both contempt and camaraderie in those who call the Great Lake city home. Just about when you might expect summer comes the insect plague, mosquitoes taking flight, the males and females each creating their own pitch, the latter more aggressive, of course. I have always been a mosquito magnet—a mystery since childhood, for they alight but only rarely draw my blood. For the first three decades of my life, I had no idea why. Now, finally, I do.

Joseph Barkeley
Transylvania

L ike many events that define life's hinges, this occurred as I sat minding my own business. Work in those days was my used bookstore. Not just your normal used bookstore, but one filled with first editions and other rarities. Even as a teenager I had a knack for spotting the rare edition in a pile of books, and developed the talent to sell in a way that made the buyer feel I was giving him a deal. My collection started in a basement until I found suitable warehouse space under the L tracks, where a computer screen and telephone allowed the world access to a guarded inventory, granting even a recluse such as myself a fair crack at capitalism. As a purveyor of old books and manuscripts, I had low volume and high margins, with handwriting- and document-authentication services supplementing my online sales.

Wed to my work, I tended to dine at counters, never a table for two. It's not as if I sprayed on human repellent; it's just that if you knew of my cloistered beginnings and limited opportunities, you'd understand why I tended to view strangers as always gathered in ranks. Ranks that were closed to the likes of me.

The call arrived on a typical late April day: The sun was promising a return from its annual three-week vacation, the temperature was trying to nudge fifty, and the Cubs were not too far out of first place. Yes, I freely admit to being a Cubs fan.

While I tended to the tedium of ledgers, the 800 line lit up. To track toll-free line traffic I had purchased an application that displays, stores, and prints incoming calls by geographic coordinates, rounded to a degree, plus the phone number. Like many calls, this one read PRIVATE, displayed 47N, 25E, and emitted the familiar delay and hiss of international long distance. I punched my pocket GPS and matched the Eastern European accent to Romania, land of my maternal ancestors, the Petrescus. I opened my computer to a foreign currency conversion Web page.

"My name is Arthur Ardelean," said the caller, "and I have been directed to you, Mr. Barkeley, on a professional matter." He rolled his r's and sounded my last name in three syllables.

"How can I be of service, Mr. Ardelean?"

"I represent a buyer who insists upon anonymity. Can you guarantee that?"

"I have made such arrangements before, yes. But I must tell

you that anonymity is usually more difficult for the buyer to maintain than the seller."

"I assure you, sir, the buyer will have no such problem." He spoke with the cadence of a formal yet stern butler and pronounced *problem* the European way: *proh-BLEM*. He clearly conveyed there would be no further discussion of identity. This is not uncommon among my clients, as most buyers purchasing rare editions enjoy seeing them in their bookcases without the public knowing of the five- or sometimes six-figure treasure resting on their residential shelves. Planned, secured display cases of bulletproof glass often followed such purchases.

"Can you stipulate to anonymity and exclusivity in a contract, Mr. Barkeley?"

"I am a member in the highest standing of the American Appraisers and Authenticators Association, my next door neighbor does not even know what business I am in, and yes, I can stipulate to such in a contract." It was true that my neighbor didn't know my business, as I operated out of an environmentally enclosed and electronically surveilled warehouse. I had no storefront, since all my business was done online. "I use sealed boxes to ship via UPS's special museum and treasures branch. For very high-end pieces, I make personal deliveries."

"Good," he said. "Personal delivery is essential in this matter."

"Would this purchase be something that is currently on my website?"

"No, it is not. Presently the item is on display in a museum in Philadelphia."

I assumed he meant the Rosenbach Museum and Library. Everyone who deals in rare manuscripts is familiar with the Rosenbach brothers, who, a century ago, played central roles in the building of America's great libraries. They are recognized as the preeminent *fin de siècle* dealers of scribed collectibles and decorative art pieces, and their former residence on Delancey Place houses treasures that would astound any serious admirer and serves as first choice for anyone wishing to display priceless written wares.

"I have done authentication work in the past for the museum."

"Very good. Are you currently under contract with the Rosenbach?"

"Not at this time. They inquired about my availability to examine a manuscript in anticipation of an auction at Christie's. My contract will be through the auction house, and logistical arrangements coordinated with the Rosenbach. Perhaps we are speaking of the same manuscript?"

"Abraham Stoker's original manuscript of *Dracula* and notes thereon." He pronounced it *Drah-kyula*.

"The rarest of treasures," I said.

"Indeed, sir, the rarest." Mr. Ardelean paused. "Please hold a moment."

"Of course." I assumed he was speaking with his principal.

"My apologies, Mr. Barkeley. The buyer wishes to purchase the entire display without . . . unnecessary exposure to the auction and handling process."

I happened to know that Christie's expected the manuscript to start at a million dollars and escalate to roughly twice that. "But

I am sure you are aware that the Stoker family has an expected starting price. To keep it from the gavel, the offering price would have to exceed even the most optimistic of bids."

"The buyer is willing to pay whatever it takes to prevent the manuscript from seeing the light of day."

"I see."

"That is why it is essential that your buyer's agreement is both exclusive and anonymous."

"I understand."

"You, of course, would be compensated *most* generously . . . an amount not to be discussed over a telephone line."

"My fees are generally set on a per diem basis, plus expenses."

"I assure you, Herr Barkeley, your compensation will exceed your per diem rate. Now, are you willing to discuss the details?"

"I am seated with pen and paper."

"You are to make immediate arrangements with the Rosenbach to authenticate the manuscript and all accompanying documents. It is most important that the entire display, notes and all, are part of this purchase. If the family does not intend it to be part of the auction, make an ancillary purchase."

I hesitated. "Are you asking me to authenticate *and* negotiate the purchase on behalf of the buyer?"

"That is correct. That is the only way to guarantee anonymity at this end."

"I see." I paused. I had traditionally prepared for auction as an independent third party. Being an agent would remove my independence and change the nature of my relations with the auction house.

"You are trying to decide, Mr. Barkeley."

"Go ahead . . . I'm writing."

"No copies are to be made of your work, not a single page, and no pages are to be removed for chemical testing."

The normal course of authentication would include a page sampled at the lab in Chicago, but I have never had a lab test reverse any of my rulings. "That should not be a problem."

"I must have your guarantee."

"I'll put it in writing."

"The buyer has done extensive research on Mr. Stoker's manuscript and is aware that the *original* manuscript included a prologue and an epilogue, and that neither was included in the printed editions."

"I will note that as I examine the documents."

"It is imperative that those two chapters be included in the purchase."

"And if they are not?"

"Then it is not the original. In such case you shall be paid your usual fee, plus expenses of course."

"And if it is the original?" I asked.

"Then you are to travel here to assist in the planning of its placement in the museum."

"May I ask where *here* is?"

"Forgive me for not explaining in the beginning, but the buyer is donating the display to the new museum in Dracula's Castle in Romania."

"Transylvania."

"Yes, Mr. Barkeley, you are familiar with it?"

"Yes." An electric jolt, a zinger, traveled my body, one that would surely spike lie-detector needles, for I was born in Romania's Transylvania region. "Do you have a curator for the museum?"

"Not yet. The castle renovation is in preparatory stages, and we will be relying on your expertise to determine how best to display such a treasure."

"It will need to be under glass in a controlled and secure environment," I said.

"We shall be converting the old wine cellar."

"Normally a good place. I will be honored to assess its new habitat."

"Arrangements will be made for your travel to Bucharest and connections north, and some local currency will be included in the envelope with your itinerary. I have prepared a contract for your execution with the details we have discussed and will e-mail it after our conversation."

"I'll review it immediately."

"One more thing, Mr. Barkeley."

"Yes?"

"I will be including something in the envelope from the buyer. It is for you to wear, a special gift, something to recognize you by. You are to wear it about your neck."

My mind conjured an array of images from a string of garlic to an embroidered ascot. "Thank you," I said uncertainly.

"Like the two missing chapters, this item is of vital importance. Do you have any questions?"

I thought of Christie's. "I do. As part of my own due diligence,

I will need to represent to the auction house, and ultimately to the Stoker family, that I can vouch for the buyer's financial where-withal."

"The details are in the contract, including my e-mail address should you have further questions."

"Do you have a cell phone number?"

"There is no cell phone service here."

We closed the conversation and I sat back in my chair, elated . . . and a little stunned.

2

Douglas Carli headed my due diligence list of contacts. A venture capitalist who worked on Michigan Avenue downtown, he once told me he could secure verbal commitments on six million dollars with a few phone calls if a guy had a good business plan. Sixty million would take a couple days. He worked in the DiPietro Building, and his corner office faced the lake. Whenever I called on him the family portrait seemed to have grown by one, and with each greeting he inquired about my marital status. My response always defended the idea of no rings, no manacles, but in truth I always saw intimacy as something reserved for the screen or the page. Doug's wife said novenas on my behalf that I might meet a respectable woman. Catholics have novenas for everything.

About ten years ago I received a call from Doug inquiring about a first edition of Michener's *Alaska*. Not only a first edition—it had to be autographed as well. He was one of my first online customers. Fortune winked my way because I had three *Alaska*s in my collection, one international edition from April 1989 and two Ballantine editions from July 1989. One of the latter was autographed. Regarding authenticity, I told him he had two options: the one included in the price of the book that came from me, or the formal Association-stamped certificate that costs four hundred dollars, payable regardless of outcome.

The Association convenes right there in Chicago and has templates of thousands of original signatures. Being a member, I had walked in, looked at Michener's signature against the book's, and seen two flaws. First, the second *e* of his last name looked like it was written over a disturbance. Considering he did not sign the jacket, I held the page the way he would have during signing and felt an irregularity on the inside jacket where the pen likely would have hit a bump. Secondly, the *r* looked like it was written over, normally a flaw that would guarantee an appraiser's rejection. But under closer scrutiny, I could see the ink was distributed and absorbed simultaneously at signing. See, ink does not lie on top of paper, but rather is absorbed into the fibers depending on which chemicals were used to make the paper. I can tell if ink was applied later to worn paper, as it absorbs differently.

This I relayed to Doug, that I could be reasonably assured it was authentic, but it would not stand the test of certification. He was thrilled to receive it and pay under a thousand dollars. I delivered it to his office, and he showed the jubilant simplicity of a birthday boy, hugging his treasure and showing it to his staff. Thereafter he offered financial advice gratis. Though I had not leaned on him that way before, on this deal I felt shaky flying solo. So I dropped in on Doug with a gift, a first edition *Thinner*, by Stephen King before he wrote under his own name.

Doug was a man of stern demeanor, but easily disarmed by simple gifts. As he thumbed carefully through his new book, I walked to his wall and looked at his latest photo, another family shot, this time gathered in front of some sort of museum.

"Another charity you support?" I asked.

"Yeah, the main charity," he said with a laugh. "My family."

"I meant . . ." I pointed at the building. "A museum?"

Doug smiled and nodded. "That's my house."

I laughed out of embarrassment, but in truth hoped he thought I was joking. This was the stark contrast between his life's station and mine—where he sat at the captain's table, I belonged in steerage.

He pointed to my ring finger. "The novenas working yet?"

I opened my mouth to tell him I was raised by nuns in a Catholic orphanage, a saltpeter experience if ever there was one, but something stopped me. I did not want all future encounters to be underpinned with pity. Instead I said, "My brother says prayers to counter your wife's. So yes, *his* are working."

"Behind every man, you know . . ."

"Is a shadow," I said, "and mine's quiet."

He held up his gift, smiling. "Thank you."

"Actually an exchange," I said. "The easy kind—just to bleed a little knowledge out of your brain."

"Oh, good," he said, and put his reading glasses on. "Name it."

"How do I verify legitimacy of a Swiss account?"

He pushed his reading glasses up his nose. It seemed to be part of his thought process. "Due diligence on a buyer?"

I nodded affirmatively. "Big transaction on a museum piece."

"Got a name?"

"Just the agent. Buyer's demanding anonymity."

"The agent's name might point to the buyer. I deal with Zurich bankers every week . . . Make the call for you?"

I hesitated.

"Look, it's big money, and you're out there walking the moors on this one, right?"

Again I nodded.

"Did the guy say his confidentiality extended to the buyer or to the agent and buyer?"

"Just the buyer."

"So what's the agent's name?"

"Ardelean."

Again he pushed his glasses up his nose. "Romanian."

"Arthur."

"You know, I get a call every six months or so to JV deals there. Seems they're sitting on serious untapped oil and natural gas in the southern region."

"The Wallachian Plain," I said.

He nodded.

"But you've taken flyers. How come?"

"Communist residue. When the Iron Curtain fell, the people hugged and celebrated the fact that they were free. But free to do what? Unless you were taken out and shot, you likely continued doing what you were doing the week before. And so the red tape lingers."

These things I knew. Nothing changed overnight. "A country led by professors instead of doers."

"Let's just say their political cycles are shorter than the time it takes from drill to tap, and nothing's done in that country on the free market."

I nodded. "The agent gave me the bank contact information."

"Then the banker will be a personal banker. He'll be formal, let you know only what you need to know to complete your transaction. Expect him to speak English, French, and German at a minimum, maybe Dutch, plus the client's native tongue."

"I'll make the call in the morning."

"Get me the routing number and I'll verify it's that bank."

"You don't have to do that," I said.

He pointed his nose down and squinted over his reading glasses. "You don't leave things like this to chance. You wanna do big deals, you don't leave the small stuff on the table. That's why it's called due diligence."

Perhaps I had told him too much.

3

I am nocturnal by nature, and at two A.M. placed my call to a Mr. Gunther Dietz at the bank in Zurich. He was, as Doug predicted, formal and awaiting my call. With a flat voice and Germanic accent, he vouchsafed that the amount in question would be honored and invited no further questions.

Promptly thereafter I pinged one of my best customers, Mara Sadov, with an e-mail and arranged for a meeting later that day. Sometimes a collector for her own volumes, more often on behalf of others, Mara fancied herself a vampire expert. Apparently others did as well, enough to provide her a living out of dispensing knowledge about the mythical creatures. Her website boasted Gypsy lineage and offered advice on vamp lifestyle and accessories, including books. It claimed she frequently spoke at vampire conventions. (I didn't know there was such a thing.)

A couple months back, when I was asked to authenticate Stoker's manuscript at the Rosenbach for auction, she offered to prep me on what I could expect to find. As with any big project, my authentication work includes not just examination of documents but the study of their place in history, from the authors' background to intended audience. I also consider historical dates and other events in order to spot potential anachronisms. I had a long list of research items for Mara to clarify.

I try to schedule my research as close to examination date as possible, then prepare a list of notes to study the day before, but the buyer's call had just accelerated my schedule. At that point I needed Mara to condense what I would have had to sift through the Internet researching, as well as fill me in on the details that I would not find on the Web.

Once before I had visited her modest woodsy cabin in lower Wisconsin not far from Lake Geneva. The April weather suggested an early summer, warm enough to lure out some greenery and attach a few bugs to my windshield. I drove a Ford Mustang, circa carburetor production era, with a 289. I think. (I'm not a gearhead. I just like the look of the car.) I pulled into her dirt drive and rode the dual ruts' crown to the rear of her parked Jeep.

Mara met me at the door. She had the countenance of the tenth Solomonari: aquiline features, puckered mouth, and abbreviated reading glasses that lent her a wizened appearance. A paranoiac by nature, Mara questioned the source of all inquiries, including my own. *Dispense* might adequately describe what she did with her knowledge, as she looked over her glasses at you and pursed her lips as if sipping a straw. "Why?" she would say, pronouncing it *vie*, always a cautionary preamble to her responses.

In my opinion, Mara took herself far too seriously, like a costumed theme park employee always in character. For example, when she greeted you she stood inside her doorway, but did not invite you to enter, waiting to see if you would see yourself in. According to convention, vampires do not cross thresholds without an invitation, and this was her way of checking vamp credentials. Yes, it seemed that even mass murderers, however fabled, had a code of conduct.

I stepped past her, inside her house, and Mara followed, satisfied.

"Good to see you, Mr. Joseph," she said. It had been decades since she lived in Eastern Europe, but she had the voice, with *z* substituting *s*.

"Always a pleasure."

To enter her house was to prepare for an invasion of the senses, notably scents. Of course the garlic prevailed, lots of it, and rose petals in every room. There were crucifixes everywhere. She also had an extensive thousand-volume library of everything vampire.

"So you wish to enter the world of the undead," she said.

"Actually, I'm trying to get my usual due diligence done on the Stoker manuscript—when and where he wrote it, for example, and the events around the first and second editions."

"To immerse in this is to invite the undead into your life."

Mara lifted an eyebrow over her reading glasses in that way the fortune teller asks if you really wish to know of your days ahead.

"Well, we all have to earn a living somehow, Miss Mara."

"By the time you understand my warning," she said, "it will be too late, and they *will* be in your life."

"It's just a manuscript."

"It is an invitation." *Eet eez an invee-tation.*

"I plan to inspect the documents and, if authentic, deliver them personally."

"Deliver . . . personally?" Her voice amplified. "That changes things."

"I am contractually bound to keep the buyer anonymous."

"Old money, Europe." Her eyes squinted. "Balkans, the corridor of war."

I shrugged, nodded.

Her fingers looked like spinning wheel spokes, and she pointed one at me. "You will need to know certain things."

"Such as?"

"How to survive."

"Well, in the meantime, what I'm looking for is the original manuscript: the prologue, all twenty-seven chapters, and the epilogue."

"Before I tell you these things," she said after another long pause, "promise you will heed my warnings." *Vornings.*

As she took herself completely seriously, I had no choice but to answer in the affirmative. "Sure. But I'm not clear what you mean."

"Listen," she said. "Just listen, my young friend. To survive, you need to know the world you're entering."

I nodded, but she saw me trying not to chuckle. It was her turn to shrug. "It's your soul." She pushed her glasses up the bridge of her nose and spun toward a stack of books on a shelf. "Here." She handed me a biography of Bram Stoker. "First you need to understand the author and his work, then the story, then the villain." She waved the back of her hand my direction. "Keep it."

"I'll read it on the way to Philadelphia."

"The problem"—she pronounced it the same way as Mr. Ardelean, *proh-BLEM*—"is how this man who was busy running a large theater—"

I interrupted, "A man who never wrote anything else of note."

"Yes." *Jyezz.* She nodded. "So, how could such a man come up with the most successful horror genre piece in history?"

"Indeed."

"Some speculate that he had help."

"Dictated or edited?" I asked.

"I think that is part of your coming journey."

I said, "Archibald Constable and Company published the manuscript in 1897."

"But you should find notes dating back to 1890."

I nodded, made a note. That meant it coincided with the administrations of Benjamin Harrison, Grover Cleveland, and William McKinley. I had authenticated some personal correspondence sent by William McKinley to his invalid wife, Ida, on his trip to Buffalo, a trip from which he never returned. In doing so I'd learned that the 1890s were a time of great invention. The decade started with the third of the great European migrations to America and served as the transition to the modern technological era.

Mara leaned toward me. "But Constable's London facility burned right after the first printing, a complete loss, *all* first editions gone. The publishing house almost went under, and it took Stoker a couple of years to get it out of the courts and published. Fortunately, the original typed manuscript was returned to Stoker's widow. I trust you will find that in the museum."

"Along with his handwritten notes."

"Yes," she said. "*Their* notes."

"Tell me about the missing chapters."

"The first edition had a prologue, where the character Jonathan Harker journeys from Munich and ends up in the wrong cemetery on *Walpurgisnacht*." When I failed to react, she shook her head as if I should know the severity of his error. "Then the epilogue was left out, and Stoker shortened the ending to have the count slain and turned to dust."

"Any idea of the last chapter's content?"

"I've seen a copy of the outline—the family put that part on museum display—and it was supposed to have a long battle scene, dramatic death, and much detail of the count's burial."

"Why shorten a glorious battle scene?"

"Perhaps another part of your journey, Mr. Joseph. You'll just have to come tell me afterward." When she smiled, it looked more like a challenge.

"Where was the count supposed to be buried?"

"Rumor has him in several places," she said. "Perhaps they are all correct." Another smile. "Come," she said, "let us break."

She made tea and we moved to her porch outside. The day was abuzz with the season's first visiting insects, and while butterflies negotiated the afternoon breezes, we sat on rocking chairs facing the woods.

"I understand Stoker did not invent vampires." I knew of the 1819 tale by Polidori entitled *The Vampyre*, the author being Lord Byron's doctor.

Mara turned her head my direction and stared over her glasses. Her black hair came to precise points in front of her earlobes, and her pursed lips foretold of a nunlike correction. "No one *invented* vampires. They have always been with us, in every era of written history. You may find Stoker's source material. From Kali in India to the Loogaroo in the Caribbean, every continent has its vampires. Stoker just happened to mass publish in the modern era."

"*The Un-Dead.*"

"*The Un-Dead*, yes. His intended title until Constable changed it." Mara stopped and pointed at my arm, where a mosquito landed. "Ahh," she said, motioning for me not to swat it. "Observe."

"You females sticking together?" I knew only female mosquitoes bite for blood. This one seemed to be deciding whether or not to bite.

"To understand the mosquito is to marvel at the creature. Right now she is probing your skin. She has two sets of blades that work like electric carving knives to cut through and insert her fascicle. Her tiny gland will inject you with a fluid that desensitizes and prevents clotting until she is finished."

I noticed the insect swell with blood and turn red, and felt its intrusion.

"She has sensors that tell her when to release. Afterward, she'll separate the water from the blood and excrete the blood proteins to nourish her eggs. They'll be in water somewhere in a tiny little boat-shaped vessel."

When the insect finished, it labored to flight and bobbed in the air before heading to the porch railing, where it appeared to stop and rest.

"Little vampires."

"Yes," she said, intoning that I was starting to catch on. "Vampire teeth are more than simply long canines." She leaned and reached into her handbag and produced a book, unpublished, bound like a journal. She opened to her intended page before turning the journal my direction, displaying a hand-drawn sketch of a creature opening its mouth like a python. I recognized her handwritten notes beside the drawing.

"Ah," I said. "So the lower jaw unhinges from the jawbone."

"Mm-hmm. And this is how they hunger." She turned the page, and another sketch showed the canine teeth. "The empty stomach collapses like a drained hot water bottle, signaling the brain that it is empty. This cycle takes about twenty-one days."

"Time to eat again."

"Almost," she said. "It takes several more days before the moon's gravitational pull lifts the fluids in the brain and releases the chemical signal to eat, among other things."

"Like high tide," I said. "Full moon."

"Sometimes a day or two prior. Don't be out those nights."

I nodded, continuing to indulge her. "You said 'among other things.' What are the other things?"

"Pure adrenaline."

"To give it strength, speed?"

"Yes, to prey." She pointed to another sketch, a drawing with two arrows pointing toward the upper lips. "Two prominent glands above the teeth along the jawline, barely detectable under facial hair. Causes the canines to protrude slightly."

"Fascicles. Like the mosquito."

She nodded. "Small knives rubbing together to slice into your neck. Once inside, the probe finds the artery, while the gland produces an anticoagulant to allow free flow to the stomach. Takes only seconds. Once the stomach lining stretches, it sends a signal to the gland to start producing a coagulant to close up."

"So the victim gets a little vamp fluid in exchange."

"Most unfortunate for the victim, I assure you," she said in that schoolmarm voice. "The vampire must leave right away and rest a few hours to begin his digestive process. He has a semiporous stomach that separates the fluids from blood proteins."

"Again, like the mosquito. So then he, or she, will excrete the blood proteins to—"

"No." She shook her head. "He has no orifices."

"Through the skin, then?"

She nodded and wrinkled her nose.

"Thus a smell," I said.

"Like a decaying animal."

I pointed to a braid of garlic she had hanging on the porch. "What's with the garlic?"

"It is more than just an aromatic," she said. "What happens to you when you slice an onion?"

"You mean the tears?"

"Yes. Just a few floating particles get on his skin or in his nostrils," Mara said, motioning with her fingers toward her nose. "It's like pepper spray."

I nodded. "What about the flying?"

"They don't," she said flatly.

"Then what's with the bats?"

She looked at me as if I should know the answer. "What do bats eat?"

"Mosquitoes!" *Of course.* To a bat, the vampire would smell like a giant female mosquito swarm. "But don't bats use echolocation?"

"That is true," she said. "They navigate and locate by echo, but they are still mammals and use their senses of smell and hearing to identify their prey."

"Then vampires are not shape-shifters."

"That is the fictional part of the legend," she said. "However, because of their adrenaline, they do move so fast that they can be a blur to the human eye."

"So don't challenge one to a fencing duel."

"Do not challenge one outside his box." She was not amused. "And do not attempt to sneak up on one. His strongest sense by far is smell. He can smell a warm-blooded animal thirty feet away, and it triggers an image in his sight. The warmer the animal, the brighter the glow."

"Like night vision goggles?"

"Precisely. He smells your emotion because how you feel releases certain hormones, and they all carry signatures through the blood. He will sense your fear, your failures."

"Some people must really stink," I mused.

Still humorless. "When he smells blood"—she pointed to her gums over a canine tooth—"his canine gland becomes active." Mara drew a breath through clenched teeth to demonstrate.

"You keep saying *he*," I said. "Do you mean in the collective sense?"

Again she shook her head as if I should know the answer. "All the survivors are male. The breeding females, the *strigoiace*, are all gone. Otherwise they would have multiplied and made us all human slaves." She leaned in. "That's what the wars were fought over."

"What wars?"

"Wars between the *wampyr* families." She used the ancient term for their species. "They fought to kill off the breeders—one breeding matriarch per family."

"Like a queen bee."

"When brothers fought, they tended to capture the other's wife and entomb instead of kill her."

I shuddered at the thought.

She added, "To keep from going extinct."

I did not want to consider the specifics. "So what exactly is the danger for a human? Do they turn us into undead, like Lucy Westenra in the story?"

"They don't. But there is just enough fluid exchanged that a human can be turned into a slave and given extended life."

I thought of a bad movie and chuckled. "I'm sorry, Mara. You must know how preposterous this sounds."

"Which part?"

"All of it," I said. "Come on, extended lives? Human slaves? It doesn't even make scientific sense."

"How so?"

"If they're processing protein, why the long lives? I mean, mosquitoes live less than a month."

"That is a very good question, my friend. The answer has only surfaced in the last generation. Tell me, what do you know about AIDS?"

I had an entire section of books at home on diseases, viruses, and epidemics. "I know that particular virus goes in and rewrites a person's genetic code at the DNA level, somehow leaving out the immune system during rewrites."

Mara nodded her head and waited for me to get it.

"So you're saying . . . the vampire's immune system is constantly rewriting . . . except it's incorporating all the immunities from his victim's blood?"

She nodded. "And constantly healing, rebuilding, as well. Forever healthy, forever young."

"So what kills it?"

"The only ways are the old ways to defeat this creature—blunt trauma or burn them in the sunlight."

"Of course."

I could not hold a straight face, and at length she stared at me, the type of stare they teach nuns in the convent to show disappointment. "Mr. Joseph," she said, "you are a smart man. You came here not to expand your wisdom, but to add to your knowledge in pursuit of commerce."

She had me. I nodded.

"Simply reverse the two, and let your wisdom match your intellect." She pointed a finger at me. "Please consider my warnings. Then come back to me and discuss what you have seen."

I thanked her and apologized for my moments of disbelief. But as I drove away, Mara's expression did not convey hurt feelings or insult, but something resembling pity.

4

Romania in the 1980s was a tragedy unimaginable only a quarter century later. To understand how an entire country can slide into godless hands, first one must envision an entire world battle weary, with jackals waiting to feed on its carcass. World War II had ended, and while the rest of Europe experienced a rebirth under liberation and moved toward prosperity, Eastern Europe saw the pointy side of an endless barbed wire fence.

Communism settled over the land, and a couple decades later a small-minded dictator named Ceaușescu attempted to pay off massive debt to Western banks by selling his country's food supply. What scraps remained were rationed, while the government dictated what to grow. This came a decade after mandating that all married couples have at least five children. In the ensuing financial collapse, Romanians dropped off their children at orphanages until our numbers swelled to more than one hundred thousand.

I say *our* because my brother, Bernhardt, and I were Romanian orphans. In fact, in a sea of the abandoned unwanted, we were truly orphaned orphans: Our parents were dead. We had no shoes and we slept on cots, sharing a single woolen blanket for almost two years while the broken windows whistled with winter's winds, all the while cared for by social workers who treated us as if we were mutes. To call them caregivers is to misstate both parcels of the word. I don't remember much about it, perhaps God's gift of a blank slate, but I recall one day a camera crew entered our room and filmed us. They spoke English, as we had done in our household with a British father. I told them our names and that I was cold and wanted to go home.

They asked me where home was, and I told them it had burned down. A single image of the event remained with me, the sight of smoke and flames consuming our house as a neighbor took us by horse cart to the local police station. Mom and Dad had both been in the house. I was five at the time of the fire, my brother a year younger.

Within a week, Bernhardt and I were on a jet to America with a priest, and we landed at O'Hare. The priest drove us to Holy Cross in Chicago, a Catholic school run by nuns. So began our orphan days in the convent basement. It was not like a licensed orphanage; more like one long study hall until age seventeen, after which I went off to DePaul University and lived on campus until earning my English lit degree three years later. It was easy, for I had already read every book assigned.

I started collecting books in the convent basement. My life was books; a day off meant a trip to the library, my brother ever at my side. The toughest part was the journey to and fro. Not because the neighbors were mean to us, but because their dogs and cats treated us as trespassers, barking and hissing. Though we passed with as much stealth as we could, we watched leery neighbors corral their animals inside when we walked by. On the other hand, we always knew which shops held out a hand with food and kind wishes for our keepers. Those routes we frequented, dropping off holy cards and gracious words, the only things we had to give.

Church food drives always meant alms for the sisters and a bumper crop of canned goods, namely beets and lima beans. Needless to say, my brother and I hated beets. Did you ever notice that the crinkle-cut ones splash more perma-stain juice than the flat slices? And for some reason the nuns always passed on the cans of lima beans. We didn't like those, either.

Clothing drives brought bags and bags of rumpled garments, about half of them clean. Our job was to sort and fold, then iron after washing. We did get our pick of the boys' clothing, always optimistically choosing a larger size. But when it came to shoes we drew the line—only a half size larger.

I've been in Doug Carli's office dozens of times and have never seen him wear the same suit twice. One day I asked him what haberdashery he patronized, and stood there mute when he said he had his clothes tailored. As an adult who'd still never bought new clothes in a store, I honestly wasn't sure what *tailored* meant—perhaps he bought them somewhere and took them to a tailor for finishing. It just never occurred to me to purchase new clothes at a store when ten dollars buys a perfectly fine blazer at Goodwill. To this day I tend to tally a man's success by the size of his wardrobe.

I mostly blame the convent for my sequestered childhood and naïveté. For example, my brother and I went a dozen years before dining at a restaurant, and I carried my hesitations to dine out well into adulthood. I didn't just drink from the loner's cup, I carried it around, thanks to the literally cloistered existence my brother and I shared with the nuns, from morning prayers to obedience hour to evening prayers. More regimented than any military order, never in the company of other children, we took our orders from Mother Daniela, alternatively known as the Don. There was a television, but it was upstairs, and we knew nothing of its operation. What we learned of the outside world arrived via daily newspapers and a transistor radio.

Our world was not devoid of affection, but from the Don it came in the form of kind words, delivered in private, always encouraging, with the promise of a fruitful future for the simple price of paying attention and following the rules we learned there. Of course there is no substitute for a mother's touch, but the Don had a certain way of patting my shoulder that turned worry to calm. She always seemed to know when it was needed.

Summertime offered a beggar's portion of freedom and a scant few hours of play not allowed during the school year. Bernhardt and I, still confined to the convent grounds and endless chores, made games out of everything, from cutting designs in the grass to trimming trees certain shapes. At least it was outdoors, and we had the radio. Just one to share, of course, tuned to Cubs games, taking turns with it pressed to an ear. Noise was not permitted, even in summer, so my brother and I established a series of hand signals to keep each other informed. Like a third base coach giving signs, if I tipped my cap that meant the top of the inning, while touching my belt buckle meant the bottom, followed by the number of fingers corresponding to the frame. Thumbs-up meant *Who's up?* and I flashed the player's uniform number. And so on.

Later, my college years ran concurrent with Bernhardt's education and training at a seminary in the suburb of Mundelein. He moved on to wear the collar at St. Sebastyen Church in Chicago, a mere ten blocks from my warehouse. I always knew he would be a priest, not so much because it was his calling but because the church and convent were his shelter. Ever since our parents' death, my brother was frightened by things that most boys would see as challenges, like a shortcut alley or city park. His cautions seemed to be my urgings, and I tended toward troubled waters.

Needless to say, college was my escape, whereas my brother was drawn to the seminary as a safe haven. We were not different, really. As brothers we observed everything the same way, yet interpreted them differently. For example, when the Don locked the convent's front gates, Berns felt safe, while I felt trapped. It was a simple matter of differing viewpoints, mine as a collector, though never a hoarder, and his as a bridge. Bernhardt smiled when things went well for other people, and considered that things were going right by him when they were going right for others, God's graces. Conversely, when affliction landed on their doorsteps, Berns always knew it was God's home delivery, courtesy of His Will Postal Service. "God has a plan," he would say. God was forever planning.

That is not to say, by my sarcasm, that I do not believe in God and judgment, for I do. Rather, I believe what is in His book, and I prefer being a good Christian to being a good practicing Catholic.

Arriving at my brother's after the drive back from Mara's, I let myself into the rectory reception area; I had a key. I noticed that he still had the purple sash of Lent over a mirror, and as I walked over to remove it, Bernhardt entered the room. Seeing his reflection beside my own in the mirror, we certainly looked like brothers, but not twins. We were both six feet tall, but were built more to escape through tight exits than to stand and fight. We both took our parents' light eyes and hair, but Berns drew the longer face and Anglo features from our father's side while I inherited the rounder Saxon face from our mother's family.

I had e-mailed ahead to alert him of my coming trip, but had not been forthright about the details. In my absence I needed him to check on orders and return calls to those inquiring about books. Other than calling attention to the collection plate, it was the only form of commerce he knew how to transact.

"Authentication work?"

I nodded and handed him the purple sash.

"Thank you," he said. "Where to?"

"The Rosenbach in Philadelphia."

"Ah, Mecca for the parchment people," he said with a chuckle. "I have never been to Philadelphia."

"Not surprised, Berns, since it's not between here and Mundelein."

"I've been places."

I knew he had been to Rome once, plus a side trip. "In the confession booth, maybe."

"I've been around the whole world in the confessional."

"You've never told me the worst thing you've heard."

"Someone asking me the worst thing I've heard in the confessional booth."

And so it was with all our conversations—needling with smiles, a safe harbor for stupid questions, the bonded assurance that we made it out okay despite our humble beginnings.

Berns's smile vanished when I asked him how the nuns were getting along. It turned out that the convent had run out of money about five or six years ago. This was news to me, though I'd noticed that their count had dropped from a couple dozen to eight. Recently, Berns said, the diocese had purchased a four-bedroom home on the near north side for the remaining elders to live out their lives, the young ones reassigned or released from their vows. But the diocese only made the down payment and the rest came from parishioners' largesse. As we spoke, they were behind on mortgage payments.

Berns changed the subject. "So what's at the Rosenbach?"

"Authentication work." I waited a moment to see if he'd change the subject again, but he did not.

"And . . . ?"

I continued, "And if this manuscript's authentic, I'll be off to Europe right away."

A long pause separated my answer from his reply. "That's not between here and Mundelein."

I shrugged. "Only a week out of the country."

He looked at me with chin lowered, the stern posture he learned from the Don. "Where in Europe *is* this buyer? East of Munich, shall we say?"

"Yeah." We both knew that meant Romania.

He motioned for me to follow him toward the chapel door just off the rectory. St. Sebastyen was not a large church for such a big city, but it did have a small chapel for intimate ritual and prayer, often used to comfort grieving family members during funeral masses. A stone floor, three rows of pews, and a low ceiling made for cozy confines. The front hosted a stained glass image of Jesus talking to children. An offset dais of wrought iron faced the pews, and a well-worn tandem kneeling station centered before Christ's image.

My brother closed the door behind us, and I took a seat at the far end of the front pew. Berns bent his knees several minutes at the kneeling station before crossing himself and motioning for me to join him. I knelt beside him and crossed myself.

He began, "I've always worried this day would come."

"I'm not supposed to go, I know," I said. "But you did." On his trip to the Vatican, Bernhardt had taken a side journey to the homeland and returned a different person, a soul cluttered with grief and foreboding, and spoke of the superstitious old ways with newfound authority. He'd gone Ortho Euro on me.

"Today I tell you why." He began a prayer. "Our Father . . ." I expected to hear the Lord's Prayer, but as he continued looking ahead, not at me, he restarted, "Our father . . . murdered our mother."

Somehow I knew that without ever being told. But today was the first time I heard the words.

He continued, "Murder-suicide. He stabbed her, then burned the house down around them. Chained himself inside."

"You inquired?"

"This collar got me some answers at the Hall of Records."

"I figured," I said. "I've often . . ." I felt my throat swell and close. ". . . often thought about why God would place us in such a household."

The rare scenes from our early past flashed in my mind— raised voices, broken objects, and our mother's lamentations over an empty table.

"Remember, Joseph," said Berns, "God sent that camera crew to the orphanage to get us to this free land and a loving home."

I nodded. On this I agreed, except the use of his descriptor as *loving*. I would choose words like *kind*, *stern*, and *disciplined*, but I guess my idea of love differed from my brother's.

"And He gave us both the tools to begin our own lives once we reached adulthood."

"I know."

"Whenever you feel shortchanged, just remember the cold floors and those poor souls stuck there, and all the adults who got lesser tools. Someone else has always got it worse."

This I knew, but for years did not see how. What could count less than orphans?

Finally he drew his eyes down from the Lord and looked at me. "You are not to go there."

Our mother's remains, buried under her maiden name Petrescu, had been interred in our hometown of Baia Mare in the northern region. No word where our father's ashes lay. I knew Romania, and Transylvania in particular, remained a land leery of strangers and crowded with superstition.

"Our ways are not their ways." I loosely quoted Bram Stoker.

There was sadness in Berns's eyes as he spoke. "The footsteps of murderers, including their sons', stain the land they tread upon."

"I don't intend to wear one of those stickers—Hello, my name is . . ."

"And you somehow think this is pure coincidence someone chose you for this errand?"

"What do you mean?"

"Look." He raised his voice. "I told you why . . ." He calmed and bowed his head toward Jesus.

"I won't do anything foolish."

"You already did, by agreeing to go. There's danger there, a type not like here. You won't like what you see, Joseph, and you'll never be able to purge it from your memory."

"Can I have your blessing?"

"If only I could," he said. "Where you are going, God's eyes do not watch."

5

W hy, might you ask, am I called to authenticate first editions and rare manuscripts? The answer is simple: I have a certain knack. Some might call it a gift. When you grow up not knowing any differently, you simply do what you do until at some point in adulthood you learn by chance that your capability is unique. For example, I went to grade school with a girl, Winona, who corrected the teacher on a Bible passage, contesting the woman's interpretation. The teacher, a sister of the Order of the Holy Cross, took Winona to the Don's office. From that day forward, Winona kept her own counsel on scriptural construal. One day I asked her how she knew what she knew, to which she replied, "God told me."

"God speaks to you? Directly?"

She looked quizzically at me. "He doesn't speak to you?"

And so it was with my gift, each of us bequeathed our unique talent at the table of God's handouts, mine the ability to spot a manuscript or a rare book, to date paper or authenticate a signature with the naked eye, while convention would mandate chemical solutions and scientific instruments. Oh, I still had things tested at the Chicago Archive Lab, but they have yet to correct me.

How do I do this? Suffice it to say I can "see into" paper when I look at it. When focused on a piece of paper, I can "see" the structure of what I'm looking at, and much like someone whose sense of touch can identify a type of fabric, so a picture materializes in my mind of the structure before me. When I reach the requisite level of concentration, a fiber-rich piece of paper can look like a handful of hair to me, and the chemicals used look like flecks, or when grouped look like stains. Thus all paper is watermarked in some way, and I have learned to discern the marks.

Paper has always fascinated me. It all starts with the cellulose fibers bound by lignin, the substance that makes wood wood. Fibers are separated forcibly into a mass called wood pulp, which can then be turned into paper, either bleached white or unbleached. Separation is achieved by either a mechanical or chemical process, the former retaining the lignin whereas the chemicals dissolve the lignin. To recognize which process was used, I determine if the acidic lignin remains, which yellows the paper when exposed to bright light, or if the shorter fibers that indicate mechanical pounding are present.

The mechanical process was invented about two thousand

years ago in China. It began by macerating tree bark into pulp and combining it with water, placing it in a mold, and allowing it to dry. When separated from its water base, what remained was a thin fragile surface capable of absorption. For the first seventeen centuries the process yielded one sheet at a time. This is referred to as handmade papermaking.

Not until the 1840s, following the Industrial Revolution, did mass production of paper commence, before which fabrics were added to whiten the surface, the cheaper stuff mostly coffee-colored or light gray. Chemical processes came later in the century. Regardless of type, I can "see" the additives, such as chalk or clay particles, used as filler in pulp to achieve the proper absorbency level on the surface to accept ink. Different places and eras infused different fillers. I can also "see" the mesh and roller lines left behind from production, as well as the feathered edges and "laid" markings left from handmade paper. All these forensics help point me toward a source.

When I arrived at the Rosenbach Museum and Library, I had an incubating appreciation of Bram Stoker's accomplishment. Rather, *accomplishments*, for he was not of singular achievement. From the biography Mara gave me, I learned he had grown up Abraham Stoker, the son of a civil servant. He began adulthood in his dad's professional footsteps, but then as his calling to the theater rang louder than the duties of a desk clerk, Stoker acquainted himself with the accomplished actor Henry Irving. Friendship led to business handshakes, and Irving's Lyceum Theatre in London became Stoker's vocation. That was 1878. As business manager, bookkeeper, personal assistant, and production and literary manager, his job kept him busy seven days a week while he met countless actors and playwrights, worked on dozens of scripts, and found time to renovate the theater when commercial electricity became available.

So how did he manage to write a half dozen novels, only one of significance, and run a major theater without assistants? He had help. That I could see as soon as I began perusing the documents.

The manuscript was part of a secured display at the museum that had finished its final public showing. It then moved to the catacombs, the environmentally controlled area where fragile pieces are handled. Each display had a set of handling instructions, and they had everything ready for me upon arrival. The curator unlocked the display case, broke the security seal, and then stood by as I began my work.

The display contained three groups of documents: notes, a handwritten final draft, and the typed manuscript from which the first edition had been typeset. Within the notes were dozens of pages devoted to vampire traits and powers, local nautical research, typed excerpts from books Stoker researched, and about fifty pages of outlines, characters, and plot. In short, his sweeping novel was no rush job.

Bram wrote right-handed and, while always adhering to the proper capitalization of words, wrote capital letters with flair while scribbling lowercase letters. His penmanship flattened when it looked like he was hurried. On his checklists he used lines through the completed tasks, not check marks. One checklist covered suggested titles, *The Un-Dead* being the original.

Pity he did not see the public's overwhelming response to his masterpiece, for that came after his 1912 passing. Given such a time lag, I was surprised the original documents survived the first decades. For that we owe Bram's widow, who secured not only the originals but his notes and source materials. She even lived long enough to see his vision materialize in moving pictures.

Stoker appeared to use at least two different types of paper. The typewritten pages were from Continental mass production mill paper; I recognized the long strands of northern European spruce commonly used in the kraft process of that era. However, the handwritten pages were mostly on paper that came from America, handmade from local upper New England sources. I recognized the "laid" lines from the mold. In addition, scribbles and verses decorated various pieces of hotel stationery to mark the author's travels, such as a late chapter's outline on letterhead from the old Stratford Hotel in Philadelphia.

Accompanying the documents were several anachronistic accessories, such as clips, paper clips, and an old pen. It was typical of the early 1890s to punch holes in the completed manuscript and bind with a post, or even twine, for the standard twisted wire clips that are still in current use did not come under patent until 1899, and other attempts at metal fasteners were neither stainless nor anodized and would have yielded black oxidation smears. I surmised these clips were added much later by Stoker's widow as she assembled his belongings.

Per Mara's suggestion, I familiarized myself with the prologue and scribbled notes. The prologue was the story of Jonathan Harker leaving the Four Seasons Hotel in Munich on the morning of *Walpurgisnacht*, which is, as I learned, the night when graves open and the dead walk forth in revelry, a sort of Mardi Gras for condemned souls. By nightfall, against the advice of his carriage driver, Jonathan dismounts and continues afoot, finding himself in a graveyard under a fierce storm both of nature and evil forces. He happens upon the tomb of a countess, which reads in Gothic German script:

Countess Dolingen of Gratz
in Styria
Sought and Found Death.
1801

The sarcophagus is of stone construction with a marble cap, topped by an iron stake. Also written on the tomb, though in Russian, was *The dead travel fast*. Jonathan, of course, survives his attack and goes on to become a central figure in the novel. In chapter twenty-seven, the final of Stoker's published novel, Jonathan joins with his friends to ambush and kill Count Dracula while the vampire is being transported back to his castle in a box. Following a great struggle, the death blow puts an end to the villain, and he at once turns to dust.

Such was the second and all subsequent editions' version, ending with chapter twenty-seven and the count's quick disposal. However, what I was looking at was the first edition manuscript, and an epilogue followed chapter twenty-seven, clearly part of the original manuscript.

Why the change? Sometime between the fire that consumed

all first editions and the second printing came the alteration. Since the prologue and epilogue held all the value to my client, I thought it wise to commit to memory their contents.

In the long-missed epilogue, a great lightning storm descends on Dracula's Castle and turns it to rubble. A half dozen shadowy characters, referred to as *Regulats*, previously unmentioned in the novel, place the count's coffin on the back of a horse-drawn cart, and they journey north from a place called Dreptu to his resting place. The graveyard is the same as in the prologue, and he is re-united with his deceased bride, Countess Dolingen. The trip is detailed enough in both time and natural markers that one could make the assumption it was a real location, but also generic enough that it could be anywhere from Pennsylvania to rural Scotland. It read:

> *From Dreptu, they took the Ladies River to where the last sweet chest-nuts grow. It is there at Bethany Home you can see their fate at sun-rise, the wicked men know their destination. It is but five minutes that way to where the Juden await judgement. They took the batter across the first building and beyond the stone bridge, a path not to miss, only seconds now, shading their eyes in the sunrise while tripping over stones.*

I looked at Stoker's notes and saw his legend of chapters. In an earlier take, the story had been sectioned into four books, in-dicated by Roman numerals, each of equal chapter counts of seven. Perhaps he intended twenty-seven chapters all along. Then I noticed the typewritten prologue was actually on that list as chapter two, right after the introductory chapter of the count engaging Mr. Harker's firm to do business. Several corrections, scribbles, and lined-out words showed this to be a working draft, all changes in his own handwriting. A cleaner, revised page showed the novel changed to three equal nine-chapter books with a prologue and epilogue.

After reading both of the eliminated chapters, something struck me as odd: Why would Stoker change the story to preclude a meaningful sequel starring the villain count? Turning him to dust in his box ended any chance of a plausible resurrection, whereas the original manuscript placed him in his casket with a knife in his heart.

Mr. Stoker's handwriting spoke much of the man. Rarely did he write over words to correct them, suggesting a high level of deliberation before committing ink to paper, an expensive commodity at the time. With a certain flair to accompany his hurry, his capital letters stood formally, followed by a scribble that contained no spelling errors. Small spaces interrupted every couple of letters to suggest he lifted his pen midword, like one would print. People who do that tend to strive for clarity and shun ambiguity in their written correspondence.

Amidst the notes were two other handwritings. One was the same as the man who signed the contract on behalf of Archibald Constable and Company, a right-handed script providing minor suggestions that I noticed did not make the final cut. But there was another handwriting on his notes that harkened me back to Mara's suggestion that Stoker had help.

This was a left-handed writer who pressed hard onto the

page, evidenced by how the ink absorbed into the paper. He, too, would write a few letters, then lift his pen. Then I found a page of notes dealing with vampire conventions, the page establishing their habits, limitations, and powers. Normally when an author deals with the most implausible parts of fantasy, his assumptions are not challenged, for it is his prerogative how and when to leap into unreality. However, it looked as if the "assistant" wrote the characteristics of vampires and Stoker marked them off as he incorporated or agreed with them. Then there were a few with lines through them and a *No* written by Stoker in the margins. These items did not see final print.

Then at the bottom of the page the words *No Epil* were written boldly by the left-hander. At first I thought it read *No Evil*, but something told me to look again at every word on the page. Whoever his assistant was emphatically insisted on discarding the epilogue, the version detailing the count's burial beside his bride. The assistant also drew a line through *Dreptu* and boldly wrote, *NO! DO NOT USE!!*

Also among the notes was the 1897 *Times* article detailing the fire that consumed the publishing company's office and warehouse. I recognized the bulk paper as northern European stock mechanically processed, typical of all news stock because of its high-yield harvest capacity and ink-absorption quality. Another *Times* article detailed a subsequent smaller conflag at the Lyceum Theatre, separated by a mere two weeks. In part it read:

> . . . *questioned following the fire was one George Anton, an itinerant craftsman engaged by the Lyceum Theatre to install electricity at the*

playhouse, who was said to have had a bit of a row with the author on 18 May following a stage reading of Mr. Stoker's manuscript to secure theatrical copyrights. In attendance were Henry Irving, owner of the Lyceum, and Ellen Terry, an actress and employee of the theatre. Both were questioned following the conflagration, and Mr. Anton was released from Scotland Yard.

Following the warehouse fire and the publisher's setback, it took two years to get the rights out of the court system and publish another printing with Doubleday & McClure. I paused and pushed my seat away from the table when the enormity of his endeavor struck me. Gazing at the large display of material, I thought of the writer's plight. Not only Abraham Stoker, but all who toil in the craft of words—that a man should write and write and write and fill volumes with notes and drafts and typed pages, only to send his creation out into the world for inspection and judgment by humans. Any number of impediments can keep it forever in manuscript form, yet here was a project that took commercial form, only to meet with fire on the eve of success. Did Bram Stoker view the fire with a similar sense of loss as I had the last time I saw my childhood home?

Had the author not prevailed in his legal pursuit, the world might never have read his story. There's a lot to be said for persistence in the ashes.

I don't know how long I sat there staring at this piece of history, but I did notice my host clearing his throat as a reminder that my time had long ago run over. Work concluded, I returned to the Rittenhouse Hotel to construct my engagement letter and certificate of authenticity.

The first time I gave a positive certificate I later found myself defending the claim in court, not because it was a fake but because I failed to include my methods of testing, rendering doubt to a subsequent buyer. See, authentication work is not a verification process for the benefit of a buyer, but rather a representation to the entire public, both for persons known and unknown, for universal reliance thereon. Simply put, my first efforts failed the weight test. Subsequently I had learned to craft my letters much like CPA firms construct their audit reports, in the double negative stance that I performed the following standard tasks of attestation and could not find anything that would conclude it was *not* the real thing, etc.

After proofing my letter, I faced the reality that I would actually be journeying back to my homeland. Not home, for that was a walled convent. Still, the place of anyone's birth holds value. On the Internet I checked train routes in and out of Baia Mare, the modest-sized town where our mother was buried. I also noted where the Hall of Records was located if I needed help.

Next I checked my e-mails and opened the one from my brother. He said the nuns' house received a notice of default after falling ninety days behind on mortgage payments. Add to that, two of them, including the Don herself, were experiencing failing health that required care in an assisted living facility. Luckily, the property had not yet met foreclosure, which meant there was still time. I vowed to approach Doug Carli about a loan as soon as I returned from Romania.

A second e-mail relayed that he received a buyer's call for a hardcover first edition of *A Separate Peace* by John Knowles. I had two of them, a 1960 Macmillan and a more valuable 1959 Secker & Warburg London international edition I found in an estate sale for ten dollars. I wondered if he remembered when we had found that first one—high school days. I found the crackling first edition for a dollar in the liquidation stack at a closing Carnegie Library in the north suburb of Waukegan. I'd long kept it in my personal favorites stash, a shelf of books that I never intended to sell, but I told Berns to consider the sale of both books as part of the collection plate for the nuns. The Macmillan was worth about a thousand dollars. The International, however, was signed (I had done the authentication myself), and it should fetch at least four thousand dollars.

It was the least I could do for the nuns. As in most convents, they taught Catholic schoolchildren, prayed volumes, and did a lot of chores. The days of the American orphanages had passed a decade before, yet they took us in, just the two of us. I never knew why. But whereas my brother gave back in the form of his vows, I had never really given anything back. They were aging and needed help, the kind I might be able to provide. I resolved to give them a home now, a permanent one.

The last e-mail had Mara's name on it, coupled with a return-receipt-requested message. It simply asked if I found what I was looking for. I hesitated to reply, so I hoped that by hitting *Yes* to the received request she would know it was an affirmative reply.

Before I could log off, another message arrived from Mara, say-ing, *Your journey begins now. Remember that your Mother taught you not to speak with strangers.*

Two days after relaying to Mr. Ardelean that I had indeed found the notes and two missing chapters, a notice arrived from the UPS Treasures Division that I was to pick up a package and bring two positive forms of identification. While there, I shipped the Knowles international edition my brother had successfully sold for $5,500. After fingerprinting and photographs at the UPS warehouse, I left with my package. Inside was my travel itiner-ary. I was to fly the very next day to Bucharest, where I would be met by a guide who would accompany me to the castle in Bran. There I would meet with Arthur Ardelean to discuss what I had found during authentication, and if the terms were acceptable, my fee contract would be finalized.

Also enclosed was a bank account signature card with a return envelope to a Swiss bank and a wooden box secured in bubble wrap. Carefully I removed the container, roughly the size of a cigar box. It was heavy, handmade of black walnut, with a carv-ing on top that looked like a dragon standing behind a crucifix with its tail partially wrapping the bottom of the cross. I opened the box carefully to find a silk bag with a drawstring. Lifting it I could tell it was a crucifix, and carefully I removed it from its bag.

It was a six-inch tall Saint Olga cross, the type a Westerner might never see or appreciate. Made of solid silver and Slavic in design, its four ends were carved to the shape of three-leaf clovers, inlaid with an image of the Eastern Orthodox cross. The three bars were accurately placed, the lower bar angled properly left up and right down. *IC* and *XC*, the written symbols for Christ, were inscribed on the cross member, and an image of the sun shone the light of Christ above the inlay.

One additional inlaid item I did not recognize—a stunning ruby placed in the middle of the cross where Jesus's heart would be. I turned it over, and on the back was written the Slavic phrase *Spasi i Sokhrani. Save and protect.* At the bottom was inscribed a pair of dragon's feet.

The neck chain, fashioned in the same silver, was sized to allow the crucifix to suspend directly over my heart. This was the relic I was to wear at all times during my trip.

6

To understand Romania is to accept that its history is driven by its position on the globe. Assuming the head-shaped country faces west, the Carpathian Mountains are the brow and mutton-chop-style sideburns sweeping south and then west at the country's midpoint. That mountainous land is Transylvania, and it takes its name by combining two Latin words, *trans* and *silva*, meaning *land beyond the forest*. Descending the Carpathian foothills, one finds the Moldavian Plain pointed east toward Asia and the Wallachian Plain south toward the Balkans. My destination was where the range makes its turn west, to a castle in a mountain pass near the town of Brașov.

Transylvania, together with the Moldavian and Wallachian Plains, formed the three principalities that ultimately united to become Romania. The Danube River forms its border with Bulgaria to the south, and the Black Sea touches a piece of its eastern border.

Latin was our connection to home. The Carpathians were the northeast corner of the Roman Empire, and its language became the foundation of the Romanian tongue. The Roman Empire, whittled away over a thousand years of skirmishes from a long roster of invaders, slowly turned the Mediterranean over to the conquering Muslims. But as the Ottoman Empire expanded north through Bulgaria, Turkey, Greece, and the rest of the Balkan Peninsula (which Mara so aptly called the "corridor of war"), they were turned back on the Wallachian Plain and failed to annex above the Danube River. Hence Romania could claim to be the land where Christianity held off the Ottoman Turks.

I cross-referenced the lineage tree in Stoker's notes, the one written by the left-handed assistant, against two history books from my shelf in an effort to understand his story's lore. With annotations of battles and dates of rule, the tree did not appear to be Stoker's work. More likely, it seemed the author looked at the chart, picked the most ruthless of the bunch, and selected him as his villain.

Dracula's family started with Vlad I, to whom the Hungarian emperor bestowed the Crusader's title of Dracul, from *drac*, meaning *dragon*, or Order of the Dragon. He ruled the Wallachian principality with one interruption for a dozen years ending in 1447. His job as prince was to keep the Ottomans on the south side of the Danube. Vlad I had at least three known sons, in age order: Mircea, Vlad, and Radu. At that time, principalities weakened when princes died, leaving thrones open to challenge and rearrangement. Vlad I aligned himself with the Ottoman sultans when his neighbors weakened, and vice versa. Discovery of his mixed allegiances ultimately led to Vlad's imprisonment by his sultan neighbor, who held sons Vlad and Radu hostage in an attempt to sideline Vlad I. Not one to stand idle, Vlad I returned to the warpath, alienating the two sons left as captives, and finished out his rule until he was reportedly executed, along with eldest son Mircea, for double-crossing those who had bestowed upon him the prince's title.

Vlad I's second son, the Vlad who was left as a hostage, once freed, added the customary *a* to the end of his father's name, becoming Dracula, and ruled under the name Vlad III, the interim ruler unrelated to the family. Vlad III reigned ruthlessly over the Wallachian principality that extended from the southern Carpathian Mountain passes down to the Danube. Impalement was his preferred manner of execution, and allegedly one of his forms of domestic entertainment. Known to have carried into battle the poled severed heads of his enemies, he became Vlad Țepeș (or Vlad the Impaler), a name that invoked terror all along the Ottoman frontier.

His reign lasted a relatively short six years, with his remaining known life spent between battlefields and prisons. It was originally written that Vlad the Impaler died in battle the same year that his brother Radu assumed the throne, in 1476.

Why such blood skirmishes between brothers? Money and power, of course, for Slavic law does not dictate that a father's position and wealth passes either to the eldest son or even to his sons in birth order. Rather, it was open to challenge by any and all sons, legitimate or illegitimate. Allegiances thus formed between the voivodes, counts, and boyars, who fought for spoils while losers were imprisoned, killed, or left the area to regroup.

Stoker's lineage chart simply ended with the word *Plague*. The year 1476 marked its return, this time spread up through Italy.

My flight left Chicago Wednesday afternoon, and following a plane change in Munich, I landed Thursday afternoon at Otopeni. I purchased a Romanian dictionary and phrase book at O'Hare and found the language strangely familiar. I spent time reading the section about dealing with Customs, but in the end thought it safer to just speak English and keep an ear open.

In all honesty, my preconceived notions of indifference were wrong, as I was not ready for the rush of feelings I encountered looking out of the plane's window at my homeland. I thought it would be all business—a face-to-face with the buyer, a look at the new museum spot, an agreement about my fee and involvement with the purchase, and perhaps a little sightseeing. I knew visiting my mother's grave would be emotional, so I slotted it after the conclusion of business and on the way home. Instead, what I felt upon approach was how I feared I might feel in the cemetery, a certain sense of return to a prison from which I'd narrowly escaped and the secret hope that no one noticed. The comforting image of my brother's face popped into my head, and I wished for his company.

Upon landing, my watch and internal clock were eight hours off. About the size of Phoenix, Bucharest is the country's capital and biggest city, and rests comfortably on both sides of the Dâmboviţa River in the Wallachian Plain, an hour north of the Danube.

I picked up my luggage and headed toward Customs. There I realized I had arrived at the world's smoking section. Everything smelled of cigarettes: the wood, the conveyor, my shoes. Among the pre-1989 Communist remnants was the acceptance of long lines and the refusal to budge an inch, so people lined up touching one another. The man behind me pushed his luggage against the back of my leg and lit a cigarette, while a uniformed man stood by inspecting the seemingly endless queue. As I looked up from my phrase book, the customs officer made eye contact and approached. *"Paşaportul."*

Unzipping my jacket to produce my passport, my crucifix came into his view. Immediately he motioned me toward the front of the line, stamped my passport, and apologized for the time I had spent in queue.

Thank you, Mr. Ardelean.

I stepped outside to weather identical to that which I had left in Chicago—cool, breezy, humid. A young man hurriedly walked my way, extending his right hand. "Mr. Joseph Barkeley." *Yoseph.*

"Yes."

He introduced himself: "Lucian Blaga."

"Like the poet," I said.

He pointed toward the open cab door and lifted my luggage into the trunk. "You know of him."

"The tragedy of the intellectuals."

"You know your history, Mr. Barkeley. Both postwar periods were unkind to the Romanian people."

"Call me Joseph."

"Call me Luc."

I was told I would have a guide, but did not expect one until reaching the hotel. He was a thoroughly Americanized young man, down to the swoosh-brand shoes, with the kind of fair, delicate features that women favored and his English tilted slightly with accent. He claimed to be a doctoral student at the University of Tennessee on summer break and, once lettered, would return to Romania to teach English at a local university.

I decided to test his knowledge of our most famous Tennesseean. "'I ask for a warrior, they send me a poet.'"

It took a moment, but Luc smiled. "Andrew Jackson."

En route to the Continental Hotel we drove south on Şoseaua Kiseleff, a wide tree-lined boulevard that passed for a good imitation of Paris as we approached a traffic circle that navigated around the Arch of Triumph before heading toward the more dense cluster of downtown buildings, a combination of old Eastern European architecture and post–World War II buildings. Luc identified the museums, government buildings, churches, and schools. "Communism demolished more buildings than the war."

I thought it wise to keep silent my gratitude for growing up where I did, and not here.

Outside was another casualty of prolonged communism— street people. They dotted the sidewalks in all ages and both genders with cupped hands and distant stares, eyebrows down. Surely many of my fellow orphans resided among them. My emotional descent continued. An orphanage is not someplace you leave or graduate from; it is something you try to wash off yourself and hope no one notices the stain. I looked down a shopping street and saw the chief American influence, golden arches on a red background. And in a place where Christian Orthodoxy dominates, the electronic billboard landscape featured plenty of scantily clad women selling improved lifestyles to the conservatively dressed walking the streets. I thought it better to look down.

After I checked in at the hotel, Luc continued his tour guide duties as we took early dinner before a show at the Romanian Athenaeum Concert Hall, and I ended the night with a leisurely stroll through the tree-lined sidewalks in Cişmigiu Park. The time change, plus my natural nocturnal routine, found me looking out the hotel window at a church older than America—the Kretzulescu Church—when its bells chimed three A.M.

Jet-lagged, I was not my sharpest when Luc met me for breakfast and took me to the train station. Leaving Bucharest from Gara de Nord train station, the Rapid train did not live up to its name. It was roughly the same speed as the Northwestern commuter line out of Chicago, stopping in each town.

Unlike in most major American cities, where leaving the city limits means entering the suburbs, here in Bucharest you left civilization behind, one block urban, the next rural. Agricultural land sits beside unspoiled, untilled land, and both rise and fall over gentle hillocks patched with random clumps of trees, mostly oaks. The rail line cut its own path, as golden and green hills grew taller with travel northbound.

There is a color pattern to Eastern Europe that the American eye will find different. Faded blue- and red-plastered buildings stand topped with faded red-tiled roofs. Gray wooden fences loosely mark territories around tiny farms, some wrapped in the old-world basket-weave pattern. Hay stands not stacked in bundles, but twisted into steeple shapes the size of outhouses. Tiny barns with witch's-hat thatched roofs serve as storage sheds. Everywhere horse-drawn carts are piled with every transportable good, including families. Roads are really just paths loosely covered, no need for overdrive, and vehicles in four-wheel drive or low gear vie for space with horse-drawn carts.

Two hours north, the landscape on either side of the train deepened to wide verdant valleys, framed with forest-covered hills and rock outcroppings. I had reached the Carpathian foothills. None of this end of the range rises above the alpine tree line, the oaks and beech and sycamores crowding the hilltops, much like the American Blue Ridge Mountains. I was not ready for such beauty, as my youth had cast a pall over what little recollection remained of childhood. None of it felt like the home I remembered. To my adult mind, Michigan Avenue was home, the smell of Garrett's Popcorn on a cold night the ultimate sensual memory.

Three and a half hours north perched the glorious old fortified city of Braşov in a mountain pass saddle, our point of disembarkation. This was the common placement of fortresses and castles in Europe, with river-fed valleys on either side of the pass. In a typical layout, the medieval town had large churches at its zero intersections, plus a fortified monastery where citizens retreated while under attack. These great buildings had function first, fashion second. It was only after the Crusades that royal families made castles their stylish residences.

Luc guided me through the city's arched entryway into the town square, centered on a huge old Lutheran church with its four-sided clock tower supporting a tall steeple, fortified walls protecting the city entrance, the monastery in walking distance.

The square *looked* ancient, most places needing paint or stucco work, usually both, and it appeared that vinyl windows had not penetrated the local weathered-wood market. All around swirled the clomping of foot and hoof traffic, people talking, the sounds of commerce, and the smell of inviting food. Underfoot lay cobblestone and brick, grouted with dirt.

This place was old long before our Constitution was conceived, I realized. What's another century or two between paint jobs? We stopped at one of the many outdoor cafés and rested under an umbrella. I enjoyed the dark coffee and Luc's silence. He seemed to understand that I was there for more than just the commerce.

Romania is the true cauldron of European bloodlines. From around the Mediterranean, people migrated over the centuries, along with visitors from India and the Middle East. From the Hungarian west the round-headed Magyars arrived, and from the Germanic north the light-featured Saxons, my relatives. There are the pointed features of Russian descent, the heavy beards from Asia Minor, and the dark skin of the Mediterraneans, usually seen in the Gypsies, or Roma. Women of all ages wore head scarves in this remote part of the country, usually not coordinated with the rest of their clothing, and unlike in Bucharest, here the attire suggested work over stylish leisure.

It was common to hear conversation held at unacceptably high volume. Patrons sat gesturing heatedly at the café tables, and though I expected a row, none followed. The round heads tended to sit in quietude and disregard their neighbors, and Luc took to flirting with our waitress, a young lady who looked to be his age. While I tried to look disinterested, they exchanged numbers. In the States, a young couple might point cell phones at each other and punch in numbers; here they still exchanged handwritten notes.

A small bus arrived. In its window, a sign read BRAN PLATFORM. Luc, after a final exchange with his newfound friend, motioned that it was time to go. We boarded and shared a bench seat behind the driver while the bus filled its twelve seats. Leaving Braşov, we traveled a narrow path of a road and bounced and swayed for more than an hour. This took us twenty miles west to the town of Bran, where we dismounted into the old market on the valley floor.

Market is a generous term for the wood slat structures in an outdoor bazaar that gave scant cover to all things agrarian. The language sounded familiar, and there were several words and phrases that I understood. The pace seemed lugubrious, and the average face was grim.

But no matter one's placement in the Bran valley, your eyes always drew upward to the huge medieval structure sculpted directly out of stone, Castel Bran, otherwise known as Dracula's

Castle and the setting of the original *Dracula* novel. It looks as if a great solid rock disrobed under chisel, revealing a high-walled Gothic edifice beneath, its complicated roofline of red tile, and four uneven steepled corners. This all stood two hundred feet up on a spiral path that wrapped the mountain until reaching the bottommost of the castle's six stories. Turrets and flanking towers gave relief to the long-sided curtain walls, with rounded corner towers gracing the four endpoints. A centered watchtower stood another five stories above the roof.

Prior to major renovation, any tourist could approach up the path to the front door and knock, a privilege since revoked and replaced with a guarded entrance gate at the mountain's base. Luc was received by the guard, who closed the gate and showed us to a horse-drawn carriage, an open-top wagon with rubber-tired wheels and red side-mounted lanterns. A lone horse pulled us up the path. As the path spiraled up the mountain and rose above the trees, I looked out at the valley and wished our ride never to end. But end it did and deposited us at the entrance, a couple of dozen stone steps below the front door.

Of solid oak and a mere six feet tall, the door surprised me with its stunted size, allowing only a single entrant at a time. I knocked on the door . . . simply because I wanted to. Seconds later, the loud locking mechanism freed the door and a man stood back away from the light.

"Do come in, sir." I recognized Arthur Ardelean's voice.

"Mr. Ardelean." I held out my hand and we exchanged greetings.

"Kindly leave your bags to the staff, Mr. Barkeley."

If one could look like his voice, Arthur did, his face long with the jowls of an elder, eyes that turned down at the corners, hair black and retreating from a widow's peak. He was tall and thin, with long arms and legs, and wore an ascot, much like the one I had expected to see in his envelope. He wore the shoes of a working man—blucher oxfords with a heavy leather welt. His hands were large, and his handshake grip belied his apparent age.

Arthur showed me inside, and I was taken by the entrance room's smell, a mixture of old wood, fabric, smoke, and the cool breeze generated by stone walls. It looked to be a large gathering room with fifteen-foot ceilings and tall, narrow windows, sparse of furnishings but decorated with frescos and dark-colored tapestries. Underfoot a dense patterned rug led to a perimeter of wide, dark oak plank flooring. We traversed the room, a good forty feet in length, and stepped into an elevator while a young man tended to my bags. Luc took his leave and bid to rejoin us for dinner.

The elevator's accordion doors closed before us, and I faced the stone texture of the shaft as we climbed. Judging height is challenging inside a slow-moving box, but I guessed we had reached the fourth story when the doors opened to a receiving room. I signed a guest book that rested on an old board table and, while tempted to peruse the pages, followed Arthur through arched doors into a hallway.

"Allow me to show you to your room first, Mr. Barkeley, so you can freshen for dinner." He pointed me through large double doors at the end of the hallway to a corner suite, where three sides of picture window offered a startling view three hundred feet above the valley floor. Cool afternoon mountain breezes swept across the room.

Staring at the vista, I suddenly realized that Arthur had spoken.

"I'm sorry, pardon me?"

"I trust your accommodations meet with your expectations, sir," he said.

I nodded, unable to find a worthy superlative.

"Dinner will be served in an hour, sir, and you need only to pick up the telephone should you need something." He pointed to a black cradle telephone on a nightstand; it had no keypad.

After Arthur left, I noticed my bags had already been placed on the stands awaiting my arrival. Odd; it felt like we had taken the most direct route possible. A change of clothes followed a shower, and as much as I wished to explore the castle, I waited out the hour seated on the windowsill instead, looking all directions over the valley. I thought of the street people I had seen that day and, but for a fateful television documentary and the gracious hands of the avowed, how likely my fate would have followed the same path. Both stunned and humbled standing in that castle window, I finally understood how far I had risen from the stone cold floors of Ceaușescu's rubble.

C ome," Arthur Ardelean said, "allow me to show you the tourist route we intend."

Lengthy dinner concluded (Arthur had referred to it as venison Carpații, which I suspected meant *local*) and after taking proper leave from Luc, we walked the route sight-seers would track on the Dracula tour. Much of the old castle furnishings and decorations had been provided by the Romanian royal family, a combination of German baronial and traditional Romanian styles with dark stains and shadowy accents. Several sleeping chambers had beds of timber beams with taut ropes, the origin of "sleep tight."

Night had drawn its shade when we stepped out into the elevated courtyard and walked to one of several lookout vantages.

An alpine chill had claimed the earlier breeze while the western horizon squinted its last purple slivers. In the east the moon, still a couple days from full, inched over the hills toward Braşov. Fast-moving clouds flickered the moonlight's intensity.

I thought of the soldiers who, over the centuries, had stood watch along this wall. High stakes in those times, when runners and carrier pigeons arrived with skinny notice of approaching armies, when battles lost meant plunder of everything dear to the soldier—not just possessions, but life, home, and family. And for survivors, slavery.

"It is time, Mr. Barkeley."

Arthur held open a door, and we walked a hall half the length of a parapet wall before stopping at an oak door, built heavy and sturdy like an exterior door, with a double crossbar lock, also of hardwood. Arthur lifted it with ease, and I stepped through into a tall stairwell. The circular stone steps spiraled tightly down windowless stone walls, a twist too tight to see your destination. The air smelled of dust from the stones. At sixty steps I lost count. Dim lanterns cast eerie red light as we descended farther and farther, our breathing and echoing footfalls the only noises.

At the bottom Arthur lifted a lantern from a wall hook and shone it on the door, another solid oak barrier with a speakeasy window and a stout iron locking mechanism. He produced a key from his pocket, a large old-fashioned iron one, and turned it in the opening. I heard two clicks and a loud clunk, and the door eased open with a hiss and a rush of cool air.

Arthur entered the room first and felt the wall for a switch. Sconce lights on three walls clicked on and only grudgingly lit the room, revealing several large wooden picnic-style tables covered with dusty tarps. They had detached bench seats. A couple smaller chambers, both doorless, occupied the left side. As my eyes adjusted, I saw that the right side wall appeared to be solid rock. Underfoot it felt like compacted dirt. There was a certain feel to the room I could not place immediately, but I had felt it before.

"Come, this might be of interest to you," Arthur said.

He showed me to the two smaller rooms along the left side, the first one used as storage for chairs and such. They did not have wood where you might expect door frames. Perhaps they had barred entrances at one time.

"This," he said, holding his lantern up, "this is where Vlad the Third slept when he was . . . a guest in the castle."

I looked inside. "Vlad the Impaler."

"Yes." A table leaned along one wall, and an empty bed frame along another.

It dawned on me that I was in the foundation of the castle, the part of the structure built from the rock itself, and the temperature and air felt like a cave. The sound from the walls failed to reflect—dead air.

We stepped out of the guest room, and he pointed toward the dark fourth wall. "Back there is the old wine cellar."

"Which you plan on converting to display the manuscript."

"Correct."

I pointed down. "This will need flooring."

"Of course."

"Cork over poured concrete would be ideal for this application."

"So noted, sir," Arthur said. "Now, if you will give me a minute." He lifted a tarp off a table and bench for us to sit, and that's when it hit me—the smell. An awful odor, a combination of carrion and something else, wafted through the air.

"Please be seated, Mr. Barkeley, and let us discuss what you came here for."

I chose a seat with my back to the wall and facing the dark end of the room. "Before going to the museum I read the novel to familiarize myself with the story."

"It is quite the enduring accomplishment, is it not?"

"Yes, it is," I said. "They had the display sealed, and unlocked it for me, double keys on the combination lock."

"What was included in the display?"

I rattled off the list, from the handwritten notes to the gem clips, and explained what belonged and what appeared to be added later. He did not seem particularly interested, but instead he moved directly to the matter's heart.

"And what of the prologue and epilogue?"

"The prologue, which was at one time chapter two, and the epilogue were part of the original handwritten as well as the typed manuscripts. They appear to have been replaced after fire destroyed the first editions."

"Did you note their content?"

"As you specified, no copies were taken. But the prologue describes one of the protagonists going out on *Walpurgisnacht* and ending up next to the tomb of a vampire, a female. And the epilogue describes a more elaborate battle to the villain's death, followed by his burial back in the same graveyard."

"Very good."

"I was able to authenticate Stoker's handwriting from his notes to the manuscript, as well as verify the paper used as stock from the 1890s."

"Without sample testing."

"Without sample testing, yes. I . . ." I paused, sensing something in the darkness of the next room. "I did not need to give it the acid test to know it was Northern European wood pulp, kraft chemical method."

"It is obvious," Arthur said with a smile, "that the best man was chosen for the job. Did you bring your report?"

"It is upstairs." I then saw what looked like a pair of eyes set back in the dark room. Red eyes. Perhaps the red lantern light from the stairwell . . . but the wall sconces surrounding me shone an amber glow of bulbs used back in the 1890s, when the world converted from gas lanterns to electric bulbs.

From the darkness a deep voice sounded: "Come forward and let me see you."

I assumed it was the buyer and stood, awaiting Arthur's instruction.

"This way, slowly please," Arthur said.

As I stepped toward the red glowing eyes, the smell increased.

"I am honored to work for you, sir," I said.

"You were chosen for your specific talent," the voice said. All voices emanate from the diaphragm, and his had a projecting, stentorian quality I had never heard, as if it carried through the air with little effort. He drew out the last word of his sentences. "Chosen well, I see, as Arthur said."

"Thank you, sir."

Arthur motioned for me to stop. I heard the man breathing. His breaths were much longer in duration than a normal man's, more like a great-sized animal.

"Closer."

I took two steps closer, and he breathed deeply. It sounded as if he drew breaths over his teeth and made a slight hissing sound on inhale. He did this twice, the second one more pronounced. When he exhaled, it was quiet.

"Your work is extraordinary, young man," the voice said.

"Thank you again, sir."

"Closer, please."

Another two steps and I was certain he saw my nose wrinkle at the strong odor.

"I sense . . . fear," the voice said.

I managed to speak. "This is an unusual setting, sir."

"You need not fear me." I heard him breathe. "Unless you are wrong."

"Do you wish for me to proceed with negotiations with the family, sir?"

"Mr. Barkeley, that manuscript belongs here . . . with me. You are to make an initial offer of two million dollars U.S. If countered, escalate with two even amounts up to four million. If that does not close the transaction, call Mr. Ardelean for further instructions."

"Yes, sir."

"Funds will be wired to the museum's account the following day. You are to take possession of the entire display yourself and immediately transport it here."

"Understood, sir."

"Upon my acceptance of the manuscript, Mr. Ardelean will instruct the bank in Zurich to credit your account for an amount equal to the purchase price."

"I beg your pardon?"

"That is all."

"Sir?" I called into the darkness.

Arthur spoke: "He is gone."

"I don't believe I heard his last instruction correctly."

"You heard it correctly." He smiled and patted me on the back. "You are no doubt just overwhelmed."

"Four million dollars?"

"It is not just four million dollars, Mr. Barkeley. It is four million dollars in a Swiss account for you to draw at your choosing."

N o need for coffee; I stayed awake looking into the southern Transylvania night, counting dots of light while the town bedded. Below there was no traffic, no one afoot, no sign of humans save the diminishing house lights. Dogs howled and returned calls deep into the woods.

I tried to keep sinister thoughts at arm's length, because, well . . . fiction is fiction. But I could not deny Mara's list of traits: the red eyes, the odor, his smelling radius and breathing patterns, his swift movement, and his comment that he smelled fear. Or did he say he sensed it? Regardless, the eccentricities matched many of my more reclusive clients who wished not to be identified. Perhaps I was looking for those traits out of my own fears. After all, I was in the house that Dracula built.

I tried to shake the images by staring out into the night, and dared look up as the moon tracked straight above the castle. Clouds scurried eastward, shading the moon, and when it shone again the bright light illuminated the trees below along with the night's airborne predators. As a child I remember seeing skeeter hawks near the lake, birds that dive through mosquito clouds for their meals, and I now recognized their distinct diving patterns. A flock darted down and toward the castle walls, looking as if they would either crash into a door or window, only to alter course and circle back.

Several bats flew by, and Mara's comments echoed along with the novel's passages telling of bats at the window. Stoker described the vampire's flight as deliberate and straight-lined, ending with a graceful landing on a sill, but this colony winged about with much jitter and weave, and none alighted on the sill. It was the first time I had ever seen the flight of bats backlit by moonlight.

Four million dollars is serious money; not just in what it could purchase, but in what I could do. That much money meant freedom from worry and a buffer against a whimsical market. Now I would be free to work and make decisions only from a position of strength, bargaining from the top hand.

And of course I would take care of those who took care of me. I had fully intended to approach Doug Carli about supporting the nuns with a mortgage guarantee, but after the four-million-dollar offer I decided I would purchase the house outright and just let them live out their days in security. That was the only money I cared to spend in my head before receiving it.

Then I stepped back and recalled something Doug once told me: "No one goes from zero to millions without getting in bed with something ugly."

After what seemed like only an hour or two, I shared breakfast with Luc on a tray he delivered to my room. Setting up on a small table, he looked well rested. "So you met with the old man last night."

I nodded.

"Made quite the impression, I see." He poured a cup of coffee and handed it to me. "Doesn't look like you slept much last night."

"A little." I thanked him as he poured.

"Don't be too worried about the condition of the basement," Luc said. "Smells down there, I know. It can be modernized."

I nodded. "I recommended a cork floor to Mr. Ardelean, but they'd have to pour a concrete floor first. The real issue is controlling the air quality."

"Well, between you and me?" He glanced toward the door before finishing. "I think the display is heading to one of the vaults."

"Where are they?" I asked.

Again he looked toward the door. "You were almost there."

"Mm-hmm," I said. I assumed he meant the dark recesses in the basement. Many of my clients chose to hoard and protect their valuables, and as I reflected on Arthur's less-than-enthusiastic response, I suspected the original might not end up on display. Not hungry, I pushed the food around with my fork. "Have you met him?"

"Couple times." He indicated I should eat. "Takes his anonymity very seriously."

"Why do you think that is?"

"They're the oldest moneyed family on the Continent. They started the bank in Switzerland. Everything they do goes through it, and if you think about it, their secrecy is all they have. When you're that rich, you're a target, like it or not. If not for criminals, then for the paparazzi. Reputation is everything to people like that. They can't afford to let anyone near them who they don't have absolute faith in."

I let the compliment pass. "So being ultra-rich makes you eccentric?"

"I'd call it shrewd. Pretty amazing, really," he said. "Look at America—you get one or two generations removed from the great wealth builders and all the offspring are dolts."

I nodded, conceding his point. "Drug addicts and social butterflies who bad-mouth the system that feathered their beds."

"Right." Luc grinned, then checked his watch. "Better get ready."

After saying good-bye to Arthur at the front door, Luc and I caught the carriage ride to the market for the bus to Braşov. We stopped at the same café, and Luc greeted the waitress with a much-heightened familiarity. After assuring him I could make it to my destination, I left him to his pursuits and stood in line at the train ticket window. From my Internet research, I had learned the northbound train went through Bistriţa and Baia Mare before border transfers, then west to Vienna and finally Munich, my flight's layover city. I placed phone calls changing my seat to two days later on a flight to Chicago before exchanging my ticket for a northbound rail pass through Bistriţa and my hometown of Baia Mare.

The Rapid train rocked and rattled down the hill from Braşov and settled on another valley floor bound for another mountain pass. I displayed my crucifix prominently in the hopes of repelling any armrest neighbor, and it worked. Village after village passed by the window, the train stopping every couple towns, and the farther north, the more in need of paint and more agrarian the towns looked. Every municipality, including the smallest villages, hosted its Christian church, and even when the newer white stucco churches sprung from the ground, the older wooden relics remained.

Not all vegetation had achieved blossom at this elevation, and the air told why: still alpine cool, downright brisk. I passed a sheep farm and saw shorn wool hanging to dry on fences, the breezes giving the appearance of thick wavy blond wigs hung after a wash. Animals still did the work that Americans delegate to John Deere, with men in black woolen pants and suspenders leaning into their plows, their sons leading the animals. Steep thatch-roofed barns housed animals and their feed, and the farther north, the more rutted the roads. Great arrays of colors were displayed on clotheslines, enhanced by multihued barnyard birds. At least as many women worked their modest farms as men.

Roads were neither concrete nor blacktop, but rather hard-packed dirt with a series of ruts that horse-drawn carts negotiated hauling their loads. Pedestrians walked close to the tree-lined edges to avoid the muck, and where the mud had puddled the people walked on long wooden planks. It was not a place for tennis shoes.

Every mile north brought more dramatic views of the white-capped Carpathian Mountains. Foothills rolled to the feet of steep cliffs with dense forests holding up the snow. Houses dotted hilltops and promised enviable views, with an occasional snow pile lingering in the shadowy stretches. A uniformed attendant called out, "Bistriţa."

I looked at my GPS and saw the coordinates read within a minute of where the buyer's original phone call emanated, just a few miles southeast. It read 47.13 degrees north by 24.48 degrees east. I stood, and after consulting my phrase book, asked the attendant, *"Scuzaţi, cât timp este valabil acest bilet?"* *Excuse me, how long is this ticket valid for?*

He looked me over before inspecting the ticket. *"Doua zile."* *Two days.*

I disembarked and walked into town. Bistriţa is a very old city of about eighty thousand people in the Bargau Valley, one of the original seven-hundred-year-old Saxon settlements, and likely the town Stoker referred to as Bistritz, where Harker's journey to Dracula's Castle commences in the novel.

Here, Saxons had come from the Germanic north and established seven settlements on seven hills, the seven citadels. With them migrated their Gothic design and orderly society, a sense of civilization and a work ethic both frugal and prosperous reflected in the cities' designs and lives of the descendents. But its decay both disturbed and saddened me. There in the city's center I stopped to admire the huge Lutheran church, with its melting windows, faded red-tiled roof, and high-spired clock tower. It needed stucco work. The church reached back to the fourteenth century, so old it predated decorated corbels. In my typical American musing, I questioned when the plumbing, electricity, and toilets went in. It not only looked old, but exhausted.

It took two hours to reach the east end of town, the direction my GPS indicated toward the original phone call. There the road ran out of pavement, and although a couple miles of flat terrain pointed toward the foothills, eventually the road continued as a path winding its way up and over a rise. Looking that direction showed no indication of either town or traffic. Could my telephone readout have been inaccurate? It listed the town of Dumitra, but I could not find it on a map.

Then as I punched in the coordinates on my GPS and increased the magnification on the screen's map, it read DUMITRA-DREPTU. The name Dreptu rang a bell. It had led off the description in Stoker's original epilogue defining the path Dracula's body took to its final rest. It also appeared in the assistant's notes, Stoker's collaborator having been most emphatic about its exclusion from the novel's final text.

I walked back a couple blocks to a coffee shop and called out, *"Vorbeşte cineva aici engleză?" Does anyone here speak English?*

The din of palaver lowered as several patrons looked at me. An elderly man raised his hand and gestured me to his small round table, where he sat smoking a cigarette. As I approached, he pointed to the second chair. "I speak a little." *Zpeak.*

"Thank you, sir. I am looking for a place called Dumitra-Dreptu." When I said the name, several people stopped talking.

"Drago."

I shook my head. "No . . . Dumitra-Dreptu."

"*Mă numesc* Drago. Drago Svetkovich."

"How rude of me. *Mă numesc* Joseph Barkeley, from Chicago."

He looked me over. "What business is yours in Dumitra?"

It took a moment to decide if I wished to lie. "I just wish to see it."

"No one *just* visits Dumitra."

"Thank you for your time." I left the table and walked outside. It was no one's business but mine what my business was. But as I crossed the street to return to the center of town, I heard the man calling my way.

"Joseph!" *Yosef.* "American." I turned toward the voice. It was Drago. "I ask you this for your own protection."

I walked back to him. "Is there such a place?"

"Yes, young man, thirteen kilometers, three hours' walk over that hill." He pointed northeast. "There is coming weather, and no places to stay in Dumitra."

"What about Dreptu?"

"No." He shook his head. "This is not a place."

I unzipped my jacket to pull out my GPS. "It's only—"

"Where did you get that?" he said, pointing.

"Amazon.com," I said, shrugging and turning the device back and forth in my hand.

"No." He pointed to my chest and the crucifix. "That."

"Oh, a gift."

"You will need it." He made the sign of the cross. "There is a man who travels over the hill every afternoon about this time, a Gypsy. You will know him by his copper wares. He speaks no English; mention my name."

"Thank you, Drago."

"But you must find a place to stay; the forests are not safe. Look for signs, and be careful to watch the moon."

Superstitions run deep in Transylvania, cautions and cere-mony I once would have waved away like a fly on a lunch plate, but I registered his words and said, "A *cameră.*" A *room.*

He nodded and waved. *"La revedere."* Good-bye.

Within an hour the man with the copper pots drove by in a horse-drawn cart. I waved for him to stop and called out, "Dumitra?" When he failed to respond, I said, "Drago."

He halted his cart and without smiling pointed to the back, where I climbed in and made company with his wares.

"Mulțumesc." Thank you.

He said, *"Va fi o furtună."*

"Furtună . . . furtună . . . I'm sorry, I don't understand," I said.

He made a sound like thunder and motioned with fluttering hands that it was going to rain. He pointed to the north sky—thunderstorm approaching. I apologized for my lack of fluent Romanian, and his grunt conveyed that was just as well. I settled in for the ride on a folded woolen blanket and slipped a leg through my backpack straps.

The two horses needed no reins, as they knew their path home. As the cart climbed the first foothill, I looked back over

Bistrița and its organized row of red-tile roofs, and again was taken by how their cities end at a certain street, then turn to tree-lined fields. Such a sight might disarm an American developer, but it made sense there, for if a town is not growing, why force it at the seams?

Soon as we reached the top of the first foothill, the magnificent white Carpathian peaks came into full view to the north and east, and with it the chilled wind of refrigerated air. Farther northwest, dark clouds obscured the horizon. The horses led the cart off the two-lane road north and onto a smaller path, leaving the numbered road toward the mountain pass that the original Saxons had migrated over. Beyond was the Ukraine.

Within a quarter mile a small valley took shape with the heavy tree lining that accompanies a river, much as willows mark the path of water in a rural setting. We traveled a single-lane path now with no signs of life ahead. Within the hour we reached the valley floor, crossed a creaky wooden plank bridge, and assumed a parallel trek with the river. Overhead hundreds of birds followed the river as it slowly churned at little more than paddling speed. I had never experienced life at this pace, and was tempted to offer to exchange jobs with my driver.

Two hours of quietude passed, and we approached a small village, outskirted by the usual small family farm plots and weathered fencing and a cemetery in a clearing. Ahead smoke rose from several chimneys in the chilly air, and I smelled the wood burning.

"Dumitra?" I asked.

The driver nodded. Before reaching the village, he halted the cart to turn into his residence, a small fenced farm with a smithing shop out back. I dismounted and reached for my bags. He lifted a small horseshoe out of his pocket and passed it over a metal box at the top of a fence post and the gate slowly swung open. Several children—I counted five, ranging from small to teenage—ran to greet him. I wondered about the rest. They had the dark features and long chins of Gypsy lineage. There really is no such race as Gypsy, for it is a catchall category for the amalgam of Latin lineage around the Mediterranean and Asia Minor. The term is meant more to caste the people, and not out of respect.

Again I thanked him. *"Mulţumesc foarte mult."*

"Cu plăcere." You're welcome.

I asked about accommodations, and he pointed to a large isolated house across the river and up a steep hill with a vantage overlooking the entire village. Considering the climb, I hoped vacancy was no issue, especially with weather approaching. One of his young sons began carrying my bags that direction, and I figured porter's wages were the least I could do.

It was a two-story house with porches both upstairs and down on a plat of land terraced into the rocky hillside. One of the windows upstairs advertised a room for rent with a sign in both Romanian and German: *cameră* and *Zimmer frei*. Surrounded by black wrought iron fencing in a fleur-de-lis pattern, the gate had no lock, and the boy led me to the door and knocked, then stepped behind me. I paid him while an older woman answered. She quickly picked up on the situation, *"Cîte nopţi?"* How many nights?

"O zi." One day.

She showed me upstairs to the end of a hall, a simple room decorated in the traditional colorful geometric patterns with a single bed, washbasin, and a screen door to the porch. I nodded my approval. It was more than I had hoped for. Then she showed me the communal bathroom. Echoes down the hall suggested I might have it to myself.

"I bring food." She was a middle-aged round lady of Germanic features and thick hands, more manners than smiles, and rolled her *r*'s in the Eastern Euro fashion.

I washed and sat on a rocking chair on the porch and smelled the imminent rain. A lightning storm approached from the northwest, and while the wind suddenly blew the storm's introduction, my hostess's husband busied himself below with the farm animals in the side yard, gathering them to the barn for shelter. She returned to my room with a generous sandwich and a hot coffee, which I gratefully consumed while watching the coming storm.

Across the valley dark clouds quickly smothered the town as rain began to pelt the house. Close by lightning cracked and instant thunder boomed. I must admit that I flinched at the storm's intensity. Only after the half-hour tempest passed did I realize the price to pay for free irrigation was mud, washing a treacherous path down the hill and over the wooden plank bridge. It also left the air chilled.

From the porch I could see the village layout. In the Middle Ages, armies followed the worn paths and marched down main streets. So, unlike the States with our large front lawns and porches, residences in the corridor of war have no setbacks from the clay or cobblestone roads. Instead, long rows of houses connect with zero lot lines, homes with shuttered windows and no porches, as uninviting as any back-alley stroll. Yard entrance is gained via large double-arched wooden gates that open to a family's courtyard. Gardens are planted in the back behind wooden fences. What distinguishes houses along the row are the faded colors from one to the next, or perhaps the levels of disrepair, such as plaster, which peels from the ground up. Every roof appears to need some form of tile work.

My host joined me on the porch, his animals secured in the barn, bringing a coffee refill. He had a long nose and bushy eyebrows, a hint of hospitality in his hazel eyes.

"So you are American," he said in a heavy German accent.

"Yes, I live in Chicago."

He looked down the hall to check for his wife. "Oprah," he said, pointing a thumb in her direction.

"Her studio is down the street from my place."

"Here's to her last show." He smiled and lifted his coffee in a toast. "So, where you go from here?"

Lifting my GPS, I said, "I'm looking for Dreptu."

The hospitality left his eyes. A moment passed before he asked, "The river?"

"The town. My device says it's Dumitra-Dreptu."

"That is the Dreptu River." He pointed toward the water I had crossed to his property. "But there is no . . . place. Not anymore."

"Was there ever such a place?"

"Mister . . . ?"

"Barkeley, Joseph Barkeley."

"Herr Barkeley." He turned to see if anyone else was on the porch. "Who sent you to this place?"

"No one. I just . . . chose it on a map." I hoped he didn't know I was lying.

He spoke slowly, carefully forming his words. "This Dreptu River, it flows down from the Carpații, and then to the Danube, this way." *Zees way.* He pointed south and west. "There is . . ."

Pausing, he rubbed his chin.

"What?"

"There is . . . *was* a place called Dreptu upriver." He pointed toward the mountains to the east. "But is now only ruins." *Eez now only rueenz.*

"What was it?"

"An old monastery. Hundreds of years *nicht arbeit.*" *Not in service.*

The storm had cleared and a late afternoon fog descended to the valley, crawling down the hillside from the north.

"How far?"

"A few kilometers."

"Can I get there by walking the river?"

"This is not a place to go, Herr Barkeley. It is upriver, yes, but much danger. There are wolves, boars, and great bears in this forest." *Zis forest.*

I was perhaps the only human in the last century to have seen Stoker's references to Dreptu buried in his notes. Even Internet search engines failed to unearth any such place, not even a legend, just a note on a GPS reading. Yet that was where the original phone call came from. I wondered, *If Luc's right and the old man heads the oldest, wealthiest family in Europe, then why place a call from a nonexistent Dreptu? An elaborate precaution in the name of anonymity?* No, I was convinced otherwise.

I was certain there was something to the place, and recalling the words of Doug Carli, "You don't leave things like this to chance. You wanna do big deals, you don't leave the small stuff on the table. That's why it's called due diligence."

Besides, to fall two miles short after having journeyed six thousand seemed cowardly to me. What would I think when I was back in Chicago, regretting that I was too timid to follow the central clue to understanding the missing chapter? This was going to be my only chance, perhaps in a lifetime, to see the place. I had several hours before nightfall. I went to pack for the walk.

"Herr Barkeley." My host shook a finger at me. "Beware the dark."

"I'll be careful."

"*Die Todten reiten schnell* . . . faster than you." *The dead travel fast.*

9

s I walked through the village, fog rolled along the ground as if being swept, and I did my best to avoid shoe-hungry mud puddles by walking atop long wooden planks that served as sidewalks in springtime. Droplets fell from spring's early leaves as I passed under branches. The rain had cooled an already chilly day.

Dolls, the only life signs in some places, were displayed in windows to show potential suitors that an eligible girl lived there. Everywhere the smell of burning wood and cooking reminded me of my early childhood. And just as in my childhood, dogs barked and snarled and cats recoiled. Parents called their children and pets and hustled to close their gates at the sight of me. Another group of children bowed their heads and made signs of the cross as I passed. An elderly woman saw me and dropped the buckets she carried and began praying. I recall somewhere in the litany of my childhood superstitions that it was unlucky to be photographed holding empty buckets, and rural villagers associated strangers with cameras. I showed her my empty hands, but she still looked away.

At the east end of town, just before crossing the small river, there stood an old wooden church with a tall steeple topped by an Eastern cross. Inside a solemn priest stared through faded windows; he, too, blessed himself.

Once past the church and over the wooden bridge, I found a lone house that stood separated from the others, the only structure east of the water. It seemed an ordinary dwelling, notably more Western in design, all white with a porch and a simple cross on the front door. Its grass was neatly trimmed, and a healthy herb and vegetable garden flourished behind a wooden fence. Walking by, I saw a woman sweeping the porch. She had middle-aged Roma features and dressed in the traditional way of wool aprons, or *catrinţe*, over a black skirt and covered with a light wool jacket. I noticed her boots, the medieval *opinci*, leather laced to the leg around wool felt. Our eyes met, but rather than turning away, she did a double take and pushed her head scarf back behind her ears. I was far enough away that I could not read precisely her features, but she looked to be concentrating on me.

Suddenly uncomfortable, I turned away. As I did so, I heard someone call out, *Can you hear me?*

Granted, I know I had not slept much the night before, but this spoken message seemed soundless. By that, I mean that it came into my head without entering through my ears. Without question it was a woman's voice. I stopped and looked around for whoever spoke to me, but no one was within earshot.

Go back where you came from.

I looked back to the village. The street was deserted except for the priest who had come out of his church and stood praying as he looked at me. In my mind, an image flashed of looking back after crossing the Acheron. I wheeled and looked again for the Gypsy woman on the porch of her isolated house, but she had disappeared and her front window was now shuttered.

I had overstepped reality's boundary. That voice you take for granted in your head is your welcome friend . . . right up until the time it has a companion. I stood waiting for another message, looking for some woman nearby. But finding no one, after a suitable silence, I turned toward the forest. Just two miles from my destination, I told myself, I could not turn back now.

On a two-rut path I walked, the absence of footprints in the mud suggesting this was not the locals' direction of choice. As best as I could I stayed to the bisecting hump between the ruts. Deeper into the forest, the trees—beech, oak, and sycamores—clasped their tops together to form a canopy and filtered the leaning afternoon sun. Continuing east, I caught glimpses of the ambling river to my right, and took several side trips to the waterway to scout ahead. Across the water the land rose to a series of rocky cliffs obscured by fog.

Can the monastery be on the hill hidden by clouds? I wondered.

My GPS suggested otherwise, and I continued east. An hour passed as the path steepened and the river churned from an elevation change. Finally I reached the end of the two-lane path as it circled back on itself like a cul-de-sac before confronting a rock barrier. Carved into the rock were a dozen steps, flanked with a flimsy wrought iron railing, suggesting civilization ahead. I figured the monastery must be close.

Again I walked to the river's edge to scout ahead, but only saw dense forest lining the banks and an impassable canyon wall beyond. I looked up at some commotion and saw flocks of birds flying straight east. With the incline came more dense fog, now hiding the treetops. I caught sight of my first pine trees and realized it must be a thousand feet higher than the village. No wonder I was tired, for I had been climbing. The GPS coordinates now told me I had reached my destination.

Just a little more, I thought, *then get back before dark.* As soon as I stepped foot on the first rock I heard the sound of an animal scurry above. Momentarily I froze and looked around. Though isolated, I did not feel alone.

Continuing up at a mild climb, the path emerged after a hundred yards to an open field. There was just enough light to see a footpath across its mildly undulating terrain that reentered the forest a quarter mile or so across. I picked up my pace across the open field and into the forest. With every turn in the woods the terrain closed in on three sides, until I found myself in the shadows of canyon walls. I looked at my GPS again, touched the backlight button, and realized it had become dark outside. Just a quarter mile more and I vowed to turn around.

From higher ground came a yipping noise: a single dog. Or possibly a wolf.

I was just about to retreat—with intentions of returning at sunup—when a breeze momentarily lifted the fog, revealing another clearing ahead, and within it the outline of a massive structure, a fortress with huge stone walls at least twenty feet high. I stood stunned. It was a side wall so long, I had to twist my neck to see its length. Corner towers stood at both ends of the wall, supported by a flanking tower at the halfway point, connected by an uncovered parapet wall. All seemed dark within the structure.

A howl descended from the fog above. Canine in origin again, but sounding more urgent than before, much closer than the first, and not a yip.

From where I stood, the wall looked to be at least two hundred feet in length. Another breeze lifted the fog long enough to allow me sight of the structure inside the walls: a single tower several stories taller than the wall. I walked toward the corner tower and saw that the wall joined at ninety degrees. *Must be a rectangle,* I reasoned. Another corner tower stood equidistant at the far end and it occurred to me they looked like giant chessmen, with bishops in the corners, rooks as the flanking towers, and a king in the courtyard. Gray dominated its appearance; dark, lifeless gray. Yet the structure did not fit the description of ruins, which suggest a certain abandoned disrepair. No, this did not feel empty.

As I walked around the front, there were what appeared to be a set of wooden doors, shaped like the pointed-arched equilaterals at Castel Bran. I approached.

A twig snapped behind me and I quickly turned my head toward the forest. Nothing.

Continuing toward the door, I noticed it was set under a Roman arch of stone. There was no writing on the corbels or front door, and if this was a monastery, then why were there no crosses?

Suddenly it fell upon me, some sort of animal. Before my senses perceived it, I was knocked to the ground and on my back with my arms trying to shield my face from blows. My first thought was a grizzly bear. Claws scraped my front, and it bit my arm. Its strength was overwhelming. A horrible growling sound and the smell . . . awful. Another scrape across my front, and suddenly the beast stopped.

I dared open an eye, but only saw a mouth of snapping teeth. It made a most unhappy sound, a growl mixed with a hiss. And as suddenly as it had ambushed me, so it rose to its feet, two feet . . . and disappeared into the fog.

What was that? I thought. Its jaw looked inhuman, but what little glimpse I got of its body did appear human. It was not canine, as the previous sounds suggested. Was it some kind of bear that I had startled? Could my adrenaline have caused my eyes to deceive me?

Terror replaced my curiosity, and I grabbed my backpack from the ground and stood to leave. It was then that pain registered across my arms and torso, and I checked to see if I was intact. That's when I heard noises coming from all directions. I could not see far in the fog, but I did see red eyes. Several pairs. Nor could I make out their features, but they looked the size of adult men, standing erect, with their hands moving, flexing as if stretching their fingers. Almost imperceptibly they moved in closer.

Instinctively I took the crucifix from around my neck and held it up, turned in a circle, and heard them react as if disgusted. A couple of them spit.

Then, from back in the forest, a voice boomed: *"Tu nu aparții aici!"* *You do not belong here!*

"Don't worry, I'm leaving."

Quickly I walked the direction I had come, crucifix held high overhead and darting my eyes side to side into the woods. From the cliffs above I heard several canines howling, deliberately betraying my position. Back across the open field, down the steps, and onto the two-rut path, my legs kept pumping.

If the men were pursuing me now, I did not hear them, but I did hear the howls in the distance and several phantom noises in the woods. I hit a dense patch of fog and could barely see the path at my feet, bumped into a couple trees, and continued on. I kept stumbling on the uneven ground and prayed I was going the right way. Nothing looked familiar in the dark.

When the last turn of the path revealed the village, I broke into a run, crossed over the bridge, and did not stop until I reached the front of the church. There I fell to my knees on the front step to say a prayer of deliverance.

"Thank you, God, thank you."

A hand touched my right shoulder.

10

I swung my arm around in defense and struck a man on his
shoulder. When he pulled back I recognized the priest and
offered my apology. *"Scuzaţi-ma, va rog."*

"I speak English," he said with a heavy Eastern Euro accent. He looked middle-aged Slavic and dressed in the black
robes of Orthodoxy, without the round cap. He kept a clean-
shaven face. "I am Father Andrew. What happened to you?"

"I was attacked by some . . . animal out there."

"Let me see." He shone a lantern over me and moved my chin
side to side, inspecting my neck. "Anything broken?"

"I don't think so." I opened my jacket and noticed a startling
amount of blood across my chest.

"You had protection," he said.

Only then did it occur to me that whatever attacked me had torn through my clothing and some skin, only to stop when it saw the relic that Arthur had sent me.

To protect.

"Come," he said, "there is a woman who will help clean your wounds." *Voonz.*

As the priest started walking toward the bridge, I halted. He turned to me and said, "It is okay. We go here." He pointed to the lone house on the other side where the middle-aged Gypsy woman had looked at me earlier. I walked across the bridge and felt a shudder of fear with each creak of the wooden planks, and knew firsthand the fearful looks owned by the superstitious villagers. Yes, I now understood them.

The priest knocked on the door and spoke as the woman emerged. *"El s-a muscat un caine."* He's been bitten by a dog.

I greeted her. *"Sărut mâna."*

We went inside where the woman's tidy house held decorations of traditional Romanian fashion: whitewashed walls with colorful fabrics and an icon corner along the east living room wall. Immediately she retrieved a wool blanket from a closet and laid it on the wooden plank floor, then covered it with a clean sheet. I lay on it while she washed her hands and the priest withdrew.

From a cabinet she removed several items: scissors, cleaning fluid, bandages, and a sewing kit. She snipped through what remained of my bloody shirt and asked, *"Cum vă numiți?"* What is your name?

"Mă numesc Joseph Barkeley."

"Bine aţi venit." Welcome. "Sonia."

She dressed as the nuns did, in layers of redundant modesty. Her collarbone-length hair was as black as the priest's shirt, but giving way to random strands of gray. Like most women of these rural parts, she wore no makeup. Her skin suggested somewhere south of the Danube and managed to avoid the common ravages of deep lines, just a couple crow's-feet. The shape of her dark eyes suggested east, somewhere the Mongols had conquered, and gave the impression she had seen much sadness in her life. Lastly, I noticed her manicured hands and slender fingers, out of place in the land of peasantry.

"I have a million questions," I said.

Sonia carefully removed the crucifix from my neck, kissed it, and set it aside. She stared at my face while preparing to clean my wounds, and I heard the female voice in my head again.

Do not speak in the company of others.

I looked quizzically at her. *Is that you?* I thought.

She nodded. *Your first question involves your own sanity.*

Yes. I yelped when the alcohol-soaked rag introduced itself to my skin. The stinging cure felt worse than the wound.

I know who you are, and these are not dog bites. She turned my chin side to side, also inspecting my neck. *Do you know what attacked you?*

"No," I said aloud. I suspected what it might be since it looked like the drawing in Mara's journal, but one does not utter the word *vampire* while in the company of strangers in the Transylvanian backcountry.

She pulled back and glared at me for speaking.

Sorry, go ahead.

Sonia continued cleaning and prepared a salve for gauze and bandages. *Those who attacked you are evil, an eternal foe of all that is good.* She wrapped me with tape. *I did not need to see your neck to know that you have been selected.*

Selected for what? I asked.

A great mission.

I don't understand.

You have come home to right a great wrong. She handed me a towel to wrap as a shirt. *You will need wisdom.* Next she returned the crucifix to my neck and laid her hand on it. *And you will need this.*

Is it enough protection?

Depends where you are going.

She went to the next room and retrieved an old coat to replace the torn one. Taking a deep breath as if to smell it one last time, she handed it to me with a wave and made a quick sign of blessing.

"*Mulţumesc,*" I said.

The coat smelled old, but not unpleasant. It fit with room for layers and had a tad more sleeve than arm. One might describe it as a barn coat with a button front, the collar and lapel cuts not trending with recent fashion.

"Come," the priest said. He had returned without my noticing. "You may sleep in the church."

"My things are at the inn."

"That door will not be open tonight."

I had so many questions as I looked at her. *How can I thank you? You must come back.*

I wondered if I had heard her right. First she warned me to be gone. Then, after I failed to heed her, she insisted that I return. Her eyes, wiser and older than her face's appearance, sought my own. Her gaze pleaded wordlessly that I mind her this time.

Come back here? I asked.

You must return to this place. This very ground holds the answers you seek. Go now. Complete your transaction and return to me. Before she closed the door, I heard, *Many lives depend on your completing your mission.*

The priest walked me to the church and showed me inside. "They will not come in here."

Many nights can I count sleeping on the hardwood pews of churches, and after my adrenaline and elevated heartbeat subsided I slept as if embalmed. I awoke to the sound of the priest opening the creaking church door.

"It is time for you to go now." The priest handed me a crust of bread and water and my traveling articles that he must have retrieved from the inn.

I thanked him and asked to pass along my gratitude to the woman who had cared for me. He acknowledged with a nod and gave a blessing as I left: "Return to the ways of *Gott*."

I caught an early cart ride back to Bistriţa with the Gypsy. As we departed the village, several locals carried bundles of wood in the direction of the cemetery and piled it up in a clearing. I asked the driver about their activity.

"*Un mare incendiu.*" *Big fire.* He waved his hands to indicate a large fire.

"Festival?"

"*Festival, da.*"

"*Când?*" *When?*

"*Deseară.*" *Tonight.*

As much as I wished to stay for it, I equally wanted to leave. Not the most peaceful of trips jostling a muddy path and crosswinds, every jolt jabbed my wounds in protest of my decision to explore the previous night. My thoughts turned to the cautious words of my brother, and his warnings of what I might see. When I had pressed him years ago for specifics, he looked uncomfortable until finally responding with, "I've never told you anything you would not believe. I'm not going to start now."

He never again spoke of his time in Romania, but perhaps he had seen something that cannot be explained without requiring a sanity check. It is one thing to tickle the tail of the daft dragon, but something completely different to tell someone of it.

Arriving at Bistriţa, I thanked my driver. I hustled to the train station and made for my hometown, Baia Mare, a city about a hundred miles northwest. The locals pronounce it as one word: *baya-mah-day*. A sizable city of 150,000 built along the Săsar River in Romania's oldest mining area, it was the reason for my detoured plans—a visit to my birthplace and my mother's grave.

Even as I sought to put all that had happened in Dreptu out of my mind, I experienced eager anticipation of homecoming, as well as anguish over how things should have been.

My eyes turned to the landscape, where stunning green and gold foothills heave to the feet of the snowcapped Carpathians. Baia Mare was built as a fortress city to fend off Turks, and its oldest house, cornerstone 1440, still stands on the east side of the town square. I walked there from the train station and wondered if any of the sights might look familiar. When I walked into the square and saw Stephen's Tower, a twelve-story Gothic watch-tower with a steeple of green patina, the memory of holding my parents' hands returned. It seemed like someone else's life, a stranger's memory. I moved on.

In an open-air market I stopped and purchased two shirts, tra-ditional Romanian cotton, white with embroidered patterns, careful not to select two identical styles, and put one on under my new coat. The image in the mirror suggested the local I might have been become. And in that moment of piteous retro-spect, I sank to a place not frequented since the days living in the convent basement. But not for long, because at that moment God favored me with a visit from two homeless street dwellers. I placed alms in their hands and continued on with my brother's voice in my head and recharged gratitude: *Someone's got it worse.*

En route to city hall, I spotted a shop that sold religious arti-facts and stopped to look for something to accessorize the shirt I'd picked up for my brother. Soon as I walked into the store, an elderly man behind the counter did a double take as if he recog-nized me, and quickly shuffled toward me. It was the crucifix he pointed to. *"Vă rog; pot să văd?" Could I please see that?*

I asked him if he spoke English. When he nodded, I told him it was not for sale. He waved his arms as if I had misunderstood him and hurried toward the front door, locked it, and turned the OPEN sign to CLOSED.

"Please?" he asked. "It will not leave your sight."

I followed him behind the counter to his tools and lifted it over my head, presenting it with two hands. Gently he took it and moved his hand over it, then turned it over.

"Save and protect," he said. "The *drac*'s feet."

"It was a gift," I said.

"This is *argint*, silver, from these very hills. Not the highest quality." He placed it under the scope. "But *eez* very old."

I knew the area had the country's oldest mines, but the silver had played out centuries back. They used it to mint the country's first coins six hundred years ago. It was the mines that brought my metallurgist father to the area.

"This is the only one I have seen with a ruby set in the middle." He looked closer. "*Scuzaţi*, this is not a ruby." He put it under a refractometer. "Single refractive, one-point . . . seven-six. This gem is a . . . red spinel."

"They are not found here," I said.

He shook his head. "Africa or Southeast Asia, usually."

He secured it under the magnifier to look for inclusions, the small irregularities that often map its origin. "It is oval faceted, polished, not cut. Not as valuable as rubies, *natürlich*, but a fine spinel like this one is much rare . . . flaws fewer than rubies. Before optics often mistaken for rubies, as this might have been." He found something on a page that he cross-referenced several times. "They are found in Burma, Tanzania, Madagascar, and I believe this came from Badakhshan mines of Afghanistan."

"Ottoman traders?"

He nodded. "Centuries ago the king dispensed them as gifts or traded to Ottoman sultans for protection."

"It came in a wooden presentation case," I said. "Could this have been a treaty gift?"

He nodded. "Is possible."

"Is the *argint* the same as the minted coins?" I asked. If so, that would place this between 1431 and 1476.

"I am most positive. Tell me of this presentation case."

"A solid box, black walnut, with a carving on top: a dragon's tail wrapped around the bottom of a cross."

"*Drac,*" he said.

"Yes, a dragon."

"The Order of the Dragon." He rubbed his chin. "My young friend," he said, removing his reading glasses, "you may . . . I say with great reservation, of course, *may* have a rare treasure, one that belongs in a museum. The stone and material used to make this tells where it came from, and the scribing tells who it was intended for. This was very possibly an emperor's gift to Vlad Dracul."

"The dates fit." I reached for the crucifix and returned it to my neck. "Don't worry, it will be in a museum very soon."

I purchased an ornate Old Believer cross for my brother and promised to let the merchant know where the treasure ultimately would land, assuring him it would remain in the country where it belonged. Then on to city hall and less pleasant tasks.

The government building was not hard to find, as it was the largest in town. In America it is the people who work and not the government, but this building served as a stark reminder that the Romanian people still believed they were granted the opportunity to conduct business only as allowed by the government. Lines were to be expected, along with the word *no* and the blank stare that was residue of Iron Curtain oxidation.

An hour's wait found me standing in front of the guardian of menial favors, a woman roughly my age. I asked if anyone spoke English in the hall of public records. She pointed to another line.

When I looked and saw the line was longer than the one I was in, I said, *"Orfan."*

She pointed at me. *"Tu?"*

"Da."

She walked me personally to the elevator and to the third floor, offered me coffee, and introduced me to an older man who could help locate where my mother was buried. I turned to thank her and noticed she was dabbing her eyes with a tissue. We nodded to each other with the understanding shared by those with similar deprived starts.

After a half-hour search, the man returned and asked me, "Do you know where the wooden church is just north of the city?"

"All Saints?" I asked.

He nodded.

"If it is still there, then yes."

"It has not changed. She should be there."

I caught a cab there, and as I suspected the driver would not wait the requested five minutes, nor did he promise a return pickup. He did not even pull up to the church, but instead dropped me off at the bottom of the hill and left me to walk the remaining quarter mile up the drive, a dirt path with two ruts centered by a grass strip, the type of drive not used enough to maintain. The old wooden church rested on the hill's knob with a bucolic view north and east to the Carpathians and south to the city, covering about an acre and surrounded by weathered wood fencing. The structure looked to be elderly, probably early eighteenth century, with the single eave of the smaller churches and no entrance porch. A solid plain tower was crowned with a tall steeple, shaped like a witch's hat. The shutters hung crookedly, and broken windows let in the elements. The entire structure needed painting, not just the siding but the doorways and traditional trim of twisted rope and wolf's-fang-motif carved molding. The building's cornerstone confirmed my guess—1714—and listed the name of the original settlement, Riv Dom.

I went inside. With each step the wooden floors announced the visitor. Whatever wooden altar or podium was in the front had been removed, along with the doors reserved for the priests under the chancel. Gaps in the side walls let in streams of sunlight, which long ago had faded the painted fresco walls. The pews sat void of books or blankets, the telling indicators of a church no longer active. I looked up at the south chancel wall to the mural showing God's outstretched hands delivering His Son to the world, then turned and looked at the north wall with its painting of the damned crossing the River of Fire with arms reaching back toward the south wall, the souls too late to pray for.

Outside, vines grew over an old stone fence. A small arched

wooden gate lay on the ground. I stepped through and into a graveyard filled with uneven rows of Eastern crosses marked with Slavic and Romanian names dating back two centuries and more. No one had tended to the vegetation for months, perhaps as long ago as All Saints' Day, when the dead receive homage and Christian cemeteries fill with visitors. Where the growth covered the names, I moved it aside looking for either my mother's married or maiden name, Barkeley or Petrescu.

By the time I had inspected half the grave markers, I realized that I might be looking in the wrong section. Superstition held that suicides and murder victims become agitated ghosts who traveled certain nights in search of victims, and such are buried in segregation.

I looked to the north and saw an internal gate with conquering vegetation, and it was a task to clear before I could read the sign: PADOC DE BLESTEMATĂ. *The Paddock of the Damned.* I should have figured that out from the mural inside, for it was behind the north wall. I looked around at her neighbors and read their headstones. She lay amongst the suicides and tortured minds. I felt sad these souls might not lie in peace.

Finally I found it—BARKELEY. How long a journey to stand on this ground? Miles to match my tears.

It was in the paddock's far corner, closest to where the fence turned, a raised sarcophagus perhaps a foot above ground with a stone casing and a chiseled rock resting atop. More than I expected. Translated, the inscription read, *Lucia Petrescu Barkeley, a Pierced Heart from the Angel of Death.*

I was not prepared for the torrent of emotions, a battering

from all things as they should have been, but ultimately were not. Aloud I cursed my father's name and wished him the hottest seat in hell amongst the cruelest of tyrants. Oh, there was no room for misinterpretation, for when he took her he took the lives of at least two more. Not one sunset has passed that I did not contemplate what might have been, not just for myself but also for my brother.

I had always hoped to avoid that level of sorrow. I laid a hand on the tomb and sobbed. I don't know how long I knelt there, but at least an hour passed. My throat and face hurt from grieving, and when I found the strength I stood to find some water. But when I turned, there was a large man standing at the paddock gate with fist raised and a finger pointing my direction.

His voiced boomed: *"Pleacă la dracu!"* Go to hell!

"My mama," I said.

"Eu ştiu cine eşti." I know who you are. He was dressed in caretaker's clothes, with Magyar features and a heavy accent. *"Sămînţa rea." Bad seed.*

"I'll leave soon."

Solemnly, he nodded. *"Îl insulţi pe Dumnezeu fiind aici." You insult God by being here.*

My glare sent him away, and I stayed a while longer, eventually walking back to Baia Mare. By the time I passed through the city square it was dark and a great bonfire was burning, surrounded by revelers, some of them dressed in witch costumes. By the welcoming signs I realized that I had arrived in time for the celebration of *Walpurgisnacht.*

11

When I returned to Chicago I found several phone messages and e-mails reminding me that I was behind in my work. But instead of tending to obligations, I found myself mired in the swamp of memory. I remember when my brother returned from his trip to the Vatican and his subsequent detour to the homeland, he kept a distant look for weeks. I kept trying to pull him back, but all my usual jokes and jabs failed to lift the corners of his mouth. I only hoped that he had not seen all that I had.

Apparently I had taken on the same look as my brother, because as Mara opened her door, she greeted me with the traditional kisses on my cheeks, a different kind of welcome, and said, "You no longer wear the skeptic's face. Come in."

I declined her offer of tea and went directly to her library and sat. "I managed a meeting with the buyer."

"Yes." *Jyezz.* "I am surprised he showed himself."

"He didn't really show himself—he stayed back in the shadows, told me to approach him." I described the castle and the setting, and his quick departure into the shadows.

"So he was close enough to see your heat and smell you."

I nodded and described my discussions with the buyer about the missing chapters and how it appeared Stoker had an assistant help with his research.

"Whatever you told him has mobilized the families to action. How did they leave it with you?"

"He wants me to act as his buying agent to keep the manuscript from going to auction."

"What was in the missing epilogue?" she asked. I hesitated, and she seemed to read my mind. "You saw things that disturb you, things I warned you of. Now you are unsure how much to say."

I acknowledged her observation with a nod. There was much to cover, and although my instincts told me to trust her, I did not know how much I could say without appearing round the bend. "A great battle scene and directions to a burial site."

"Can you recall them?"

"They were cryptic and referenced several landmarks. The journey started in Dreptu and—"

"Dreptu?" A man's voice interrupted me from the next room. I knocked the chair backward when I stood and saw an elderly man fill the doorway. He repeated, "Did you say Dreptu?"

Mara stood and said, "Joseph Barkeley, this is Mr. Bena, Alexandru Bena." The elder held out a hand. "He asked to meet with you."

He had an elder's eyes, dark and recessed, but his skin and salt-and-pepper hair looked healthy enough. Alexandru wore the lace-up shoes of a foreigner and stood a solid but slender six feet tall with the firm grip of a craftsman.

I remained quiet, not intending to share my information with someone I did not know, as much as I wanted to get answers from Mara. In the house of the Gypsy woman, Sonia, I'd had a long list of questions and felt open to ask them, as the events had occurred right outside her door and seemed all too real. But here I felt the need to guard my knowledge. No matter how real, it seemed the greater the distance from the events, the greater the need for discretion. No wonder Mara was the way she was.

"Mr. Joseph, please." Alexandru pointed to the chair, and I returned it upright and sat. He spoke with an accent spawned in the Balkans. "By way of introduction, I would be the other bidder at the auction."

Mara nodded. "I have known Mr. Bena forever. All that I have I owe to him."

"Now," Alexandru said, "please tell me of this epilogue."

"Well, I'm not sure I can. I'm under contract."

The two looked at each other before Alexandru turned back toward me and spoke. "Young man, you've been chosen."

I thought back to Sonia's parting words, the look in her eyes. "So I've heard," I said at last.

"But you do not know what you are facing. I do." He crossed his legs and straightened his wedding ring. "That family is the subject of Mr. Stoker's novel, and there are things in that display that they wish to keep to themselves."

Much as Luc had predicted. I nodded. "Things I've seen."

"Names, locations . . ." Alexandru nodded in return. "You said the missing epilogue describes a battle scene and directions to a grave."

I hesitated before acknowledging. "It matches the prologue's description of where the villain's wife is buried."

"Do you remember the name on the tomb?" he asked.

"Countess Dolingen of Gratz."

Again Mara and Alexandru looked at each other, this time with eyes widened. He continued, "You mentioned Dreptu."

Once more I paused and decided to keep my encounter at the monastery to myself. "Yes. That is where the journey began."

Mara looked at Alexandru. "Is there such a place?"

He took a deep breath before answering. "Yes." Again he looked at me and asked, "Did you go there?"

"No," I lied, "but there was a Dreptu River east of Bistriţa."

Their ensuing silence suggested disbelief, or perhaps they realized I did not want to discuss it. Alexandru continued, "When you return to complete your transaction, this place of legend needs to be verified."

"I'm not sure I will be returning."

Mara drew a gasping breath and began to speak just as her guest raised a calming hand and said, "This is a very . . . dangerous family, as you have already surmised, my young friend, and they will stop at nothing to protect the relics of their ancestors. You have already laid eyes on what they need."

I did not need clarification of what that meant. I wished I had known before going to Philadelphia the first time.

"My family," Alexandru said, "has been at odds with that family for a very long time."

"Then why don't you approach the Stoker family to buy the manuscript yourself?"

"No," he said. "That would risk exposing both of you." He pointed to me and Mara as he spoke.

Mara added, "The seller would know that there are competing interests, and it would surely go to auction."

"Neither family can afford such publicity."

He had a point. "But right now I'm the one with the biggest risk."

"I am prepared to make a contract with you, Mr. Joseph."

I gave a prompting nod.

"It is very rare; indeed, it has been over a century since a human has been invited into the affairs of that family. You have been chosen because of your unique talents, and you need to return there to complete the transaction."

Again, as with Sonia, talk of the transaction. I sighed, audibly, I realized.

He hesitated.

"I'm listening."

Alexandru smiled; not an honest smile, but that of a player

who's calling your hand—correctly. "You are listening to hear what is in it for you."

"Among other things."

"I am prepared to match whatever fee the family has offered you."

I was not prepared to divulge that amount. "What would I need to do, exactly?"

Mara cut in. "The only way to penetrate their defenses is from the inside."

"And you are being invited inside," Alexandru said. "Find out where they live, *all* of them—where they sleep, how many subjects they have. See if any of their wives surface. Do a good job for them, get as close as you can. See how many heads pop up."

"And then what?"

"Someone will approach you and refer to me by name. Tell him when and where you wish to be picked up and removed."

"I don't plan on being there very long."

Again Mara broke in: "It might not be up to you."

"We have people there who will help protect you," Alexandru said.

"How do I know that to be true?"

He lifted his right hand toward me, palm up, and said, "They have already told me they saw the young man with the spinel crucifix."

I was reduced to silence.

"Mr. Joseph," he said, "the knowledge you possess places you in danger. You are in more danger here than there."

Alexandru excused himself to walk outside. I whispered to Mara, "I saw one of the creatures."

"A Common," she asked in statement form.

"It did this," I said, unbuttoning my shirt to show part of the wound on my chest. "I don't know what it was. I left immediately. Is there more than one kind?"

"The Nobles are the breeders," Mara said, leaning in to inspect. "The Commons are the offspring born with no reproductive parts."

I nodded.

"This creature," Mara said, "let you live. Why?"

I shrugged, keeping thoughts of the crucifix to myself. Considering all that had happened, I continued to wear it.

"Nobles," she said. Her look told me that I knew the answer.

"Nobles?"

"Nobles—the ones born with parts. But since no one has seen any female breeders in centuries, there are no new breeders."

"Are the Commons as dangerous as the Nobles?"

"Of course. They are the warriors who protect the Nobles. But don't worry," Mara said as she pointed to my crucifix. "So long as you wear that, they will not harm you unless ordered to."

As I prepared to leave, she reached behind a stack of books on her top bookshelf and handed me an untitled journal bound in a Victorian-patterned fabric with the initials G.A. written on the inside cover. It was handwritten, with several old photos and a couple letters. I recognized the paper from the Aachen region, circa the 1880s and placed it in my jacket pocket.

"Take this," she said. "You will need it to do your research."

I recalled the first time I had driven out to Mara's cabin to deliver a rare German printing of *The Vampyre*. She entertained me with tales of vampire hunters who might be able to glean clues of locations from the book. I had paid little attention, intent on hurrying the check to the bank. This time I asked, "Is he . . . ?"

"Yes," she said, as if to read my thoughts. A hunter.

I left with as many questions as I had arrived with, plus a few more, and promised to return with details.

❧

Doug Carli had left several phone messages and said he would wait for me, and after the long drive in from southern Wisconsin I arrived to find him alone in his office after hours.

"Come in, come in," Doug said, and closed the door behind me. "Please." He pointed to a chair across from his desk.

"Thanks," I said, though I'm certain I didn't look particularly grateful. "Your message mentioned due diligence."

"I took the liberty of calling my guy in Zurich about your man Ardelean there, and he did not want to talk over a landline. I got a cell call the next day, and this guy said the family you are deal-ing with is old Euro money."

"I assumed that."

"No, I mean *old*. As in older than the Swiss bank itself."

That did not surprise me.

"Joseph, that means their wealth predates the entire banking and currency system. Whoever this is," Doug said, looking over his reading glasses and wagging a finger, "do not cross them or screw up this deal."

"No mistakes. Appreciate it."

"I also made a call to one of my clients, a heavy hitter at the Field Museum." By that, Doug meant someone on the top tier of the donor list. "Guy knows the curator at the Rosenbach. Got him in touch with the family's selling agent."

It made me uneasy to think an outside party was being alerted to this transaction. "Did you need to do that?" I asked. I'm sure I sounded annoyed, because his response was a notch higher on the volume knob.

"This is how you get things *done*." He said it in such a way as to distinguish *done* from *trying*. "If you can pick up the phone and make things happen to conclude a transaction before walking into negotiations, that's getting things *done*."

I shrugged and nodded.

"As opposed to doing nothing and hoping that when you get there it works out for the best."

"So what did you do?" I asked.

"Found out what the agent thinks it will take to close the deal without letting it get to auction."

"And the curator?"

"He's not in on the deal."

I nodded. "Good—didn't want to soil a good referral source."

"So when you were here before, you figured a million or so at Christie's. He thinks the family is looking for twice that. Your buyer in for that much?"

I nodded. "Yeah."

"How much did he authorize?"

I held up four fingers.

"Perfect. What we have is the ideal scenario to consummate a deal—equally motivated buyer and seller. So here's how you play it, Joseph: You offer two-point-six . . ." He stopped. "You tracking?"

I was reminded how weary and worn I must have appeared. I acknowledged with a nod. "Two-six."

"You offer two-point-six and let the agent run that by the family. He'll suggest that he thinks he can get more. At six hundred large, he knows that you're halfway raised, and he'll talk them into three million two."

I was thinking four. "What about the rest?"

"Joey, *stunod*, your deal is for four mil. That's what you wire to the agent's escrow account. This is not like a real estate purchase, where the seller gets a copy of the escrow settlement sheet from the title company; the seller just gets a wire out of escrow."

"So . . . the rest falls to the agent for pushing through the deal."

"You're a quick study." He pointed a finger at me. "And a couple nice donations to the museums will go a long way toward your next referral."

"How nice is nice?"

"Fifty should do it." I must have looked blank, because he clarified, "Large. That would be fifty large."

My life was simple before that phone call came in, just a merchant dealing with markups and keeping dust off the jackets, tending to a closed shop with plenty of time to read. "Would I be rude to ask where your take comes from all this, Doug?"

"You don't worry about that, my friend, but I'd really like to hold that manuscript in my hands, just once. A treasure for the ages, you know."

That I would not be able to pull off unless he wanted to accompany me to Philadelphia the next day. "I'm going directly from the museum back to Europe the day after transacting, so you may have to go there if you want to hold it."

Doug shrugged. "One more thing," he said, pointing his nose down and staring over his reading glasses. "When I said family, I mean you're dealing with . . . a *family*."

I looked at him for clarification.

"What I mean is, you already made your deal. You have to go through with it."

Don't I know it . . .

I thanked Doug as heartily as I could and left.

My last stop for the day was to visit my brother, who was reading in the rectory from the front of the book—must have been the Old Testament. I didn't know if he would have a fatherly scowl for my decision or be happy to see me, and I was pleased to see him excited as I held out his gift bag. But when he looked at my face, he quickly placed the offering on the table.

"You have the widow's stare," he said. "Come in, tell me what you saw."

"*Padoc de Blestemată.*" *The Paddock of the Damned.*

He nodded. "So you met the caretaker, too."

"Yeah." I accepted Bernhardt's offer of bottled water. "A bunch of memories came flooding back in, none of them nice."

"Eight years later and I still see that place." He looked down and shook his head. "When I was there I stopped in front of an orphanage. There were a dozen or so little boys, maybe five or six years old, with their little fingers gripping a chain-link fence. They were naked and in diapers." He choked up. "I was too ashamed to stop and see if I could help."

"What could you have possibly done?"

"Same thing someone did for us once. But I failed, Joseph. I failed my test."

"You can't save everyone. Especially in that country."

He nodded. "Are you okay?"

"Yeah." I paused. "Lot of strange things happen there."

"Easy to see why those people are so superstitious."

"Yeah." I drained the water bottle, and for the first time in my life I had an off-limits topic separating me and my brother. I started to ask him if he had any other strange encounters there, but instead pointed to his gift bag to change the topic. "Go ahead."

He spread the handles apart and looked in, and the smile returned to his face. He unwrapped the cross. "Old Believer."

"I thought it fit."

"A treasure from home. A good memory."

I nodded. "The square, at Stephen's Tower."

He turned it over and over before kissing it, and his eyes watered.

"And something to wear," I said.

He reached in the bag and unwrapped the embroidered shirt

and held it up in front of him. "It's perfect. I've been invited to a Serbian wedding out in Mundelein next month. I shall wear it to the party."

"Careful, Berns, some girl will ask you to dance."

"Girls ask more than that these days, Joseph." He pointed toward his Bible. "I was just reading Sodom and Gomorrah again."

"The part where the whole town's doin' the lowdown, or the part where the lady turns to salt?"

"The part where God agrees that if there's only one righteous man . . . Where did you get *that*?"

He saw my crucifix after I unzipped my jacket. "A gift from the buyer."

"Saint Olga." He reached his hand out, wanting to see it. "This is magnificent. Nice ruby."

"A spinel, actually."

"Amazing." He looked closer and turned it over. "Serve and protect."

"Maybe the police should wear these."

"This is really old."

I dummied up. "You were saying?"

"Oh . . . yes. I've been thinking that you've been granted a very special gift, and here in the prime of your life when you have no obligations except to yourself, this . . . opportunity comes in the form of some solicitation from afar."

"And you're thinking it's no coincidence that it's our homeland."

"That's right. You didn't think that someone from the old country just opened up the Chicago directory of booksellers and landed on you?"

"No."

"It's God's way of testing you, to see if you'd go to the one forbidden place in pursuit of wealth."

I looked down. "Only a fool would dismiss the coincidence, and I . . . I didn't listen to your advice."

"It was not *my* advice," he said.

I nodded. It was the nuns who raised us that warned against ever returning there, that we would not be welcome. This was told to the Don by our benefactor, the person who arranged our immigration.

"You'd be surprised, Joseph. There are a whole lot more fools out there than sages."

"So I'm being tested."

"God tests hermits, too, you know."

I nodded. This I knew.

"Joseph, I don't go out looking for calamity in my life; it just comes into my confessional and spills every Saturday. I'm here to tell you that every single sin someone confesses is some test they failed. At first I thought it was just random bad behavior and giving in to temptation. Now I see they have patterns—a person's going along minding his own day-to-day, and *wham*, he gets tested."

"And fails."

"And fails, yes," he said. "It starts a pattern of sin."

"So what's my test?"

"You've been working on your business half of your life already, and out of nowhere comes this offer for a lot of money. I assume you're getting a large consulting fee out of this, a lot more than your standard fare."

"Mult mai mult." Much more.

"But you were told never to return there. The *one* place." He strummed his fingers in that way that told me I should have already gotten it. Just in case, he continued, "My son, I have given you all you could want, just stay away from that one tree, that one fruit."

Adam being tested; I knew what he was getting at. "I look at it another way, Berns."

He gave me a look. "Sinners always do."

"No, really," I said. "God gives me a special talent so that I don't have to live like those other *orfani* on the streets over there, and now He opens a door to give me a comfortable life for the rest of my days, not to mention helping others, like a good father who wishes better for his son."

"I see." My brother nodded. "I'm sure most people who win the lottery overlook their sin of gambling on their way to thanking God for finally picking their Ping-Pong balls."

He had a point, but this was not some game of chance; it was the result of a lot of work. Or perhaps I just didn't want to heed his advice.

I asked, "Then how would you say I should recognize the difference between the culmination of hard work versus staying away from the tree?"

"You'll know," he said. "You probably already know."

"How?"

"When things start happening that you cannot explain, things that confound humans or seem outside of natural law." They already had done that, and more. "When what comes next is evil," Berns said, "you'll know where that came from." He pointed downward.

"Maybe something good'll come out of it." I changed the subject. "Like selling the Knowles?"

"Oh, the Don thanks you very much. Sold the Secker and Warburg edition."

"Hope it helps."

"Every bit helps," he said. "They've got medical bills ahead."

12

I had never flown on a private jet before, but with business concluded at the Rosenbach, Arthur arranged logistics, including
armed guards and movers who crated and loaded the documents and display case into an armored truck bound for
the airport. There we boarded some sort of large aircraft
(I wouldn't know a Gulfstream from a Greyhound, except maybe
for the wings), and I shared a quiet cabin with the workers and
crew bound for Bucharest. I settled into a reclining leather chair
and fell asleep before takeoff.

The transaction had gone as if choreographed. Following
pleasantries and legal formalities that essentially cleared the museum of its bailment, my $2.6 million offer was countered and

accepted at $3.2 million, and I placed a call to Arthur to authorize the $4 million wire. Waiting had proved to be the most difficult part, as the international wire desks close at noon local. I spent a sleepless night in the hotel until the bank confirmed receipt the following morning.

All too soon I awoke, still aboard a jet. And as is often the case with me, worry moved in and hogged my blankets. Mentally I had not spent any of the money, since I had yet to receive my fees. I could have made it legit and insist on a reasonable fee inside escrow with a side deal, or I could have insisted on the payment being upon delivery, but I signed the contract "upon delivery *and* acceptance." Then I made the mistake of not clarifying the term *acceptance* in the body of the contract. I realized too late that I should have inserted a proviso stating it meant acceptable as I had purported it to be. As written, the contract remained silent as to what constituted the buyer's acceptance. Alas, in the eventuality of legal contest, I, like the goods, would not be in a Chicago court, but rather dealing with the likes of Escu & Escu, Esq.

I took the opportunity afforded by the long flight to commit to memory snippets from the epilogue verses that described the supposed location of Dracula's tomb:

> *From Dreptu . . . Ladies River . . . last chestnuts . . . Bethany Home . . .*
> *see their fate at sunrise . . . wicked Men's destination . . . five*
> *minutes . . . Juden await judgement . . . batter across the first*
> *building . . . beyond the stone bridge . . . path not to miss . . .*
> *seconds . . . shading eyes at sunrise . . . tripping over stones.*

Like my original impression, I continued to find the references odd, as they seemed at once both specific and cryptic, with the sequence strangely brief, as well. So much ink had spilled on the great battle that produced Dracula's demise; why so little on his interrment ceremony? No encomiums over the grave, no celebrations staged; it seemed almost as if the pallbearers wished to finish and exit with haste. What seemed more important to me as I inspected the document was that the riddle content was verbatim from the assistant's notes, and then Stoker wrote different verses in what seemed to be an attempt at metering, only to have them boldly lined through and replaced by the original words. I surmised the assistant won out on this closing page and insisted on precise obscurity, but I felt puzzled. Why in his novel's final scene would the author accede to the assistant?

The jet put down in Bucharest and, rather than approaching a terminal, taxied toward a hangar. It slowed to a stop, then one last nudge and the plane rolled inside with the great door closing behind us. I stepped outside into a spotless hangar as an armored truck backed up to receive its cargo.

Arthur was quick to extend a hand and smile. "This is an historic day."

"Indeed," I said.

In fact I wished he would have handed me a check and seen to it that the jet was refueled and homeward bound. But instead I found the open door to a black Suburban. It was not until we departed the airport grounds that I realized we had not passed through Customs, nor were we southbound toward the city, but northbound toward Braşov in the SUV tailing the armored truck.

Outside occasional rain splattered the windshield on an overcast day. They drove in a way as not to bring attention to themselves, although the armored vehicle was the only one on the road. Rather than take the road to Braşov, the drivers opted for the more direct but treacherous route up 73A at the town of Predeal. We climbed the hill past several small villages while mud splashed the wheel wells and decorated the black paint. It turned to late evening, and the rutted road snaked steeply in the woods before reuniting with a road that had a number, but still no pavement. Just as I was trying to figure out our location, the sight of Castel Bran loomed above in an overcast evening. Had I been a first-time tourist, I would have marveled at the sight.

The vehicles drove through the lower gate, and I missed out on my carriage ride. Inside I was seen to my corner tower suite and informed that dinner would be room-served within the hour. Arthur left before I had the opportunity to get clarification on the balance of the transaction.

A thin, wiry man whom I had not previously met delivered my dinner. He was malodorous and I hoped he didn't get any on the food. When he left he locked the door behind him, and despite my unease I ate like a starving man. Two hours passed awaiting Arthur's return, and I spent the time gazing out the window until all I could see was a dense cloud cover. Then the door lock clicked.

Arthur entered and said, "I trust your stay is pleasant."

"Of course." I offered him a chair in the parlor section.

"We cannot stay," he said. "The Master is reviewing the manuscript."

"I've been meaning to ask you about concluding the transaction."

Arthur smiled. Not the most convincing of looks, but a smile. "You need not worry, Mr. Barkeley, you will be taken care of."

"And the timing?"

"The Master operates . . . let us say, in his own time. Till then you are to here wait. You will receive your meals promptly."

He left and locked the door. I didn't like the idea of *meals*, as in plural. Not long ago I sat at the window in that very room wondering what blessings had been bestowed upon me that I might spend nights in Dracula's Castle as honored guest, yet now I connived my escape in a room identical to the one where Jonathan Harker was driven mad. Perhaps that account was not fiction.

Sleep came hard, both from the time change and worry. More than a week passed with only my Romanian dictionary and phrase book and a map of the country, the latter delivered with a breakfast. Several more meals came and went, and I looked upon a night so clear, it looked like fresh paint, and with only days before a full moon it appeared as if searchlights looked down into the hills. Worry and dread have a creeping effect and provoke physical responses, so I exercised by walking the room. For excitement I watched occasional rain and lightning roll through the valley and memorized the map.

When you lose your freedom of movement, the cadence of time changes, for it is more deliberate, less relative. You always know what time it is when you are not free. When all else fails . . .

"When all else fails," my brother used to say, "don't start praying. You should have been praying a long time ago."

"I know, Berns, I know." My mumble crossed the room and echoed back, startling me slightly. That was not the time to pray; that was the time to figure out what had ensnared me.

Here is what I knew: That I was perhaps the only human in the last hundred years or so to see the original epilogue, that the original had made it to first edition printing, and that following the fire it was replaced with a different ending. The epilogue obviously pointed to the burial site of the fictional character, but the deeds of the manuscript buyer suggested strongly that the site was not fictional. If that was in fact true, then the buyer was convinced he could locate the reliquary that held the remains of his ancestor, Dracula. If so, then the bones of Dracula would hold many times more value than the literary treasure. Who knew how much more value? For the buyer, the value would probably not even be measured in dollars.

But why this talk of warring families? Both Mara and Alexandru alluded to it. Could it be that I was helping only one family member over another, or even more, to find the treasure? That would certainly explain the buyer's insistence of anonymity.

I thought of Berns and wished for his counsel. What would he have been doing at that time? Probably reading Scripture. And then it hit me: The passages in the epilogue were similar to what I had tackled in Bible study, the King James Version. It was written in similar style to what my brother had taught me—that the dates, structure, and form were equally important to understanding the meaning of a passage. So I decided to try to decipher what I could of the directions. The trick to these was not necessarily to start at the beginning, but anywhere you can solve, like a crossword puzzle. Just get one piece of it down on paper and build from there.

Where the Juden await judgement. I noticed that the assistant left out the middle *e* in *judgment* in his notes. But Stoker's spelling, by contrast, always followed British convention, which included the extra vowel. Maybe a clue, maybe not; I filed it away in my head.

Juden is the German word for Jews, and where they awaited judgment would be in a cemetery.

The grave lies in a Jewish cemetery?

Commonly in European history, Christians refused to be buried alongside nonbelievers. One could often find Jews and people of other religions interred down the road from a cross-filled ossuary. Unlike Christian burial grounds, which often encircled their wooden churches, the Jewish cemeteries took the form of a classic potter's field: no caretaker, and only periodically tended to by volunteers. So it made sense that the workers in the epilogue could perform their task and flee without being seen.

Most directions dictate generalities first, leading the reader to an area, followed by specific directions involving landmarks, such as a natural outcropping or some other geological feature that should last for at least a couple centuries. If the direction-writer wrote in the present tense it referred to something he was looking at, whereas if he wrote in the past tense it normally meant a place that history had landmarked.

I also reminded myself that if the author chose singular he meant singular, and plural meant plural.

Finally, I thought, when the author uses an action verb, it is important to visualize the act.

Shading their eyes in the sunrise. They, plural, are looking east.

I heard the door unlock, and a grim-looking Arthur walked toward me. "The Master is not satisfied."

"I cannot give the documents a stronger opinion of authenticity than—"

He interrupted. "That it is real is not at issue. That he can use it matters only."

Having begun the treasure hunt myself, I knew exactly what he meant, and guessed that the buyer was stuck on the directions. I shrugged. "Perhaps I can be of assistance."

"I shall return," Arthur said.

He left and returned within an hour, instructing me to follow and bring any reading glasses I might need. Down the long hallway to the wooden door, again descending the stone stairwell with the red lanterns to the earthen basement, I stepped inside and was immediately assaulted by a horrible smell—carrion. The wall sconces again dimly lit three of the room's boundaries. On one of the large wooden tables lay the original manuscript open to the epilogue. Beside it was a detailed topographical map of Romania and a lantern.

Arthur directed me to sit with my back to the darkness. "The Master wishes to know the place described."

"Okay . . ." Caution suggested I pretend only to understand what Arthur wanted as he revealed it, since making copies had been forbidden from the start. Playing dumb, I turned the page.

Arthur cleared his throat. "There is no need to view the other pages."

I put my hands in my lap and looked up at him. "It might help if I knew some backstory."

"We seek a singular place."

I simply stared back, thinking it best to stay mute and wait for clarification. I did not have to wait long. At once I sensed someone standing behind me. My blood rushed, and my nose confirmed it just as the deep voice spoke.

"I am a very patient man." The voice was without question the one I had heard on my first trip, this time within inches of my right ear, speaking just above a whisper, annunciating each syllable formally. "I have waited many . . . many years for this." He breathed through his mouth with a detectable hiss. "No longer will I wait, for if you cannot tell me where this is, I have no further use for you."

"I understand," I said, not turning to look at him. I didn't need to be told that "no further use" meant disposal.

"I do not think you do," he said. "I smell in you . . . hesitation. You know something, *orfan*." I wanted to speak, but could not. He whispered close enough to my ear that I could feel his breath. "Tell me what you know."

I pointed to the page. "To be clear, you are looking for the burial site described here."

"Yes."

"*Where the Juden await judgement.* Whoever it is is buried in a Jewish cemetery."

His hand touched my right shoulder and gave a squeeze. "This much is clear." He patted my shoulder. *"Continua."* There was no heat to his touch, nor was there cold. My blood pulsed so hard that my ears rang.

"And here, *shading their eyes in the sunrise*, they are facing east."

"Good. Very good." His finger traced a line across my shoulders as he stepped around me to the opposite side of the table to sit. The wood did not creak when his weight alighted.

I did not know what to expect in his face, but it was long, very long, with a perfectly rounded lower jaw devoid of the jowls one expects when seeing a man past middle age. A thin, trim mustache covered the area over his lip. His skin was smooth, yet gave no hint of surgical enhancement. He had a straight Roman nose, bony cheekbones, and straight dark hair. No widow's peak. It might have been the light, since the lantern shone directly down on the paper, but his eyes looked red and were positioned an odd distance away from the bridge of his nose. His skin was pale, most noticeable against a long woolen coat of black with the collar turned up.

"I believe I can do business with you," he said. "Continue."

The Book of Isaiah flashed into my brain, and the story of how aspiring prophets were charged with interpreting the king's dreams, rejects tossed to the potter's field. I looked back down at the page. "I believe the first couple passages direct the reader to a general area. Then it gets more specific, until finally *tripping over stones.*"

His hands came into view in the lantern light as he placed them on the table. The fingers were long and perfectly manicured. His could have been the hands of an eye surgeon. The nails looked longer than men wear, and appeared to be filed to points.

"Tell me," he said. "My first tongue is not of English; what is this . . . Ladies River?"

"If the name of a place does not match anything on a map, then look to names in neighboring countries or words that mean the same in the language of the native land." I thought of words for *ladies*. "*Femei . . . doamne . . .*" I thought of Latin. "*Dominae . . .*"

"*Da,*" he said, lifting a hand to stop me. "*Rivulus Dominarum.*" He closed his eyes and took a long deep breath through his nostrils. "I know it from my youth. That is original name of—"

"Baia Mare." My own place of birth. I knew it when he said *Rivulus* and recalled the church's cornerstone engraved with *Riv Dom.* "*Where the last sweet chestnuts grow . . .*" A five-centuries-old grove of chestnut trees grew near the city, I knew. The trees were locally famous, the farthest north of the Mediterranean these trees grew, and the city even hosted an annual chestnut festival, which I had once attended as a child.

He nodded, no smile. "And what of this Bethany Home?"

I leaned my forehead on my right hand, shading my eyes like a visor, and stared at the paper in thought. If it was a home or a house, it was a structure. What structure was there a century and a half ago that was expected to survive the millennium? Historic buildings . . . variations of *Bethany* . . . home . . . *heim* . . . *doma* . . . *casa* . . .

"Casa," I said. *Bethany. Beth?* "Elisabeta."

The remains of a castle sat across the square from Stephen's Tower, where I had stood only weeks ago. It was the oldest structure in town, dating to 1440, and the site of a castle some Transylvanian prince built for his wife, Elisabeta. These days the building, Casa Elisabeta, housed art exhibits.

"You have a brain worth keeping," the Master said. I still did not know his name. "Continue to use it."

I read the page again, now focusing on the use of the word *sunrise*. *"You can see their fate at sunrise . . ."* I intoned. "Looking east is Stephen's Tower. Was it ever a prison?"

"It was used as many things over the centuries," he said, "and most likely a prison at some time."

I was stumped on *wicked men know their destination*. Did it have something to do with the tower as a prison? As I tried to make sense of it, I was reminded of my own insight about the author's use of action verbs. *You can see*. What do you see when you're at the casa looking at the tower? It is a simple stone structure topped with a tall steeple and . . . a cross. An Eastern Orthodox cross.

The top crossbar of the Eastern cross is for the head. The second crossbar, the long one, is for the arms, and the bottom crossbar, tilted at an angle, is for the feet. The bottom bar is tilted from upper left to lower right to the viewer, and it is believed that the souls of good men are pointed upward, but the *souls of wicked men* point down.

The next line read *It is but five minutes that way.* So in all likelihood the cross was pointing in a specific direction.

I said, "The cross at the top of Stephen's—"

He raised his voice: "I do not wish to hear of this cross."

"It points . . ." I tried to visualize but could not. "I don't know what direction it points."

"Enough," Arthur said. "The object points in some direction from there. Let us continue."

I continued, *"It is but five minutes to the Jewish Cemetery."*

"That would be in town," said Arthur. "One does not get far in five minutes."

"And it would depend on the mode of transport," I said. My concentration was interrupted several times as the Master's smell assaulted my nose. I stood to pace the room.

"I smell repulsion," the Master said. His demeanor clearly conveyed *Get used to it.*

I tried to focus on the clues again. Five minutes in any direction put you still in the heart of the city, and no cemeteries lay inside that radius, only concrete and buildings and walking areas. Walking . . . walking . . . distance.

"Distance in minutes," I said, returning to my seat. "Minutes of arc."

"Da," said the Master, betraying his excitement with his speedy response. "One-point-eight-six kilometers per minute."

"That would be at the Equator," I said. "That's the formula for zero degrees north, but it would be less distance at the forty-seventh parallel." I looked at the map and estimated six miles in any direction from Baia Mare and found it to the east. "Baia Sprie, if the marker points east."

"Foarte bine." Well done.

"The rest of these directions are specific to local landmarks," I said, "and I have not been there."

"You will," he said.

And in the time it took to stand, he had disappeared into the dark end of the room.

13

There is something unsettling about meeting a creature not human. Equally disturbing is recognizing that what you experienced belongs to the outliers of acceptable conversation, perhaps more aptly reserved for late-night radio call-in shows. It was hard enough to convince myself of what I had seen. The notion of trying to explain it to another was unthinkable.

This I pondered while sequestered in the castle tower for two days. My thoughts no longer dwelt on contractual acceptability and payment, but instead on how I might survive long enough to escape. And yet my mind and emotions adapted over the long hours to the point where I had, if not a plan, per se, an approach to my precarious situation.

On the third morning, Arthur walked into my room and told me I had ten minutes to get ready.

"Bring your jacket," he said, "and your device."

My GPS. Of course.

I followed him down the stairs to the front entrance where the black Suburban waited, and we sped in the direction of Braşov, turning north on Route 1, the main highway—loosely defined to be sure—through the Carpathians. I suspected we were bound for Baia Mare to resume the search for Dracula's tomb. Clearly on a schedule himself, our driver aggressively covered ground by muscling out lesser vehicles and horse carts, disregarding caution signs. Late afternoon we approached the city. The weather had cleared, still breezy and cool, with only a hint of disturbance hovering north over the Carpathians.

Pulling into the city center, we parked in the square facing Stephen's Tower. The driver stayed while Arthur and I walked toward Casa Elisabeta. No longer a grand residence, it still retained the impressive air of ancient nobility. I moved to its entrance, the same as where the author would have stood, and turned toward the Tower.

"It is as you thought?" asked Arthur.

Stephen's Tower was an impressive, lofty, square structure of stone and arched windows, with a tall mansard roofline and four corner turrets, each raising a cross at its peak. In the middle of the roof stood two additional large Eastern crosses. All six crosses faced east–west, with the bottom crossbars tilted upward on the sunset side, downward on the sunrise side.

Wicked men know their way—east.

"Baia Sprie," I said.

"How far?"

I consulted the GPS to confirm. "I would say five and a half miles."

"Good," he said. "You should make it by nightfall."

I looked at him, and he gave no expression. "You want me to walk?"

"No," he said, handing me a flashlight, "but the Master does."

"Forgive me for asking, but does the Master have a name?"

"Yes," he answered, and walked back to the Suburban.

At some point, if you're human, you can't help but wonder if your hardships are worth it. I glanced at the Suburban, then at the local people in the vicinity, and I thought of my brother and knew what he'd say, even now: *Someone else has got it worse.*

I started walking.

Baia Mare spreads across a valley split by the Săsar River in a region that resembles much of West Virginia. Softly sculpted with thick forest cover, Baia Sprie is the next town ascending the hills to the east via the river road, Route 18, as it climbs in elevation, a modern, two-lane, twisting blacktop road with sporadic guardrail protection. As in most of Romania, the alternate parallel route was the original connecting road between towns, barely more than a path, and the route of choice for horse-drawn carts. I knew that if I was looking for an ancient cemetery on an old road, it would connect to the older path and not Route 18.

A half hour into my walk, I sat and rested on a roadside rock. The day continued sunny and cool and, being pale-skinned, I was grateful the late afternoon sun was shining on my back and not in my face. I looked back to the west over the valley and saw the giant chimney stack, the city's tallest structure, a brick cylinder several stories tall, the former site of the old smelter. My father had worked there. Other than his harsh domestic outbursts, that's about all my memory holds of him.

Another hour's walk and I saw a *troiță* and decided to stop for another rest. Picture a weathered ornate crucifix roughly five feet tall, topped with a chalet roof, complete with protective shingles and a place to kneel and leave notes, sometimes light a candle. That's a *troiță*. Travelers often leave photos of passed loved ones, or simply pause and pray for safe passage. I knelt and prayed for protection; there would be no one to leave my picture.

The sun had subsided enough in the western sky that only its curved light made it over the trees, and though the weather remained clear, the temperature ratcheted down several degrees in that elevation. No one had passed me on the road in over an hour; as I progressed up the gentle incline, my legs burned.

As shadows followed sundown, I heard the drone of mosquitoes and stopped to look around. They sounded close, but seeing none, I continued hiking. Again I stopped, for it did not sound right. Whereas mosquitoes travel slowly, these sounded like large swift-moving swarms, and the pitch of their sound was clearly female, no males. Males always accompany females, yet I heard none. Eventually the sound passed, but within minutes the skies filled with birds by the thousands, perhaps tens of thousands, sufficiently startling to stop and take notice.

When I was almost to my destination and walking along the crest of the old road, a horse-drawn cart sped by westbound.

The frantic driver was doing all he could to control his galloping horses, and he called for me to take shelter as he passed: *"Adaposti!"*

Take shelter? Where? I continued my trek into the dark. According to my GPS, I had not quite reached the five-mile mark when off to the east I heard a few dogs bark. Immediately other dogs responded with howls from all directions, much like the sounds in the hills around the castle. *Wolves.* I picked up the pace.

Within minutes I reached the point where the old road diverged from its parallel younger sibling and served as the original approach to town. It was time to look for landmarks in earnest.

They took the batter across the first building and beyond the stone bridge.

I looked for any signs of an old structure, any building, or even a rock outcropping resembling a building. The evening was dark enough that I couldn't see ahead because the moon had not yet breached. More mosquitoes, but none landed. An army of something seemed to be marshaling.

A large haystack stood to my right in a clearing. I paused at the property's edge. If I was to encounter houses and farms, I would have to determine by age which was the first building. That simply was not going to happen.

My GPS works in decimal points off the degree instead of minutes and seconds, making the device accurate to within a thousand-foot tolerance. That's the better part of a quarter mile. As my instructions probably needed to be followed to within a couple hundred feet, I was reduced to hunches and guesswork to supplement my gadgetry.

Nearing the haystack, something told me that it looked too tall. I walked into the field, approaching it, when suddenly a great racket sounded all around me. Wolves howled, the mosquito humming increased, and I thought I heard shrieks—one or two at first, then dozens. Armies at war. I looked up just as the first rays of moonlight illuminated the sky, and I saw a flock of small birds flying and diving into the woods. Not just birds, but also bats, more bats than I could count, thousands and thousands of them swarming until the sky blackened above the field where I stood. I unzipped my jacket and lifted it to cover my head as they dived and whirled all around me. One brushed by my arm. Along with the leathery sound of their flittering, they squealed.

They passed on, clearing the sky and letting the moon light the haystack before me. Only it was not a haystack. It was actually an old structure, perhaps part of an old stone wall that had once adjoined a larger building. It just happened to be shaped like one of the tall spun stacks. I smiled despite myself; I had found the first landmark.

Several more shrieks ascended from the woods, sounding similar to bats, except louder and agonized.

Time to look for the batter. *They took the batter across* . . .

From an old Milton poem I knew that *batter* was old Gaelic for *road*, so I looked for the first road across the highway.

A path not to miss. That meant take the first one. By the construction of the passage, the warning immediately following the description, it seemed to be an admonition, like *Careful, don't miss it.*

Immediately I saw a narrow path angling toward the river, almost directly across from the old stone structure. I crossed the road and entered a single path with woods and underbrush on both sides. About a quarter mile ahead I heard the sound of a river flowing over rocks. Cautiously I approached and saw two short wooden posts with signs warning of an unsafe bridge.

Beyond the stone bridge . . .

As I bent to look at the structure, I heard more mosquitoes pass by. Stone pillars held up the rickety bridge made of wood and metal. This was the bridge from the epilogue.

Only seconds now.

I didn't know if that meant seconds of the arc or counting on a clock. Regardless, a second's distance is only a hundred feet, and the cemetery could lie anywhere to the east, or right, side. Cemeteries normally are not placed at the same level as water, especially an old cemetery that had survived the centuries, so I expected to encounter a rise in terrain away from the river.

A loud shriek from the woods nearby frightened me, and I stopped. It sounded like the wounding of an animal and lasted several seconds. After it subsided, I heard the buzz of mosquitoes before a thousand bats descended toward the noise.

I picked up my pace and soon encountered uneven rocks underfoot where the path began its climb.

Tripping over stones.

I was almost there.

14

At the top of a small rise were traces of a two-lane path leading north off the road and through a dense row of trees to an open field beyond. I knew I was not alone, yet saw no one. I had saved the flashlight for just this part of my search, and I clicked it on.

In the clearing I found a cemetery. No crosses adorned the headstones, and the engravings were clearly in Hebrew.

The Jewish cemetery, *awaiting their judgement*.

So ended the trail of clues. Was it enough that I had gotten there, or was I supposed to guess which tomb hosted the unholy guest? And were the Master's people watching as I tried to decide what to do next?

I turned off the flashlight in the hopes of reacquiring my

night vision. It appeared the cemetery occupied about an acre of scrubby land, neither flat nor sculpted, boundaried on two sides by a loosely wired fence, with trees lining the roadside to the west and a wall of rocks and stones providing a natural northern barrier.

If I were in a hurry, doing something wrong in a place without welcome, where would I place the casket?

I looked back south, across the river and down into Baia Sprie, where the brightly moonlit twin steeples of the Catholic church rose against the uneven outline of mountains crowning the valley. A noise began to build behind me from the tree line. I clicked on and pointed the flashlight in that direction, only to see the tree limbs and branches filled to capacity, not with the dense foliage as I had assumed, but with perched birds. Past their bedtime, they certainly must have been waiting for something. I tried to refocus on the puzzle.

Would it be unmarked? Or might it have a scrambled name, either a character in Stoker's book or one I saw in the notes?

My search continued. Something told me I was not using my head. *Think, think.* If the object was to get in and out quickly, I would . . . not want to dig. I would use an aboveground sarcophagus. My search narrowed to only elevated crypts. I passed by one because it had a cross at its head, but passing by it a second time, it occurred to me that the cross was exactly what did not belong here.

I returned to the spot and looked it over. The tomb stood by itself, a stone box topped with a large slab about belt height. It had a smooth top, unadorned except for the design of a strap forming the shape of a cross as one looked down upon it. Engraved in the stone was a name—LOREENA BRAITHWAITE. No dates.

Why should I know that name?

Then the light flickered. I checked the flashlight, but it was still strong. The interruption seemed to come from above, and when I looked up, I saw that the moon had been eclipsed. The sky was filled from horizon to horizon with bats, as if every bat in Europe were receiving its calling that night. I pulled my jacket over my head, covering my face as they swarmed and dived all around. They squealed like rats on water, and all at once all the birds lifted from the branches and shrieked a war cry. I peered out from under my coat; it looked like two men were fighting near an oak tree only ten yards from me. Both men appeared to be the same size, lean and quick, grabbing and lunging at each other and making banshee noises as the bats bombed and bounced off of them. They moved so quickly that I could only see a blur in the darkness.

I turned my flashlight toward them, and when the light hit one set of eyes, the man froze. In his moment of hesitation, the other one bit down on his forearm. The victim let out a howl that sounded half human and half dog. A quick swipe of the aggressor's hand ripped open the side of the screaming man's neck, and a second later blood pumped out like a squeezed fountain pen. The victor grabbed the wounded man's neck with one hand, an arm with the other, and pinned the victim to the tree. A third man joined the fight, also moving as a blur, and grabbed the victim's other arm. The pair yanked to pin his arms around the tree trunk, exposing the man's front as he cried in pain, blood now running freely out of his neck.

A fourth man entered the scene from behind me, walking a hunter's conquering stride. He wore a long black coat with its collar turned up. Two long knives sparkled in the moonlight from his draped sleeves as he stepped to the tree. The defeated man spat at him futilely as the hunter lifted both knives head high and plunged them in the victim's chest.

One last loud howl drained from the dying man as he slumped forward, head lolling. The hunter then reached deep into the wound on the dead man's neck and yanked. I heard a sound like a branch snapping, and the victim's head fell onto the ground. I shone the flashlight down on the man's grimacing face, revealing two prominent canine teeth and dim red lights in his eyes that were slowly extinguishing.

The hunter turned and walked toward me. It was the Master from Castel Bran. He breathed hard, not from exhaustion, I thought, but from excitement. He grabbed a bat in midair that had bumped into him, snapped its neck, and tossed it to the ground as one would crumple and discard a paper cup. He stood on the other side of the tomb I had been looking at.

"I am Dalca," he said, "and I have come to reclaim my family."

I opened my mouth to speak, but nothing came out.

He raised his voice. "Tell me what you found."

I thought a moment. "This tomb is marked *Loreena Braithwaite.*"

He looked down at the sarcophagus, and when his eyes saw

the stone cross standing at its head, he swung his right arm toward it and smashed the crucifix to the ground.

His eyes glowed red. "Explain."

The directions in Stoker's original epilogue led to the cemetery, but to no specific tomb. Nor did he write it, for he was never there. I concluded that the assistant picked the name off a headstone, altered it, and gave it to Stoker to insert somewhere else in the novel. Two other chapters in the original manuscript mentioned names on tombs, *Dolingen* being the most obvious and thus not likely. I recognized the woman's name as a derivative of another one in the novel.

"A Christian," I said, referring to the cross, "with a Scottish-Irish name does not belong in this cemetery." I sensed the Master's impatience and spoke quickly. "In Stoker's manuscript, there's a fictional character in the Whitby cemetery named Braithwaite Lowery."

He looked at me, looked at the tomb, then reached under the stone cap, and with a great exhale heaved at least two tons of stone from its mooring. It tilted my direction and slid off as I jumped backward. I shone the flashlight toward the open tomb. Inside lay the skeletal remains of a person—a woman, I think— clothed in a wedding dress with hands folded over the midsection holding a candle, a coin, and a rosary, the traditional burial garb of an unmarried woman. Around the neck rested a crucifix on a chain. Dalca reached into the tomb, grabbed a handful of remains, and threw them at me. I ducked, but a bone hit me and knocked me to the ground.

"This is not my wife!" His growling voice was so loud, I

plugged my ears while kneeling. Had I not I would surely be deaf today, because he let out a primal scream inhuman in volume lasting a good ten seconds. Birds scattered and bats retreated. Finished, he walked over and yanked me up with one hand and spoke with his coffin breath in my face. "Imbecile. I lost three warriors tonight." He shook me. "Those are my *copii!*" *Children.* He dropped me to the ground and instructed the other two, "Take him."

Each of the pair took an arm and roughly led me toward the road from which I had come. They walked faster than I could run, my feet skipping along the dirt road, across the flimsy stone bridge, and into the black Suburban. They threw me inside and pinned me to the floor as the vehicle sped off.

Only minutes later the vehicle stopped and the door opened; roughly was I lifted and set on the ground. Outside the city where no lights burned, it took several seconds to recognize the wooden church lit only by moonlight—All Saints. Dalca was there waiting and instructed his two guards to bring me. At his command they grabbed my shoulders and dragged me at running speed toward the gate. The Master didn't bother to open it, but kicked it off its meager hinges and walked directly toward the Paddock of the Damned. He stopped at the side of my mother's tomb while the guards shoved me next to him. Dalca reached under the lip of the lid, just as he had with Braithwaite's tomb, and lifted the cap off the crypt, sliding it onto the grass.

"Look," he said. Grabbing the nape of my neck, he shoved my face toward the vault. "Look!"

In the dim light, I saw a shriveled, headless, unrecognizable corpse draped in ragged, burnt-blackened clothing. A shard of wood stuck out of my mother's chest. Her head, detached, lay at her feet.

"I should put you in there." He adjusted his grip to my neck and lifted me, pulling me within inches of his face. "She belonged to us, until your *tată* took her." *Father.* He shook me. "How do you think you got your eye for paper, *orfan?* You think it is your gift. It is from me. My blood . . . to her . . . to you. You owe me, you *and* your brother owe me."

He threw me to the ground and ordered his guards to take me back.

15

Days passed back in internment in the confines of my room in Castel Bran, silent room service my only interruptions. Now I knew what *acceptance* meant and needed no imagination to know how this would all end. What was it that swung this normally God-fearing man to one who plots the demise and destruction of another? When Dalca announced that both I *and* my brother owed him, I knew he meant to splatter the blood of one of us so the other would see.

There were other realities, as well—my injuries throbbed, it took five days before I could retain any food, and my vision jittered as if I had consumed too much coffee. At times I fantasized that I had been drugged or infected.

But most of all, a single question pulsed in my mind: *Could that have really been our mother?*

She had been murdered—correct that, *destroyed* by way of the centuries-old disposal of the undead. My father was either deranged enough to believe she belonged to them or he had witnessed something that spurred his attack. When I peeled away the horror surrounding the truth, certain things became clear, like why dogs and cats reacted toward us the way they do, and why mosquitoes think I'm one of them. It was because of the smell of our blood.

Certain questions stirred about: Why did my father do it? Did he have sufficient reason? And most of all, if my mother was involved with the undead, why did they have children? I kept hearing Dalca's words invading my mind: *my blood . . . to yours.* As much as I wished not to be so, I did have an inhuman gift of sight, one that could not be explained away by mere science.

Further, I questioned if my brother had found out, and if it was the source of his stern warnings. I did not know how I would broach the subject.

Rummaging through the bottom of my suitcase for a clean set of clothes, I found a small book, Mara's journal, which I had packed and forgotten. Lifting the protective crucifix to my lips, I kissed it in gratitude, for I knew that every time I had been in real need, God had always sent me a tool. I prayed now that some answers lay therein.

The page fell open to the jaw structure Mara had shown me, and instantly I recognized what I had seen at the monastery and cemetery. Another page had a three-tiered pyramid of boxes, similar to a corporate org chart, with two boxes at the top of the pyramid labeled *Nobles*. The middle row showed several boxes with solid lines up to the Nobles, labeled *Regulats*, the Romanian word for *common*, and must be how the offspring came to be known as Common Vampires. Below that the bottom row, labeled *H Slave*, was connected to the Commons boxes. To the side of the Nobles were several *H Slaves*, plural, perhaps denoting a harem arrangement. This helped clarify for me what Mara mentioned—that the Nobles were the breeders, and that their children were either other Nobles or Commons, the latter born without reproductive parts. The Commons served as protective forces around the Nobles, thus Dalca's reason for scolding me for the loss of his children in battle.

Human slaves were the people supplying regular nourishment to the vampires, and appeared to be assigned in pairs to each Common. Nobles maintained several humans for nourishment. Again thoughts of my mother invaded. If she was, in fact, supplying blood to vampires, it was no wonder my father would be furious and destroy her. But no matter how many times the evidence suggested that reality, my reason and heart dismissed it as too far-fetched to consider.

Another couple pages dealt with lunar phases and what Mara had told me about the full moon's gravitational pull on their bodily fluids. The last five days before a full moon were highlighted with the word *adrenaline*. Perhaps that constituted the distinct glandular smell I sensed in the cemetery, the hormone secreted during their warring period, the source of his superhuman strength.

Another page listed methods of killing vampires, including burning, cooking in the sunlight, decapitation, or skewering, either by wooden stakes or metal lances. Drawings included two knives to the heart, a wooden stake much like the one in my mother's tomb, and a detached head. The silver bullet was not recommended, for the creatures moved fast enough to avoid any but the closest gunshot, pouncing on the shooter before another round could be fired. One other crude drawing showed a handheld device emitting squiggly lines, like a weapon shooting heat waves toward a closed coffin. I did not immediately understand what that diagram meant.

Aside from the obscure electrical device, my options were limited to centuries-old technology, namely blunt trauma, just as Mara had indicated, followed by dismemberment.

A family tree centered the journal, with Vlad Dracul at the top and four sons, not three as the history books suggested, listed below in order of birth: Mircea, Vlad, Radu, and Dalca. Somehow Dalca had managed to escape the pages of history, or else he'd disappeared into the Plague years just as his brother Radu assumed voivode status. If this were in fact him, then the Master would be at least six hundred years old.

One more page caught my eye, something about sunshine. A drawing illustrated sunlight rays with arrows pointing at an arm, with another illustration showing a larger view of the arm and the arrows penetrating the skin, the words *Vit D* written above the arm and *anaph shock* beneath it. After some thought I concluded that the journal was telling me that vitamin D, created in the body by exposure to sunlight, could curdle the vampire's blood, causing anaphylactic shock. This page happened to be in Mara's handwriting.

Much of the rest of the book contained miscellaneous drawings and unrelated sketches, none of which looked like weapons, and a list of travel dates and destinations, plus references to certain contract numbers. When I noticed the writing was sourced from a left hand, it dawned on me who'd written the bulk of this journal—Stoker's assistant.

Unmistakable.

Quite the journey this little book had taken, I thought, from London over a century ago, to Mara's in southern Wisconsin, and now to Transylvania in my possession. Just as I finished perusing the journal and returned it to my suitcase, the telephone rang, the red phone that had no keypad.

With hesitation, I answered. "Hello?"

I heard the long distance hiss and my brother's voice. "Joseph?"

"Bernhardt?"

"Where have you been?"

I looked about the room, thinking who might be listening to the call. "Visiting relatives," I said.

"You're supposed to be home by now."

"I've been delayed." I paused. "The buyer is still doing his . . . due diligence."

"Where are you calling from?" he asked.

Of course, I had not placed the call; someone within the castle must have dialed my brother's number. "Castel Bran," I said. I wanted him to know my location.

"Have the police come to speak with you?"

"No, why?"

"There's been a murder . . . two murders, actually."

"Someone we know?"

"Your friend, the businessman from downtown, Doug."

"Doug Carli? You sure?"

"The police were here looking for you, want to ask you a few questions."

"What happened? Why would they want to speak to me?"

"Seems your friend took a leap off a building downtown and impaled himself on a fence."

"Doug? He would never kill himself . . . Wait, why speak to me?"

"You met with him that day, and you were his last appointment."

"He helped me with the due dili—" I remembered who might be listening. Anonymity.

"Joseph . . . Joseph?"

"You said two. Who else?"

"The same day, neighbors of your friend Mara found her body up in a tree."

I was too stunned to speak.

"Joseph?"

"Mara Sadov? Near Lake Geneva?"

"Yes, I didn't know her last name," he said.

"I visited her the day before I left. I . . ." Words failed me. And I did not want to mention Alexandru Bena.

"So you saw her."

"Of course. She was fine."

"Some neighbors gave a clear description of your car. It doesn't look good, Joseph."

"You said she was hanging in a tree?"

"Not hanging."

"What happened?"

"Joseph, you need to get back here right away. The police want to question you. You might want to talk to an attorney first."

"Sounds like more than just a person of interest."

"Jo—" The line clicked off.

Just as I hung the receiver on its cradle, an envelope slid under the door. I walked over, picked it up, and tried the door again—still locked. It was a handwritten note on personalized Castel Bran stationery. In perfect penmanship, it read:

To Mr. Joseph Barkeley,

The honor of your presence is requested at a birthday party tomorrow night, Friday, at 23:00 until just before sunrise. Dress is casual, meals will be served, transportation and entertainment to be provided by the host. Be ready to be picked up by 14:00. Location is at my residence in Dreptu.

Dalca Drakula

16

Sunrise Friday arrived with a newspaper, an aging *Chicago Tribune* carrying the story of Doug Carli's death on page two, including the obligatory smiling family portrait, plus another of the death scene—not the impalement, but the bloody aftermath. He had plunged more than ten stories. The article chronicled his financial rise and recent economic setbacks, plus a quarrel with a client earlier in the day, no names listed.

Details of Mara's death followed on the opposite page. Neighbors apparently checked on her after seeing visitors leave her property and discovered her slain body, as my brother said, up in a tree in her backyard. However, my brother left out the detail that the treetop had been whittled to a sharp point and Mara placed thereon. The trunk had passed up through her body into her brain stem, and she was found in a sitting position like an angel placed atop a Christmas tree, with her arms wrapped around a weighted shoulder yoke.

I slumped in the chair and let the paper fall aside. Once the shock of the details passed, I realized I had had meetings with both victims the day they died, and both articles alluded to that detail without divulging my name. But that was not all, as only two surviving people knew of my mission: my brother and a stranger named Alexandru Bena. If Alexandru could not keep Mara from harm in Wisconsin, I concluded that I was on my own here.

Somehow I needed to warn my brother. But even if I had a way of contacting him, what could I say that he'd understand or believe? Graveyard encounters with warring vampire families, or our dismembered mother with a stake in her heart? Not likely.

One might hope that the murders of Doug and Mara would be compelling enough to force Berns to believe anything I told him. Yet Dalca's people had cleverly framed me as the prime suspect. Doug could not have known how close to the truth he was when he suggested the term *family* in my dealings with the buyer, and the family was tying up loose ends before they became *too* loose.

I sighed and shook my head. In Illinois they send murderers to Stateville in Joliet, but they send the criminally insane to a place even the Stateville inmates fear.

At two, the door opened and Arthur led me through the halls, down the elevator, and out the front door to the waiting Suburban. It had been cleaned, and I took a backseat and watched the scenery pass, sites foreign only a week ago now familiar. Once in Bistriţa, we continued to the east end of town and parked beside the highway. On schedule, the Gypsy arrived with his copper wares heading home to Dumitra, and Arthur got out and flagged him over for a conversation. Money changed hands and Arthur nodded my way, and as I climbed on the horse cart he informed me that this was my transport there and back, and that he hoped to see me again.

The ride over the hill was a silent one, while guilt only compounded my despair. Of course I had not impaled my friends, but I was the only reason they had died. I, who had deliberately lived a sheltered life, wishing to insulate my heart from such loss, now felt the full blow of it.

Traveling along the river, the Gypsy halted the cart and slowly reached back under his canvas tarp to retrieve something. The look on his face and a finger to his lips instructed me to silence. He pulled a crossbow from under a tarp, and with his other hand, reached behind his seat and produced an arrow from a leather pouch. Silently, quickly, he armed the bow, lifted it to his shoulder, and took aim at a small deer. In America it would be referred to as poaching. In remote Romania it is referred to as feeding your family. A single shot put the animal down. Observing the silent weapon ignited my curiosity, and I asked him several questions, as best as I could in Romanian, about its operation while he field dressed the animal. He was forthright with his answers, as much as our language barriers allowed, and with typical Romanian hospitality offered to instruct me in its use.

I helped him lift his conquest to the back of his cart and cover it with the tarp. Nothing more was said of the event.

The Gypsy stopped just as he turned into his drive and lifted his horseshoe to open the gate. He turned and pointed upward and said, *"Este lună plină."*

"I know," I said. "Full moon. *Mulțumesc.*"

He made the sign of the cross and continued up his driveway.

I called to him and pointed at my watch to see what time he would be leaving in the morning. *"De dimineață?"*

He waved me off; it was Friday. *"Luni." Monday.*

I walked through the village of Dumitra and received only sideways looks as adults corralled their children. Just as before, doors slammed, dogs barked, and everywhere the villagers made the sign of the cross. Even the dolls had been removed from their windows. The priest blessed me as I walked by, and while traversing the bridge I noticed that Sonia's doors and windows were shuttered. It was only minutes from sundown, and I walked the stride of a man resigned to the gallows and swift judgment.

The hike toward Dreptu seemed farther than the first time, likely because of my diminished pace. The deeper into the woods I walked, the louder the sound of wolves, while birds by the thousands flew just over the treetops. Several times I heard the sound of female mosquitoes like the ones near the Baia Sprie cemetery, their hum a higher, faster, more rhythmic pitch than the males'.

I was jolted from my woolgathering by what looked like lights dancing in the trees in front of me. Realizing the light shone from behind, I quickly moved to the shadows and stood behind a tree. The engine sounded like a heavy truck, and as it passed I saw that it was an old school bus filled with people laughing and carrying on as if celebrating. Perhaps that was what Dalca's invitation had meant by a birthday party? The passengers did not see me, but one man looking out a window appeared familiar. It was but a moment, yet I placed his face—the merchant who had identified my crucifix and its gemstone and sold me my brother's gift.

The vehicle barely fit the tight path as tree branches scraped the roof and sides, bouncing along the uneven ruts. I followed it at a growing distance, smelling the trailing exhaust.

At the end of the path, I cautiously approached the turn-around circle, where the bus sat silently. I called out before stepping up inside to check for occupants. Empty. When I turned around to descend the steps, I was startled to see a man in a long coat standing in the shadows watching the door. He had a large jaw and red eyes, and without saying a word pointed a long spindly finger in the direction of the path toward the monastery. He grunted in disgust at the sight of my crucifix.

Up the stone steps and through the woods, the noise grew louder. When I reached the open field I heard laughter and shouting ahead, and saw thousands of bats joining the birds overhead. Through that last stretch of woods, light was coming from the direction of the monastery. Wolves howled above from cliff to cliff as the walls closed in on the box canyon. All about me the sounds of movement in the woods encroached; I was sneaking up on no one.

When the monastery came into view, it was not dim or fogged in like it had been on my first trip, but rather it appeared lit from inside. Red flickering firelight illuminated the center tower the way torch fire might. The moon had just crested the eastern Carpathian peaks and lit the outline of the great structure as the sounds of celebration continued to rise.

I smelled evil and stopped. Every sense I had said to leave. But I knew that if I was to defeat Dalca, much less extend my brother's life expectancy, I would have to go inside.

A low voice sounded behind me: "You are expected." I spun to see a man with a white beard and Caucasian features, his neck wrapped with a leather bandanna. He pointed at my crucifix and said, "You no need to show that since you arrive."

He did not have red eyes. "Who are you?"

"*Gardă.*" Guard. "I am caretaker here. This time I show you inside."

I recognized his voice as the one that had chased me away on my first trip to Dreptu. The guard opened the door and held it for me. I passed through the arch under immense stone walls and tried to grasp what I was looking at.

I stepped into the bailey, a great courtyard filled with tombstones, and saw the massive cylindrical tower in the center. Approaching it, I saw that its base sat not at ground level but at least three stories—perhaps forty feet—below ground in a huge reinforced hole lined with stone walls wrapped with a staircase. The vast structure did call to mind a chess set, with an enormous king lowered into a concrete pit. At the tower's base was an opening, large double doors about a quarter of the way around the foundation. Next to the tower was a seating area with several tables facing one head table and one large seat, a throne. Hundreds of torches lit the area, and next to the seating area stood what looked like a dense cluster of flagpoles.

The guard walked me down the wrapping staircase that hugged the stone wall until we reached the bottom, where he pointed me toward the main table. Dust kicked up with each footstep from a layer of dirt over cobblestone, while above great clutsters of birds flocked and dived about. I smelled the burning torch oil and heard the flames dance in the breeze; it sounded like flags flapping. And I was mistaken about the flagpoles. Closer inspection revealed them to be black wrought iron spikes fifteen feet tall, set a meter apart and planted in a semicircular pattern about the base of the tower a good ten meters, or thirty feet, out. I counted the rows—thirteen. Looking up I could plainly see the spike pit was positioned directly below a balcony some eight stories high. A great cloud of bats blotted out the full moon momentarily, and when the light returned, large double doors opened to the balcony above. It felt like walking into a medieval ritual.

The guard ushered me to the seat closest to the throne, not ten feet from the pit. Of heavy wood construction, the seats at the large rectangular head table and the benches at the smaller subordinate tables all faced the pit, except for the oak throne, which faced the audience.

There I sat for several minutes until a pair of men exited the tower doors and took seats at one of the small tables. I tried not to stare, but it was hard not to when their chins looked to be splashed with blood. Both men were tall and slender, with long straight black hair, thin mustaches, and aquiline noses. They appeared, even allowing for the ambient red lamplight, to be flush-faced.

Soon another pair and then several others much like them moved to their seats. They all looked to be fatigued, red eyes aglow, with stained chins. None looked happy to see me at their table.

Regulats? I hazarded a silent guess.

From inside the tower modern music from some sort of speaker echoed about the courtyard. I looked up and saw the torchlight glowing from within the open balcony doors.

My wonderings ceased when the Regulats all stood at once and quieted, for their master had arrived, his presence and power preceding him as he entered. Dalca strode by them and gave nods to each table, and though he kept licking his lips like a dog after dining, his face was clean. He approached the head of the table. "Regulats," he announced, motioning with an open hand in my direction, "my guest, Mr. Joseph Barkeley."

They nodded, not in approval but grudgingly, at the same time that a conga line of revelers danced out the front doors and snaked their way toward the pit. An ungainly overweight woman led the way, holding a boom box in the air as forty-year-old disco music blared into the night. As the visitors approached the tables, the celebration seemed to turn sober. The music switched off and the revelers formed a reception line facing Dalca at his throne. One by one the partiers solemnly approached the throne, each filing directly past me on their way to offer homage to the Master. All extended their hands to take his and kiss it.

"Master," each said with a deep bow, and then peeled off to wait behind the tables. When the man who I recognized earlier passed, he made a quick nod in my direction—yes, it was the jeweler from Baia Mare. Another beady-eyed man handed the Master a small envelope and whispered something.

As the last supplicant walked away, Dalca stood and announced, "Lasting memories on all your birthdays." He waved them away. "Carry on."

Again the music struck up, the conga line re-formed, and the dancers shook and wiggled past the tables and toward the tower and back in the main doors, their music tailing them inside and up the stairs.

Dalca looked my direction and breathed deeply. "I smell . . . confusion. You wonder what all this means."

I nodded.

"Our guests, they work for me . . . have for many years. They increase my wealth, and in return they enjoy good health and wealth far in excess of their limited talents, certainly more than they could have done for themselves." He stood from his throne and moved to the chair next to me at the head table. "As for this, a simple party, a gesture of my gratitude."

"Master," I said, "I do not know why I am here."

"You have proven yourself rather adept at your craft, I might say." I had not noticed until then that his tongue was red, and pointed. "But do you see these young men here?" He motioned to the four dozen or so Regulats. "These are my children, and there is now an empty table because *you* directed this army to the wrong battleground, and they had to lay their brothers to rest." Dalca was calm, but I could see several pairs of red eyes burning in my direction. "Your job . . . is to find my wife."

Dalca stopped speaking when a man approached pulling a cart heaped with containers covered with linen cloths. He stopped at each table and delivered a pair, serving the head table last. The server, a man of Indian descent with a long pointy beard and white gloves, placed a cloth-covered box in front of Dalca, and then slid a silver domed plate in front of me. No utensils.

"Dessert, Master?" the server asked.

Dalca nodded, and the server lifted the linen cloth, revealing a cage, and awaited approval. Inside sat a large, live rat. Dalca nodded his approval, stood, and opened the cage top. The rat hunched; the Regulats groaned approvals. In a blur Dalca grabbed the live rat and attached his mouth to its chest. I turned away . . . just in time to see the Regulats open their cages and do the same.

Feeling queasy, I turned to retch, but with an empty stomach nothing emerged. Overhead the music blared out the tower window.

"Human," said Dalca. I looked back and saw he had tried to wipe his chin clean, but splatter remained. "We know you do not eat live animals, so we made yours special." He pointed to my plate. "Please, eat."

I looked at the plate, still covered, and did not comply.

"Human," he said again, lifting the dome off my plate, "I said . . ." It was a dead rat, quite uncooked, and he shoved it toward my face. ". . . eat."

A moment later I heard a loud thump and felt the spray of warm liquid. I looked up to see, not fifteen feet in front of me, someone impaled on a pair of spikes. It looked like a man, body limp, shoved halfway down two stakes, one of them sticking out of his back and another through his lower pelvic area. He had a fresh pair of puncture wounds on his neck. Apparently the revelers had donated some blood to their hosts, but enough remained to make a mess of the spikes.

I looked at my arm and saw a splash of blood and some other chunky substances. Instinctively I wiped at it, but my efforts only served to soil the back of my hand—same when wiping my other hand across my face.

Dalca looked at me and pointed to my face. "I see you are getting into the spirit of things."

A scream came from above as a woman plunged into the pit, her legs kicking all the way down. It looked like the obese woman. She fell onto a different set of spikes, and one of them caught her throat and silenced her. The impact left her head to dangle until falling off seconds later, a last spurt of blood shooting from her neck.

The Regulats murmured approval.

Next, a couple flew out the window and down to their deaths. The impalement ripped the woman in half, while the man landed backward and with his last breath arched his back with a spike sticking out of his torso as his body shook. Captive to the spectacle, I continued catching the spray of blood and bits as reveler after reveler descended to his death.

"Come now, Mr. Barkeley," Dalca said as he slid an envelope in my direction. "Go ahead, look."

While the sounds of screams and bodily impacts continued, I

opened the envelope. Inside were a half dozen photos taken by an instamatic camera. *Thump.* More spray, some of it landing on the photo in my hand. I stared at the picture of Doug Carli draped over a railing with a fence post sticking out of his back. A second photo was taken from ground level looking up at his contorted face. Both appeared to have been taken at night.

The next three photos showed Mara in a tree in her backyard. She looked to be sitting upright, but upon closer look the whittled trunk had impaled her, blood everywhere. She wore the yoke about her shoulders, her wrists tied to make her look as if mounted on a cross. Her head hung limp. In another picture a ground-level shot captured the agony on her face. Seeing those photos invoked sadness in me matched only by kneeling beside my mother's grave.

"That one"—Dalca pointed to an impaled man—"delivered those photos. So feel no pity, human."

I looked at the man and felt nothing.

Periodically the Regulats pulled bodies off the spikes to make room for others. Piled with the rat carcasses on pull carts, they were taken outside the monastery walls like trash and fed to the wolves.

Another screaming woman landed on the closest row of spikes and sprayed blood on us, the last of the revelers. Overhead the balcony doors closed. Dalca looked at his right bloodied index finger and licked it clean. "Now you know what's at stake, Mr. Barkeley." He licked his other fingers. "Pun intended."

17

One finds shelter in the cloistered world of the cloth. The priest gives his life over to his parishioners' welfare in hopes that his efforts point them and him toward eternal peace. He has faith that the other side of the great curtain holds not only just judgment, but also something that will reward those who have shed earthly pursuits and suppressed their natural desires, in essence serving mankind at life's buffet table while starving themselves. Underwriting such convictions is the assumption that God is always there, always watching.

Sustenance for the servers comes from daily routine, for as the Don used to say, "The grateful heart, sure of its fate, invites contentment." She stressed that with material pursuit comes restless discontent, and when one relegates God to part-time, one invites calamity. Such is the difference between those who serve and those seated at the table.

It is perhaps human nature—designed and given by God, mind you—that enables us to believe that if we do our best, project good thoughts, and pursue only that which God approves, then His protective grasp will keep us safe, so long as God is the overseer.

But God was not out there in that forest. No, like the other side of the Acheron, it was a place where the dark one rules and God's hands do not shape events. Oh, what a skein of events had I spun to invite such calamity into my life.

Trying to stumble my way back to this side of sanity, I bent to wash in the Dreptu River, but could only clean my exterior. Slowly I came to realize that my stained clothes would announce a murderer's arrival back in civilization, so at daybreak I walked out of the woods and, recalling Sonia's last message to return to her, approached her house. I knocked softly, and she opened the door with neither surprise nor hesitation. She was already dressed for the day.

I greeted her in the formal way. *"Sărut mâna."*

"Vă rog." Please. She walked me to the back of the house to the bathing tub and patted a small stack of towels. She left me a change of clothing and pointed to a basket on the floor and said, "Clothes." The clothes fit, just as the others had, and I joined Sonia in her living room.

Her front door was closed. Where Eastern Orthodox Christianity reigns, so does the Middle Ages superstition that evil spirits ride the breezes. Those prone to such fear live behind closed doors, even in summer's heat. But Orthodoxy allows no closed-door privacy between unmarrieds, so I stood before the door.

"Would you like the front door open?" I asked, unsure of which would be best.

"No. We speak with no audience," she said aloud.

I sat on a wooden bench across a table from her where a Bible separated the space between us, the English King James Version.

"You have questions," she said. I must have looked surprised. "Many years ago, I speak your tongue. Go ahead, ask your questions."

"*Îmi pare rău.*"

"Apologize not to me." She pointed upward. "To Him."

I made the sign of the cross and kissed my crucifix. "I should have listened to you the first time."

She smiled and shrugged. "*Tu eşti . . . om.*" *You are a man.*

I pointed toward the woods. "What are those creatures out there?"

She nodded and turned the Bible in my direction. "Read."

I opened it and noticed its age, all handmade pages of Euro stock predating 1830, and handled the old book delicately. "Which book?"

"Start at beginning."

To Genesis, the story of creation. "'In the beginning God created the heaven and the earth.'"

"Is first man there yet?" she asked.

"No."

"Continue."

"'. . . and God said, Let there be light, and there was light.'"

Again she asked, "Is first man there yet?"

"No. Day and night is day one."

"And day two?"

"Firmament," I said. "On day two He was preparing a place for man to live. On day three, heaven and earth and all that the earth bears. Day four, the sun and stars."

"And all these things good," she said.

"On the fifth day He creates animals."

"And all these things good."

I nodded. "On the sixth day He creates man and woman— Adam and Eve."

"No," she said. "Read per words."

"Verse twenty-seven: 'So God created man in His own image, in the image of God created He man; male and female created He them.'"

"He gave them dominion over earth and living creatures," she said. "Read last verse in chapter."

"Verse thirty-one: 'And God saw everything that He had made, and, behold, it was very good. And the evening and the morning were the sixth day.'"

"Where is first man . . . Adam? Read on."

She was right, for the sixth day of creation did not mention Adam and Eve by name. I looked ahead. "Chapter two, verse seven: 'And all things were in place, and the Lord God formed man of the dust of the ground, and breathed into his nostrils the breath of life, and man became a living soul.'"

She stopped me. "So Our Lord plants garden and places first

man there, from whom first woman formed. On day six He make male and female creature referred to as man, and saw it was very good, then rested."

"So it's all good up to this point."

She nodded and smiled, as if I was starting to get it. "All these things in six days were mere thoughts, and they came to be."

"He made it so just by thinking it . . . thus creation . . . something from nothing."

Again she nodded. "But first man"—she motioned as if kneading dough to form bread—"*formed* from dust and breathed into life."

"The living soul!"

"*After* creation," she said. "Formed."

"So chapter two is not a detail of what happened on day six of creation."

She pointed to the page. "Read again."

I did, and clearly Adam and Eve followed the day of rest. The Bible stated that man and woman were part of creation, but then after creation man was formed from existing material and got a living soul breathed into him. "So who are this man and woman back on day six?"

"Another creature in His image."

I looked at her. "Just not one with a living soul," I said. "Why would he make a manlike creature and not give it a soul?"

"Perhaps He wanted first to see how they behave."

"So these creatures might have been a test of sorts, to see if He wanted to make more?"

"Perhaps." She pointed to the book. "Move to chapter six."

"The descendents of Adam and Eve are multiplying, and . . . verse four: 'There were giants on the earth in those days—'"

"Giants," she interrupted, and paused before continuing. "Creatures look like men with great skills. Do things humans cannot. Read next two verses."

"Verse five: 'And God saw that the wickedness of man was great on the earth, and that every imagination of the thoughts of his heart was only evil continually.' Verse six: 'And the Lord repented that He had made man on the earth, and it grieved Him at His heart.'"

"So soon?" she asked. It was more like a leading comment.

I closed the book and laid it facing her. "Which man was wicked, the giants or the living souls?"

"If it was important, it says so. But point is it grieved Him."

"He's sorry He made mankind."

She stopped me with a gesture, then placed her own thought in my head: *He regrets making the living souls while the original creatures remained.*

"*Femeie înțeleaptă,*" I said. *Wise woman.* "How is it you can read my thoughts and project yours?"

She covered my hands with hers and patted them twice. "Like you, Mr. Joseph, I was given a gift . . . soothsay . . . How you say English?"

"Soothsayer? A fortune teller?"

She nodded. "My gift was to receive thought, to perceive." She pointed from her ear down to her stomach.

"To hear thoughts in your head?"

"Close." She looked away to find the words. "First in head, then below stomach to . . . seal." She motioned like closing an envelope.

"So you hear thoughts in your head . . . then a certain feeling comes to confirm."

"Confirm, yes." She tapped her temple, then pointed to my eyes. "Must have eye contact or be close to person to receive thoughts."

"And you project your thoughts only if your feelings are confirmed."

"Yes. That is how connection made."

She sounded like Mara.

"You grieve her loss greatly."

I nodded. "Mara."

"You may feel at fault, but God does not."

I straightened back up. "How did you learn English?"

"My gift . . . my husband take me to America." She made the sign of the cross in his memory. "To World Exposition. I work."

"You worked the Expo?"

"Both. Gheorghe an electrician, I was . . . soothsayer?"

I nodded. "Can you see future events?"

"No." She shook her head. *Of course not.* "I read thoughts and tell them what they concerns."

"I bet you shocked a lot of people."

She nodded. "They stop talking and listen. I tell them to work hard, pray hard, and stop doing bad things that invite misfortune."

"And your husband?"

"He was taken from me there." Her dark eyes turned from soft to cold. "By them." She pointed to the woods toward Dreptu.

"Sonia." I leaned toward her. "What did I witness out there?"

She spoke in a whisper. "They select humans with unique skill." She paused and pointed to the Bible. "You, for example . . . see the pages, determine age, just like that man."

The image of the jeweler flashed in my head.

"Yes, him." She pointed to my crucifix. "He sees the metal, *argint*, at same level you see paper."

"To the fibers." That explains why in the shop he told me about the metal's age with an unaided eye.

"Yes. The way the Regulats see."

"The Common vampires."

She nodded. "That is how they . . . respect your crucifix. They see the object and know it is from their master."

"My protection," I said.

"Yes and no. You cannot go anywhere and hide so long as you wear it, but you need it for safe passage. Regulats serve the Master and get their nourishment from the slaves."

"The human slaves?"

"Yes." She made the sign of the cross. "These . . . slaves work for Master in exchange for wealth and long life."

"So those were human slaves sacrificed?"

"Yes. Some live this village."

"But why kill them? It seems so . . . wasteful."

She shook her head. "They were being retired. Either services no longer needed or reach . . . the age."

"What age would that be?"

She did not answer outright. I thought of my own situation: services no longer needed.

"Do not worry." She covered my hands again. "Dalca will make sure you stay alive at least until he is certain he has found what he seeks."

"I understand the human slaves exchange blood monthly with the Common vampires," I said.

"Windows left open full moon."

"Last night was a full moon."

"Once a year, *iunie,*" *June.* "The thousand-year ritual. The Rose Moon."

"Birthday parties."

"Yes. Each group of slaves gets invited every fifty years, starting on their fiftieth birthday. Stay together."

"So to them it's a reunion. They don't know what's coming."

Again she nodded. "The *wampyrs* gorge on blood of slaves, let humans think they are at party."

I was almost too embarrassed to ask, but I knew she'd read me. "They also had . . . animals there."

"The rats."

I was too ashamed to look her in the eye, and stared at the wooden plank floor.

"*Copilul meu.*" *My child.* I looked up to see her eyes watering with tears. She continued, "I see him pushing this thing in your face."

Dalca had tried to force me to eat the rat, and I could not discard the smell, taste, and feel of it. I shuddered.

"I see animal blood on your face." Sonia brought a tissue up to my face and dabbed as if wiping it clean. "My heart sinks with yours," she said before making the sign of the cross. "Let us pray. *Gott sacți ascunde amintirile.*" *May God hide your memories.*

A long stretch of silence passed while she allowed me time to speak without choking up or losing my place. I stood and walked to the back of the house and ran water, scooping it to my face and toweling off before returning to the living room. She had left the room, and while awaiting her return, I looked at a couple photos on the wall above her reading chair. One picture was at least a hundred years old, but with the layer of glass between it and me, I couldn't date it by seeing it. Someone who looked a lot like Sonia stood smiling next to a man with Slavic features, also smiling. I noticed the woman wore the traditional footwear, the *opinci*, same as the ones in the corner on the mat. On closer inspection of the photo, it appeared they had pigskin bottoms, same as Sonia's. Pig's hide had gone out of use early in the twentieth century in favor of rubber.

She reentered the room and I pointed to the photo. *"Bunici?"* *Grandparents?*

She did not answer. As I wondered why she refused to answer simple questions, she said, "It is the order of things."

Several minutes of silence passed. Not an awkward silence at all; Sonia seemed to understand that I had a courage reservoir in need of periodic refilling. She always felt present and supportive, even when refusing to speak. Her responses did not imply that I had asked an out-of-bounds question, but rather that I would learn the answer in due time.

"Sonia," I asked, "why me? Why was I chosen?"

"You were selected," she said. "They must have observed you for many years."

"Dalca's human slaves?"

She nodded. "The same ones who watched your friend, the woman."

"But if I succeed and Dalca finds what he's looking for . . ."

Again she read my thoughts. "Yes, your fate, too, will be like theirs." She pointed toward Dreptu.

"How did they know me?" I asked. "And how did he know my brother?"

"That image you carry from the graveyard," she said.

The sight of my mother's dismembered body became vivid. "My mother . . ." I tried to say *human slave*, but she saved me the embarrassment.

She nodded. "Since before you were born. She had already exchanged blood before she had you, so you and your brother have a portion of *their* blood. You are born of the house of the Master."

"Then they can smell me, recognize me," I said.

"And your talent matched what he wants most; that is how you were selected."

I imagined what my father did and what he must have endured on his way to his decision. Until that moment I had never thought of my father as a hero.

Sonia said, "He was a slayer, a man of courage. Like you."

So he'd done what he did to protect Berns and me. And others, as well. And just maybe to spite Dalca. He also knew there was no place he could hide. I shook my head. Even as her words confirmed my earlier inference, it was a difficult line of thought to travel.

"Your father did it to end the bloodline."

I could tell from Sonia's eyes what she wanted, what would come next: My father's legacy now fell to me, not just because of my family lineage, but because I answered the call into their world. That was precisely what advantaged me over other humans, for that invitation could get me close enough to Dalca to form an attack. Yet I had no idea how to pull it off. *I am no match for him,* I thought. *For them.*

"But will you do it if you get the chance?" She knew I was torn, for I did not have a warrior's heart.

"At times I've felt inserted here," I told her, "at this moment to defeat him, like it's my mission, and I intend to fulfill it." I recalled the conversation at Mara's, and Alexandru Bena's insistence that I had before me a great mission. I was beginning to understand. "And other times I feel like finishing this, finding what he wants, and going home."

"Joseph, you *are* home. You and your brother are sons of the soil." She spread her hands in welcoming fashion. Her eyes softened. "You are not a coward. Remember, even the greatest among us asked to have the cup passed from him."

So I was to hunt Dalca. A lunatic thought, it seemed. Be that as it may, however, I resolved to try to think like a hunter, starting with understanding my prey. More specifically, what it was that Dalca wanted.

"Why is Dalca looking for his wife's remains?"

"She is buried somewhere in Transylvania."

"And he thought I would find her from what I read in the manuscript."

"Yes." *Jyezz.*

"What is he going to do when he finds her?"

"He will try to resurrect her and breed again."

I was bewildered. How could he do *that*?

"Like certain *insectă*," she said. "They go . . . suspended very long time."

"Hibernation," I said.

"Yes, in a way." She thought for a moment. "Dormant, I think is word. The vampire can survive asleep, dormant, for very long time. So long as body is intact."

It clicked then why killing vampires so often involved dismemberment.

She affirmed my thought. "Yes."

"How do you know these things?"

"Tell me your intentions first."

"I want to kill him. I have to kill him. But I don't know how . . . I mean, I know with a stake or two knives to the heart. But how can I hope to succeed, unless he's unguarded in his sleep?"

"He will be guarded," she said. "But if you could lure him somewhere and place the knife in his heart, would you?"

"Yes," I said without hesitation.

"Then you must, Mr. Joseph. And here is how: You must find his wife and allow them to couple. In that moment he will not move. They will be locked as one."

"Won't he be guarded?"

"The Regulats are not allowed to look upon the Master's nakedness. Nor do they want to hear the sounds."

I thought it over.

"You will do this?" she asked.

I nodded. "I will try."

"No. If you only try, then that is all you will *do*," she said. "But if you *know* you will do it, only then can it happen."

As I said, she was wise. There was much to admire in her.

Across the river a handheld church bell clamored, a call to services, followed by the distant chant of the *Rugăciunea pentru morți*, the service for the dead, as Christians commemorated loved ones. But I knew such bells would never toll for me. At most there'd be a few silent prayers from my brother, and with his end would go our lineage. That would be good for mankind, considering what I had just learned. Perhaps I would join my mother in the Paddock of the Damned. Then what would God say to me if I somehow managed to kill a creature He chose not to?

"*Două sute.*" Two hundred.

I turned and looked at Sonia. "Pardon?"

"Years," she said, and in my head the words formed: *You asked about the birthday party.*

"They let the human slaves live two hundred years?"

"Is that not long enough?" she asked.

I stood and walked toward her kitchen to look out the window and pondered living two hundred healthy years, from the Jefferson Administration to George Bush, from horse-drawn everything to the space shuttle, and of course losing friends or relatives in every war the country fought. I quickly dismissed the thought of outliving my brother, the only companion my cheated life was granted.

No. I turned toward Sonia. "Do not blame God for the womb He placed you in, for He makes no mistakes."

"We just read that He resented making humans, some more than others, I'm sure."

She looked solemnly at me. *He gave you tools to do this job.*

I don't want this job. I didn't ask for it.

Maybe you did. Her stare continued, but the outer corners of her eyes turned downward to reflect sorrow. Several silent minutes passed. "Come," she said, walking toward the back door. "Let us walk. Daylight, it is safe."

"You worried about your neighbors seeing me with you?"

"Come." She held out her hand. "There is much to discuss."

We walked upriver, and while I heard demons amongst the trees and trembled at every small creature's sound and scamper, Sonia wandered slowly, deliberately along the path, stopping occasionally to reach for flowers. When we arrived at the spot where the river began its rise, we crossed by jumping from rock to rock and returned on the opposite side. She may have appeared at first to be middle aged, or perhaps it was just her attire, but she moved with the agility of an active person my age.

"Tell me about your time in America."

She stopped and looked at me, then looked around. In my head popped the word *Chicago.*

I smiled. "That's where I live."

"That is where the Fair was. My husband was electrician in charge of grounds lighting."

"Gheorghe?"

"It was big job, months to set up, never done before."

I must have looked puzzled.

"There was no power at the time," she said.

"When *was* this?" Chicago hasn't hosted a World's Expo since . . .

"It was terrible financial time. Your president was man named Cleveland, like city. He was not good speaker."

I stood there staring at her, and she read my thoughts. Removing her scarf and pulling away her collar, she showed me the sides of her neck—nothing, no scars.

"Healed?" I asked.

"Yes. I was young and so in love. Gheorghe was great man, great mind, always trying to harness electricity. He seemed not to age, which I think is strange, so I ask his secret."

"He was one of their slaves," I said.

She nodded. "He exchange long life for work."

"And you?"

"I wanted more than anything to stay young and beautiful for him." She looked down in shame.

I thought about why she carried no scar.

"The Regulat assigned to me was killed in battle many years ago. I resume aging process."

At a slower rate, I assumed. "When did you become a widow?"

"Your president was McKinley. I come home from America

and wait for Gheorghe while he work with Tesla. He never come home."

"Wait. Who did you say he worked with?"

"A great man, great inventor, Nikola Tesla."

I had read biographies of Tesla and knew a little about him. For one thing, Tesla had received the contract to install and showcase AC power for the 1893 World's Fair in Chicago, arranged by George Westinghouse, I recall. It had bested Thomas Edison's DC power proposal. It was the biggest thing to ever happen in Chicago until Michael Jordan arrived.

"As I recall, though, Tesla worked alone," I said.

"My husband take notes. Only one who could keep up with Tesla's words. Gheorghe understood what Nikola working on. Not many did."

Gheorghe sounded like *George*. A thought occurred. "Your husband wasn't George Westinghouse?" I asked.

"No. I met Mr. Westinghouse there, but my husband's name was Gheorghe Antonescu."

"He must've been busy; that was a huge event."

"Yes. My husband said I met Stoker, the author, and his employer, Henry Irving, but I not recall the meeting."

The World's Fair display had been such a success that eastern cities ordered AC power plants up and down the Hudson River. "Did your husband stay on with Tesla during the growth years?"

"Gheorghe install power in the royal residences and palaces all over Europe."

"An electrician," I said.

"Yes. He put in the electricity at Irving's theater in London."

"The Lyceum?" I asked.

Sonia nodded. She appeared to want to say something, but did not.

"What is it?" I asked.

"Gheorghe rescued something . . . from the fire."

"The fire at the publishing house or the theater?"

"The theater," she said.

Immediately my thoughts raced to the epilogue, and she must have picked up on it, because she responded aloud: "Yes, the missing epilogue."

I pointed to her. "Do you have it?"

"No," she said. "He kept pages in a safe place. And you must go find them. This is part of your mission."

"Where are they?"

"He took them back to America to Tesla's lab. They are with the inventor's scientific papers."

Of course, I thought, *the safest place to store documents for posterity would be in the inventor's great volume of research files.* After Tesla's passing in 1943, a prodigious inventory of work, including his papers and drawings, were moved from storage in New York and New Jersey across the Atlantic to Serbia and to a museum in the inventor's honor.

"The Tesla Museum in Belgrade?" I asked.

"Yes," Sonia said. "If the chapter survives, it will be in Tesla's files."

I had a hundred more questions for her. "How did your husband—"

She interrupted me by lifting her hand, then spoke. "First you go find the chapter. Then return and I will answer the rest of your questions."

18

Monday morning I left Sonia and walked through the village toward the Gypsy's house, while the residents waited for sunrise to unshutter their homes. Father Andrew nodded and blessed me as I crossed the river back to the land of living souls. Considering what I had witnessed on Friday night, these Dumitra villagers had every reason to keep barred doors and loaded weapons between me and their loved ones.

Past the village the Gypsy waited at the end of his driveway, a waving family sending him off to Bistriţa with his copper wares. I hopped on with a nod and stretched my neck to show him it was free of puncture wounds or scars. He shared his coffee with a grunt, and I watched the town disappear into the landscape.

Though I could not see the far end of the village, I felt Sonia's parting look, one that said she was proud of me.

The morning was cool, with humid air raising woolly columns of steam off the river and an abundance of deer foraging. And while birds sang, I listened with all the concentration I could muster, trying to discern a pattern, anything that might indicate a sinister motive for participating in the ritual. Such are the missteps on the other side of the bridge to unreality. Returning to this side, I noticed wildflowers of yellow and purple decorated fields that only three days earlier had been bare. Summer had finally arrived.

I fended off ugly images with more pleasant memories featuring Berns and found myself tipping the bill of my imaginary cap and holding up fingers when I noticed the Gypsy turn to look at me, no doubt a sanity check.

"Do you like baseball?" I asked.

He shook his head, equally, I think, to reject the sport as to reject the question. I smiled and thanked him again for the ride. How I wished for a different fate than the one before me.

At the edge of Bistrița, where I had been dropped off on Friday, Arthur waited in the black Suburban. The horse cart halted, and another sum of money was exchanged. My companion Gypsy did not return my call of gratitude, only gave a farewell nod. Arthur opened the back door for me. Inside was Luc, whose stony expression clearly conveyed that my surprise side trip on my first visit to Romania had caused him a spot of grief.

Once in the vehicle, Arthur tossed me a copy of the weekend newspaper, the *Bucharest Herald*, its pages folded to reveal the

Maramureş section, the county where Baia Mare and Baia Sprie reside. The article spoke of ritual sacrifice, not at the monastery but in the cemetery I'd found, with townspeople reporting great noise and plague-sized invasions of bats. Graves had been disturbed, and there was speculation of a possible connection to a murder in the United States of a Romanian ex-pat named Mara Sadoveanu. No corpses were found in the graveyard, but plenty of blood had been spilled.

I recalled Sonia mentioning last night, during a wide-ranging discussion of the life cycle and habits of vampires, that they always remove their dead from the battlefield, even the enemy, because they cannot afford to have humans autopsy their bodies. The species also has no fingerprints, so it is tough to place them at crime scenes. *Not so for frightened foreign visitors,* I thought.

Arthur turned from his front seat to face me. "Seems you have created a bit of a *strica*, Mr. Barkeley. It is not wise to be destructive when you carry a passport."

"You know I didn't do anything wrong."

"Ah, but I am not a judge, you see, and here, let us say, our ways are not the ways of your land. Juries of peers are an American invention."

"I don't intend to be tried."

"Over the weekend I received a call from the *poliţie.*" Police. "They queried your whereabouts and suggested I contact them as soon as I once again meet up with you."

My silence prompted him to continue.

"Mr. Barkeley, I took the liberty to schedule an appointment with an *avocat*, a lawyer, in Braşov, since it appears obvious that you will be in need of such services."

Immediately my worries mounted. Did they have something similar to the Fifth Amendment? Would I be innocent until proven guilty? Was there attorney-client confidentiality?

We stopped at a small office complex and parked, and while Luc and the driver remained in the car, Arthur showed me through the doors of a law office. Annemarie Pope was the lawyer's name, and she commanded the top-floor corner office in a modest space. I learned there are no private law firms in Romania, that *avocaţi* group together to form a *barou* as part of a union. The offices lacked the panache of an upscale American white-shoe firm, but the guest chairs were comfortable leather and invited one for a long stay. Arthur and I were shown to her office without delay.

Annemarie Pope carried the air of money in her stride. She dressed entirely in shades of gray, from her mock turtle blouse to her thoroughly Western pantsuit and pumps. She wore no wedding ring.

Pointed, harsh, and purse-lipped, she looked ready to pounce. "So you are the ex-pat stirring these suspicions from here to Chicago." She spoke perfect Midwest English and pointed to a chair after shaking my hand. "Please call me Anna."

I looked at the letters framed on her walls, including a degree from the University of Michigan Law School to complement her Romanian degrees and certification. "Ms. Pope." I sat across from her large dark-stained oak desk.

She nodded. "So you have decided to seek legal counsel prior to answering questions as a person of interest."

"Yes. I didn't know what happened until my brother phoned me here."

"When was that?" she asked.

I looked down and started counting on my fingers. It all seemed like one long day since I had arrived. "I don't know."

"Mr. Barkeley," she said, "you will need to account for your time since the . . . unfortunate incidents, all of it, if you wish to appear credible."

I looked up at her. "Should I write it on a calendar?"

"However you recall it, you must secure it in your memory."

I nodded, though I no longer trusted my memory.

"Let me tell you a few things I know of this case, Mr. Barkeley." She looked down at her notepad. "When Mr. Ardelean engaged my services, I placed a couple phone calls back to the States, and I must tell you that things do not look good for you at this point."

"Ms. Pope, I don't even know when these murders happened, so I don't know what days to account for."

"Let me begin again," she said. "I am not the person you need to convince of your innocence. What this initial consultation is intended to accomplish is for me to ask you certain questions, queries you are likely to face either during questioning or a trial, so that I can advise you of your options. Is that okay?"

"Yes, ma'am."

"What day and time did you arrive at the airport in Bucharest?"

I thought it over. "The first or second time?"

"This latest trip."

I gave her the date.

"Is that what your passport stamp will verify?"

"Yes," I said reflexively, then remembered that the private flight had taxied to a hangar and we left with the cargo and by-passed Customs.

"May I see your passport?" She held out her hand.

"No."

"I may not see it, or the stamp will not verify the date?"

Silence stole several seconds of airtime before I answered. "Both."

"Are you prepared to testify how you entered the country without the approval of Customs?"

I sat mute.

"When you left Romania the first time, did you travel according to the itinerary Mr. Ardelean here provided you?"

That seemed like such a long time ago. "No." I thought of Luc sitting outside.

"Where did you go?"

"From Braşov I traveled by train north to Baia Mare and on to Munich. I caught the same number flight home, just a couple days later."

"Was Baia Mare your only other stop?"

"Yes." I recalled my purchases from the merchant.

"And what was your purpose in visiting Baia Mare?"

"I was born there." I glanced down. "Wanted to buy my brother a souvenir gift . . . and visit my mother."

Ms. Pope squinted at me; she knew better.

"Visit my mother's gravesite."

"And did you do both?"

"Yes." I'm sure she saw the sadness in my eyes, because she pushed a box of tissues my way. "I had to go to the Hall of Records to find where she is."

"*Orfan?*" she asked.

"Yes. Both parents . . . in a fire."

"So you *were* born here."

I nodded. "Spent two years in the state-run orphanage before being rescued by the Catholic Church."

"And they uprooted you to Chicago."

"Yes."

"Tell me about your childhood."

A lot safer than my adulthood is turning out to be, I thought, and recalled the Don's face. "The nuns did the best job they could, considering . . . and I will always be grateful for being reared in God's ways."

"Did God tell you to murder those two people?"

"I did not murder those two people," I said, "and no, God does not talk to me directly."

"Indirectly?"

I didn't give her the satisfaction of a response.

"Are you engaged in any cultlike behaviors? Belong to any associations?"

"No. And the only association I belong to is professional."

"What would that be?"

"Appraisals and authentication work, based in Chicago."

"Are you well-known in your field?"

"Yes, I would say so."

"What would your associates say about you and your work?"

I thought a moment. "That I never make mistakes."

"Do you own any vampire books?"

"Yes."

"How many?"

"Hundreds. I have—"

"Any books on the occult?"

I nodded.

"Please state yes or no."

"Yes." I could tell where this was going, and it was not purgatory. Someplace lower.

"Are you familiar with Vlad the Third?"

"Yes. He was a fifteenth-century Wallachian prince and warlord."

"What was he known for?"

"Vlad the Impaler," I said. "Stuck his victims on poles and threw others onto spears."

"Just like the two murder victims."

I shrugged my shoulders as if I didn't know.

"Mr. Barkeley, what do you do for a living?"

"I own a warehouse full of rare and first edition books that I sell online to collectors. I also provide authentication services when someone needs verification regarding a book, a letter, or a manuscript."

"I see," she said. "And tell me, what did the authorities find when they raided your warehouse looking for you in connection with these crimes?"

The thought infuriated me. "Books, I imagine."

"Including many books on vampires and the occult?"

I thought of the inventory, including a hundred or so first editions on all things vampire, since they are always in demand.

"Mr. Barkeley?"

"Everything in inventory is for sale; it is *not* my private collection. Yes, there are several vampire books, because that genre's fans are fanatical and collect first editions."

"Is that how you came to meet the deceased?"

"Mara? Yes. She purchased several first editions."

"When was the last time you saw Ms. Sadoveanu?"

"I went to see her the day before my Philadelphia trip."

"What did you discuss?"

I couldn't think of anything that I wished to divulge, and shrugged my shoulders.

"Was anyone with her?"

I refused to react. "No. She lives alone."

"And from there?"

I decided that if no one had seen me at Doug Carli's office, then I would not offer that I had been there. "The next day I worked at the Rosenbach Museum, and the following night flew to Bucharest."

"What flight?"

"It was a private chartered flight."

"What time did it leave?"

"I don't know; it was nighttime."

"I mean, was it just after sundown, or closer to midnight?"

"I don't recall."

"Was there anyone with you on the flight?"

"Security guards."

"Guarding the manuscript or guarding you?"

I laughed. The question sounded funny in a morbid way.

"I was not being funny, Mr. Barkeley."

"I know, Ms. Pope. It just seems odd . . . I was transporting extremely valuable cargo and arrived late the next day in Bucharest to present it to the buyer."

"And who is the buyer?"

Arthur interrupted, "I am acting as the agent on behalf of the family, madam. And Mr. Barkeley is a guest at the family residence in Bran."

She nodded.

"Without telling me who, Mr. Barkeley, do you know who the buyer is?"

"Ah, no."

"Where were you on the night of May fifteenth?"

I thought a moment. That was the night of the battle in the cemetery. The real answer would get me a spell in some mental institution. "I don't recall."

"Then why might your fingerprints be on the tomb of Loreena Braithwaite in the cemetery just outside Baia Sprie?"

I looked down and away. It was all too preposterous to contemplate, much less explain.

"Okay," she said, "here is how I see things." The attorney glanced again at her paper, looked at me, and sighed. "I don't know you, have never met you. What I am about to say is not personal, but a professional legal recommendation from my years of working in the criminal justice system, both here and in the States."

This did not sound like it was going to go well.

She reminded me that my brother had not phoned me, since he did not know where I was staying. She must have received that information from Arthur.

"You absolutely must know your time line, Joseph, and not in some memorized way."

"I'll work on it."

She went on to say that the lack of an inbound passport stamp would suggest to a court my dealing in black-market traffic, regardless of whether the manuscript story was legit. My reasons for deviating from the original itinerary as a guest of Mr. Ardelean were understandable since it was my first time back, but demonstrated poor judgment. Next she called me on failing to divulge my side trip to Bistriţa and Dumitra the first time, obviously revealed by Arthur.

She warned me to be careful of my word choice. For example, she quoted me: "'I did not murder *those two people.*'" Judges listen for what you don't say as much as what you do say and how you parse things. I should have said that I never killed anyone, that I did see Mara the day before I flew to Philadelphia, and left with the promise of souvenirs. I was to avoid references to God.

As for my saying that "I never make mistakes," she reminded me that the criminal mind invests great effort attempting to pull off the perfect crime, and modesty would suit me better. As for the questions about my books, I was to refer to them as part of my unsold inventory. And when speaking of the occult, she suggested I use the word *them* to create separation.

She continued, "You showed emotional volatility when I asked you about the raid on your warehouse."

"Well, the thought of some jerks breaking down my doors and stealing my life's work sort of pisses me off."

"Next time, try to look hurt instead, just like you should work on your response when asked if you know who the buyer is."

"I don't know the buyer," I said.

"Visually, that was not what you conveyed."

"Yes, ma'am."

"As for your fingerprints on Miss Braithwaite's tomb, I suggest you recall the facts along with your mode of transportation and where you stayed, as well as your motive for being there."

I nodded. That pretty much covered all her questions and my responses. I was impressed that she had recalled all of our exchanges without the aid of notes. It gave me confidence in her judgment, even if I didn't like her bedside manner.

"Allow me to summarize," she said, pausing to take a deep breath. "This does not look good."

"I know."

"I believe that if you give a seasoned detective answers to the same questions I posed, even if you worked on your responses, you would immediately turn from a person of interest to the prime suspect."

I looked down again.

"During questioning they would say you were not being detained, but they would start delaying your release until they could secure a warrant for your arrest."

"Is that here or there?"

"Either," she said. "In high-profile cases like this, a law enforcement official could be sent from the States. Extradition papers would be drafted, and they would delay you until they felt secure charging you."

"Anna . . . my two friends were murdered. I didn't do it, you know that, Arthur knows that. How can I be charged with murder when—"

"Mr. Barkeley," she cut in. "You were the last person to visit both of them before they were brutally murdered in similar ritual fashion. Your accounting for time and activities since those events has holes in it. A good prosecutor could adequately paint you as an antisocial loner with a troubled childhood, the classic sociopathic killer profile. Frankly, if you were not in the custody of one of our country's leading citizens"—she nodded toward Arthur—"you'd be fighting extradition right now."

I never thought I would ever ask this in my life, but I did: "What are my options?"

She rubbed her forehead and looked again at Arthur. "You could fight extradition."

"You mean refuse to go home?" The very thought inspired a wave of panic.

"This country, along with others in the EU, will not extradite its citizens to any country where a conviction could bring the death penalty."

All I heard was *death penalty*. She said several more things after that, and I asked her to repeat them.

"Repeat what I said from what point?"

"'Death penalty.'"

"There has not been a death penalty in Wisconsin since the first half of the nineteenth century, but there is one on the books in Illinois. It's been suspended under executive order by the last few governors, but it is not abolished."

"So I most likely would not face extradition."

"Unless there is a plea deal with a promise not to seek the death penalty," she said. "Do you understand this?"

"Yes. Joliet."

"Stateville, that's right. Certainly your name and profile would be instant national news even before you arrived back in the States. Your business would be gone and your name forever linked to cult killings even if you're found not guilty."

I sat shaking my head.

"You would get a nickname. Considering where you were born, it would be something with *Transylvania* or *Impaler* in it." She waited a moment before adding the obvious. "And your brother would be targeted."

This I already knew, but the reality hit harder when someone else said it. "Ms. Pope, you said *its citizens* . . ."

"You were born here, Mr. Barkeley; you are of Romanian blood."

"I am an American citizen."

"Yes, but while becoming an American citizen you were a

minor, and as such never renounced any other citizenships. You have not renounced any as an adult, have you?"

"No. I never thought about citizenship."

"Romanian law recognizes that since you were born on this soil to at least one Romanian citizen parent, you are by birthright a Romanian. In the case of someone who leaves as a minor, all you have to do is sign an official document that states you intend to resume your citizenship and you are thus recognized."

"Does the document include renunciation of my American citizenship?"

She paused before answering. "Yes. It would have to in order to avoid extradition."

I felt a net drawing around me, held by Dalca and Arthur Ardelean, who sat there without expression. Danger might be described as when you're caught behind the eight ball. But real danger is when you're caught behind the eight ball and didn't even realize you were at the billiards table.

"I'd like to think about it."

"Mr. Barkeley," she said, leaning toward me, "if the *poliţie* are out in the lobby, you are extradited."

If so, I could escape the inevitable confrontation with Dalca.

Arthur spoke up. "*Avocat* Pope, would it be possible to have your client sign such a document in anticipation of filing?"

She nodded.

"What does that mean?" I asked.

"We have the forms in this office," she said. "You could sign the renunciation forms, and I would hold them in anticipation of your call to file them. You will have to carry a copy of them with your U.S. passport."

"But you won't file until I call?"

"That's correct. I will do that . . . for Mr. Ardelean, of course."

It took the better part of an hour for me to read the forms, interpret, and clarify before concluding our meeting and putting my signature on the documents. Romania was my home for the foreseeable future. My world shrank to the size of Oregon.

"Please notify Mr. Ardelean of your whereabouts at all times, and know that only the neighboring countries have complete reciprocal agreements with Romania regarding citizenship laws."

I shook her hand and thanked her. *"Mulțumesc."*

Ms. Pope gave me what must have passed, for her, as an empathetic look. "I am not going to tell you that it's all going to work out or be okay."

Like I didn't know that. I nodded and returned to the vehicle while Arthur concluded his visit with Pope. The driver opened the door for me and I took a seat in the back, next to Luc.

"So," he said, "we sit beneath the same old oak tree."

There is an old Romanian fable about sitting in the shade of an old oak tree and watching the walls of your coffin grow. Such fatalisms being the staple of Romanian lore, I knew what he meant—that our efforts shared a common end point.

"Don't worry," I said, "it's an old-growth forest."

I hoped.

19

The drive back to the castle was uneventful, quiet, paranoid. Every vehicle looked suspect, as did the one I was riding in, the only large black American SUV on the road. Certain phrases circled the drain in my mind: *death penalty, ritual killing, occult killer, Joliet Joe the Impaler.*

Back in Castel Bran, my escorts led me to my guest quarters in the corner tower, and when Arthur asked if there was anything else I needed, I told him I wished to visit with Dalca to discuss his ultimatum. He replied that if there was a meeting to be called, it would be at the insistence of the Master, and that my wishes were as insignificant as the *sânge* (*blood*) of slaves. Further, I was to address Dalca with the title and formal diction befitting a prince.

"How does he wish to be addressed?" I asked.

"He does not wish, he insists on *Master*."

Luc remained with me after Arthur departed. His look had not softened the entire day, and he explained why. "Look, Barkeley, you had your itinerary and tickets in hand. When you left me and chose to run personal errands, did it occur to you that I was in charge of getting you to and from the airport?"

"No," I said, "it did not. And I paid for the ticket changes myself."

"Well, in case you hadn't figured it out yet, you got me on the wrong side of the Master with your stunt, and now I have to stay with you for as long as you're here."

I knew the consequences of outliving your usefulness to the family, and as long as we were stuck together I thought it wise to apply a little salve. "I'm sorry I didn't discuss my plans with you. I didn't know you had anything at stake. I just wanted to see my hometown."

Luc did not exactly accept my apology. "I don't mean I have to stay in the same room, or even the same building. But I have to be able to locate you at all times."

"Okay." That loosened things only slightly.

"Look," he said, sitting back in his chair, "not every meeting with the Master is hostile. Some can actually be pleasant . . . even invigorating. He is patient, and sometimes he can be pretty open about things he's seen over the years. And he can be very, very generous."

"Maybe when he wants something. Everyone has it in them to be pleasant then."

"My point exactly," he said, pointing at me. "So as long as he thinks he can get something from you, and you don't disappear, then I still serve a useful purpose to him."

"I got it," I said. "Your neck is tied to my ankle."

"As long as we understand each other."

"In the meantime, can you see about getting me out for a few walks around the neighborhood? I need the exercise to stay sharp."

Luc shook his head. "It's not up to me." And he left.

A night passed and then a day and another night was in progress when I awoke from a sound sleep just after midnight. Someone had entered the room, and my nose recognized the odor. The strongest link to memory is the sense of smell, and I knew it was Dalca before adjusting my eyes to the shadows and streaming moonlight. A pair of red eyes emerged over in the parlor section of the suite.

His strong voice reached across the space. "I wish to discuss my proposal."

Sitting up in bed, I slipped into a robe and shoes and moved to the seat across from where he sat. I could see no more than his outline and eyes, which shone a lesser shade of red that evening.

"Yes," I said. When he did not respond, I added, "Master."

"Cover yourself."

I looked down to see if I was exposed and realized my crucifix was in full view. I tucked it into my shirt. *"Scuzaţi-ma."*

I waited for him to start the conversation, and in a dismissive tone he said, "Pity . . . about your friends."

Immediately my blood pressure soared.

I heard him breathe deeply, his nose in the air and mouth open, a long finger tracing his chin. "I smell . . . fury. It crowds your fearful heart."

I took it as something of a compliment. No one was more surprised than I at my newfound ability to harbor such rage. And that anger spawned a sense of calculation, for I instinctively knew that I had to buy time, not just to find his answers, but mine as well. Still, how does one manipulate a man who embodies cold calculation himself? A monster whose heart never entertained empathy or remorse?

"Know, Christian boy, that your friends' lives are on your head. When I insisted that you keep your mouth shut, did it not occur to you that it might be for your own good as well as your client's?"

"No." I looked down. "It did not."

"And once you knew what you were looking at, did it not occur to you there may be powerful competing forces that would be willing to go to war for it?"

For a brief moment I wanted to believe what he was implying, that I had been taken for a fool—and my friends' lives literally taken—by someone else.

"Here I invite you into my house, even into my sanctuary, extend a financial offer more generous than you could ever attain in your lifetime of work. Yet you fail to adhere to the most rudimentary of demands—simple silence." He breathed in again. "And now you feel . . . *prost*." Foolish.

He tried to sound convincing, yet he was anything but.

Dalca continued, "You already have the blood of my family flowing through your veins. Once you have completed your mission, I am prepared to offer you my own blood, the Noble blood . . . of eternal life."

I felt insulted. Briefly I recalled the Don's message: "Your soul is the only thing that is yours eternally. Protect it." With that, I felt the strength of proclaiming my faith and love of God, and reached to my chest and revealed the crucifix. "Only my Savior gives me eternal life."

His red eyes flared and he looked away. I returned the cross to its place, and Dalca stood and strolled over to the window. Looking out at the night, he pointed to the valley floor. "My family and I watched your Christian Crusaders march through this very yard on their way to slaughter infidels and sack great cities in the name of this God of yours. Oh yes, they were all dressed up with their painted shields and amulets and pointy sticks, eating their way through the land like locusts and thinking their little crosses would protect them. Just like you there. And for what? A disagreement over whose book was right? Fools. Dead fools."

"This crucifix cannot hurt you," I said, subtly redirecting the conversation to put him on the defensive. "Yet the sight of it repulses you."

"That thing holds no power over me." He dismissed it with a wave.

"Does the sight of God remind you that you were born with no soul?"

"Christian!" He spat out the word. "A dead man hung on a

cross in shame by humans. You think that is the face of your Creator?"

"You will never see His face," I said.

"What is this God that watches wars and does not lift a finger to stop them?" He drew out God's name under a heavy breath, as if it pained him. "What is this . . . *thing* . . . that creates superior mortal sons, then flaunts His new . . . beloved . . . creation? What reaction would you expect, human?"

"So you resent our Lord."

In an instant Dalca was standing behind me, bending toward my ear. "Every sense given you, my kind is superior. You are slow, stupid, pathetic. It takes you years before you can even feed yourself."

"But we were given souls."

"Only to force you to behave or else suffer eternal torment. I would rather be destroyed." His voice was just over a whisper, going back and forth behind me to each ear.

"God grants eternal companionship to those of us who love Him."

"And for those who despise Him?"

"Eternal death," I said.

"There are differences, *orfan*—you are awake in your eternal death, forever tormented. But you . . . you have the opportunity to choose your fate. Not I. What kind of *loving God* would create life without such a chance?"

"So you choose to destroy that which He loves."

"I *hate* Him." He drew out a full-breath *h* on *hate* as he breathed on the back of my head, parting my hair. It smelled. "And I hate you, human . . . simply because you exist. I want to *hurt* Him. I want to know He cries watching His children lured to the other side and dying in torture, freely choosing evil. He spurns my children; I reject His equally."

"If you are already condemned, then you are lucky to be mortal."

"We were not condemned until your kind came along."

I stiffened as he sniffed the back of my neck.

"I smell . . . pity. I forbid pity."

I turned around and looked at him, his eyes glowing a brighter shade of red. "You think you know me. You think you know what I feel. Pity? Not for you. Fear?" I shrugged. "I might fear you, but I don't fear death. I know God will be just to me."

He lifted his lip to show his long sharp teeth and sound a low growl. Through a clenched jaw he hissed, "Don't threaten me, human. I could force you to *not* die, to live as my personal slave. Until I choose otherwise. And don't challenge me, *orfan*; you have already seen your fate."

"It's only a matter of when," I said, "and since I don't want it to be tonight, I accept your ultimatum, but not your offer of blood."

"Oh, come now," his voice soothed, and he ran a hand down the side of my face. "Ultimatum sounds so . . . Ceauşescu. Now, let us discuss your progress."

I said, "There are notes throughout the manuscript, as you know. Some direct the reader to places where more clues might lie, and then to other places. Whoever assisted Bram Stoker had knowledge of events and did not want them handed off to your family. The paper he used provided as much of a clue as what he wrote."

"So what is it you want?"

In that moment his leash loosened ever so slightly, for it was the first time he ever asked me a question. Up to that point he had only given me statements and directives, and I knew I needed to make it convincing. "My research will take me to where I think those clues are. First to Belgrade. I'm not sure after that."

He nodded. "Just remember, I am patient only so much, boy. You will be protected, of course." Then he pointed to my chest. "As long as you wear your little pagan amulet."

With that he walked swiftly and silently toward the door.

"Thank you," I said.

He looked at me, then spat on the floor and left.

20

Just before sunrise, Luc met me in my room, and with a
new, more rigid, comportment, escorted me down to the
waiting carriage at the front door. My overnight bags in
tow, I climbed aboard and took a seat and watched Arthur
mouth last-minute instructions to Luc at the door before
releasing him to join me.

I looked to the east just as the dawn's first rays illuminated the
castle walls, and as we pulled away from Castel Bran I loosely
quoted the poet of Luc's namesake: "At dawn, when the ashes of
night are gone, taken by the wind to the west . . ." I offered to let
him finish the verse, but his face showed a stolid indifference.

From Bran we traveled by bus to Braşov and then by train
through Bucharest and on to Serbia, where we took a taxi to the

Excelsior Hotel. The next morning, we walked from there to the Tesla Museum at Krunska 51 in central Belgrade. Luc briefed me on the rules I was to obey under his watch—mainly no side trips or changes of plans. I was to meet him at the appointed time to break for lunch and he said he'd return promptly at the museum's closing hour. Relieved that I would be working alone, I promised there would be no deviation.

I stood outside the museum and said a silent prayer that what I sought was within its walls. Built in 1929 as a residence in a villa style of arched windows and entryways, with two stories plus a partial underground basement, the building since had been converted to a small, single-themed museum housing only articles of legacy from the prolific inventor.

I arrived just before opening and was greeted by a doleful-looking attendant who let me in early to browse the open displays. The public viewing portion occupied the main floor, a counterclockwise tour of seven themed areas wrapping a central enclosed stairway and ending back at the entrance foyer. The top floor served as offices, and the basement as archive storage.

I stepped into the first area, a classically designed room of hardwood plank floors and twelve-foot ceilings. Indirect lighting added an elegant touch, with large life-size photos of Nikola Tesla and his family, some friends, and scenes from his place of birth used as wallpaper. I was struck by the intensity of Tesla's look, the inventor's face pointed with the usual Slavic features and a direct stare, as if the cameraman had just posed a challenge.

In the second room a dozen glass curio cabinets held his personal objects, such as a black hat and traveling bag, tickets to events, invitations and evidence that his social life was as active as his scientific one. Tesla was a man married to greatness, but he bickered with her instruction, and the two remained asymptotic. Correspondence decorated the walls, letters from such luminaries as Mark Twain, George Westinghouse, and Lord Tennyson. A dozen or more small inventions rested in the cases.

At the far corner of the first floor, in the third room, rested Tesla's ashes in a golden spherical urn hoisted on a marble pedestal. And at the tour's completion, near the museum's entrance, his death mask stared back at his unfinished work from inside a glass case.

The curator, a man of few words and fewer smiles, pointed toward the stairwell, where I descended past a locked interior door and into the large archive room. Immediately the air temp and humidity told me this was not the proper place to store valuable documents, nor were the contents cataloged or secured in weather-safe containers. The concrete floors spelled moisture. A quick look at the basement windows shook me with the realization that one small flood through the street-level windows would destroy more than a hundred thousand irreplaceable documents. Above the windows were mounted surveillance cameras.

In broken English the attendant asked if I knew which documents I sought.

"Laboratory notes and personal journals from the 1890s, including notes taken by assistants."

"We try best to organize by dates," he said, pointing toward the middle stacks. "Most volumes come from last two decades of that century . . . seem to be in these."

"Thank you. I'll return the boxes back precisely."

He left with a nod and resumed his duties upstairs, and I paused to look around. Finding myself again in the bowels of a museum, much like the Rosenbach, alone this time, a sense of urgency pushed me toward a strategy of how best to search systematically. Though I wished to inspect each document, there was insufficient time, and turning to the process of elimination I listed what I was not looking for—drawings, accolades, legal correspondence, and anything written in the twentieth century. Things written personally by Tesla were likely not pertinent, except as it established the relationship between the inventor and his assistant, Gheorghe.

More specifically, I was searching for the lost epilogue and any notes attached to it.

I had already seen the southpaw handwriting of the assistant, as well as Abraham Stoker's, so at least I knew the size and shape of the needle I sought in this haystack. As the attendant had purported, the stacks were loosely arranged by decade, so I began by lifting a box from the nearest stack and carried it to a large working table. The contents of the box had that unmistakable chemical smell of paper's acidic composting that, if not protected against air's natural assault, would first discolor, then adhere, and finally lose its absorbency and disintegrate.

The first batch included correspondence between Tesla and the U.S. War Department in the Woodrow Wilson era, in which he proposed to build remote-controlled submarines and demonstrate them in the Hudson River. The same box also held similar proposals from the Taft Administration.

Wrong century and subject, as it turned out. To mark what I'd already viewed and rejected, I noted contents on a yellow pad and placed the manifests inside the boxes, scribing the outsides of boxes with small numbers denoting the years covered. Three hours into my task, I had reviewed an entire row of boxes before taking a break. The work was heavy and dusty, but my heart ached for the fate that most certainly awaited these decaying documents, for although they saw the end of the last century, they would not see another. I mentioned this to the curator as the day ended, and he commented that it was a matter of resource priority and his government had a long list above it.

How offensive, I thought, to lose treasures that belong to the ages because of budget casualties. The very idea of an archive is to preserve, not to set in motion the process of decay.

Ending the day, I was confident that by the week's end I could inspect and mark every box. Unfortunately, that first day had yielded nothing on the topic I sought.

As I left the museum, Luc was waiting for me across the street. He did not say much and did not appear to be fielding questions on his day's activity. He did, however, seem to sense that I needed to do something more than just return to my hotel room, and we detoured toward Pionirski Park for a lengthy walk. Ours was a brisk pace among the strolling couples and lounging seniors who enjoyed the summery warmth that brought the gardens and trees into full bloom. As sunset approached, we headed back to the Excelsior Hotel for a late and mostly silent dinner.

Luc mostly pushed his food around his plate with his fork before asking, "Making any progress?"

I shrugged. "I won't know until I find something."

"Look." Luc pointed his fork in my direction. "I have to check in with the Master every couple days. Give me something to report."

"It's a mess down there."

"That's all you got?" he said, shaking his head. "Let me help you then. Maybe it will help us both. What are you working on?"

I could not divulge my assignment.

"Barkeley," he said, continuing to point his fork in my direction, "I know what you're working on. I just don't know how Tesla ties into it, except the time frames overlap."

I thought about how to say something without saying anything. Of course Tesla had nothing to do with the novel or its creatures, but his assistant, Gheorghe, obviously knew that the famous inventor's research papers would be archived after his death. It must have seemed a safe way to hide them without destroying them.

"You're right," I told Luc. "The connection is the time frame. Tesla's electrical company had a contract to convert Bram Stoker's theater from gas to electrical lighting. They archived correspondence grouped roughly by decade. I'm going through every piece of paper and note during the 1890s."

"But why? You think some of Stoker's documents got mixed up with Tesla's during that time?"

I shrugged.

I knew this was the tricky part of answering, because I had to tell him something that could be verified, but also tell him something to keep the leash long. "No. I think some documents were *taken* so they would not get published in the book. And whoever did it replaced it with something that would instigate conflict within the family."

"Well, that certainly did happen," Luc said.

"Possibly with the idea to see who surfaces."

"Interesting conjecture, but that last part I won't put in my report." His look suggested he was pleased with my response. Then he asked, "So what do you think you'll find?"

"Whatever is hidden in there is meant to be found, so I suspect it will point to actual events and where they took place."

"Thank you," Luc said, "that's better. Some form of that I can report. Let me know if I can add anything by tomorrow night."

Dinner ended, and I promised Luc I would stay the entire night in my room.

⊰⊱

On my third day in the basement of the Tesla Museum, returning from a midday break, I opened a box in a new row and found what turned out to be the introductory correspondence sent by the inventor's assistant, Sonia's husband.

21 April, 1892
Belgrade

Dear Mr. Tesla,

We first met ten years ago at the power station in Strasbourg when you came under the employ of the local authority to repair the damage caused by an explosion. I am the man you entrusted to be your laborer. We again met in Paris in 1889. Since those days I have given great preponderance of thought to your Alternating Current theories and agree that this will be the practical solution to the limitations imposed by Mr. Edison's systems.

I am not a learned man of letters, but as you might recall, I do give complete attention to my tasks, and by my measured observance of distance degradation from the source, I estimate Mr. Edison will need to place generating stations at two-mile intervals, and not ten miles as posited by his proposals. On the basis of the latter, the local officials are proceeding with plans to install commercial power sources throughout the city at ten-mile intervals, and most certainly will have exhausted the city's coffers before realizing their failure.

I speak German, English, and of course my native Romanian. If I can be of service to you either here on the Continent or in the States, I will be your most faithful assistant.

I shall present myself to you upon your lecture visit this June to Belgrade, where I hope you will allow sufficient time to discuss your alternatives with the city officials.

> *Sincerely,*
> *Gheorghe Antonescu*

I sensed my blood pressure surge at finally connecting physical evidence to that which I had only spoken of with Sonia. I wished she were there at the moment to hold it.

The box further yielded a half dozen such letters prior to Tesla's hiring his assistant that year, 1892. This began the greatest acceleration toward modernism the world has ever seen, for the harnessing of electricity and its cheap production ended the slow plod out of agrarianism and into the age of convenience.

I paused at a letter from George Westinghouse that challenged the inventor to consider electrical-powered appliances in every American home, not just the moneyed class. It dawned on me then that the world of modern invention had been waiting for electricity as much as electricity spawned modern inventions. And though I might have savored an unlimited dig through the historical documents of our greatest inventors, I had business to attend to, so I moved on.

Several more letters from George Westinghouse to Tesla followed, one offering to purchase Tesla's power-generating machine patents with a royalty that eventually would have funded every idea he could ever conjure. But next in the pile came Tesla's rejection letter, which would surely rank among history's worst business decisions. Instead, Tesla chose to undertake self-guided expansion with very limited capital, thus a shoestring staff, including one Gheorghe Antonescu, who worked for Tesla repairing Edison's generating systems in Europe. Countless nights Tesla spent in his lab in New York City while his engineering staff babysat flimsy infant power systems. Then, later that year, George Westinghouse won the contract to provide electricity for the World's Fair in Chicago and tasked Tesla with installing it in only eight months. Immediately the inventor sent for Antonescu, exhorting him to grab the first available boat and join him as a long-term assistant. I found Gheorghe's response letter filed with Westinghouse's congratulatory note.

1 August, 1892
London

Dear Mr. Tesla,

How pleased I am that you have chosen me to join you in this historic endeavor. Am departing from Southampton on the first berth I can secure.

Recently, my work here in London has been near The Strand in the Theatre District, and in that endeavor I chanced to meet the owner and operator of the Lyceum Theatre, Sir Henry Irving. He claims to have met you at your lecture before the Royal Society of London and insists he knows sincere from acting when he sees it. I believe I have convinced him to travel to Chicago's Fair for a firsthand demonstration, and he agreed to schedule his entire company for travel, including the actress Ellen Terry and his operations manager, Mr. Abraham Stoker.

There are no fewer than two dozen theatres within walking distance of The Strand here, Mr. Tesla, and I am confident that as one house, such as the prestigious Lyceum, converts, the others will queue with impatience.

My wife, Sonia, will be accompanying me, and although she does not speak the language she has begun taking lessons in anticipation of working at the event.

Congratulations again and I
look forward to seeing you soon,
Gheorghe Antonescu

That was how Sonia and Gheorghe came to America. He worked eight months, day and night, beside Tesla to build the AC-generating station on the fairgrounds, erect poles, string wires, and run cable inside buildings. Sonia learned the language and worked the event in her soothsaying tent. Tesla won his contracts when buyers observed firsthand that his newly invented systems were safe.

Among the papers I found a list of London theatres, written in Gheorghe's handwriting, with check marks beside those who signed contracts to convert from gas to electric lighting systems and purchases of electrical stage lights. First on the list was the Lyceum, and a contract executed by Sir Henry Irving rested in the box.

Following the Chicago Fair, Gheorghe and Sonia returned to Europe and modernization work began at the Lyceum. In the file box were dozens of drawings and crude schematics of the electrician's work, plus several notes exchanged with the operations manager, Bram Stoker. Mostly the notes covered supply purchase orders and work schedules, but others spoke of their outside meetings on "that other topic."

The next box contained the original contracts signed by Tesla to provide power stations and transformation plans for several palaces, grand residences, and government buildings across Europe. Three such castles were located in Romania, one of which I had already stayed in. The dim lights in the basement came to mind.

I located several documents tracking Gheorghe over a four-year period around Europe and back and forth to New York City.

He was Tesla's most versatile employee across the Atlantic. Finally, in 1897, Tesla invited him back to New York to assist him by taking notes in his laboratory, to which I found this response letter:

14 April, 1897

London

Dear Mr. Tesla,

I will be honored to take the position of lab assistant with you, though I am briefly detained in London at the Lyceum with a most pressing issue, one that cannot see my departure before resolution.

As soon as such matter is resolved, I shall at once return. My most conservative estimate would be that resolution shall occur within thirty days of this postmark.

With Sincerest Gratitude,

George

I understand I was a little slow connecting dots, but when I saw *George* written and registered the date, I realized why I should have identified him earlier. I recalled my authentication work at the Rosenbach: Included in the documents were articles of news clipped from London papers chronicling the fires at the Lyceum and those that consumed the Constable publishing house. The person questioned and released in connection with the theater fire was an itinerant tradesman, an electrician by the name of

George Anton, the Americanized version of the name Gheorghe Antonescu.

Mere weeks separated that letter and the fire at Constable, where all of Stoker's first editions were consumed. George was there for both events.

I then looked closely at the handwriting on the correspondence sent from George to Tesla. Though I had immediately recognized that the penman wrote left-handed, it took until that moment to realize that the same hand that penned those letters also wrote the notes on Stoker's manuscript. Undeniably, Sonia's husband George served as assistant to both Tesla and Stoker.

That raised a question in my mind—why would Sonia give me only half the truth?

21

I took a moment to inventory what I knew, a mental list connecting dates with people. It all started in 1890 when Bram Stoker began composing his novel, based upon ideas gleaned from that era's gothic plays, which had often been staged at the Lyceum Theatre. The story took a material change in 1894, when the electrician charged with installing AC power at the theater provided Stoker with numerous details of Romanian and vampire-related lore, events, and locales that Stoker could never have known on his own. Yet the assistant, Gheorghe, had clearly not intended for Stoker to include all these details in a book destined for international publication. In fact, based on the notes I'd read in the original manuscript, I gathered that the two had a falling-out when Stoker included confidential details as the book went to press. This was followed by the warehouse fire, and a total loss of the first editions—perhaps a desperate attempt by Gheorghe to prevent the dissemination of sensitive information. Second and subsequent editions of *Dracula* included only the content that Gheorghe had approved of.

Yet at some point much later the secrets were bound to surface, as they had when I'd gained access to the original epilogue in Philadelphia. Still, the location clues there had led me to the wrong grave entirely, one the assistant deliberately inserted, whose discovery led to a familial war between Noble vampires.

It was confounding, as I knew the who and when, but not yet the real where, how, or why. It was like cobbling together a puzzle, but the last few remaining pieces did not fit the available spaces. They must be in a different storage box. I was sure they were somewhere in that basement.

Now that I was getting closer to finding what I needed, my mind turned to practicalities—specifically to conducting some petty larceny. I started by casing the perimeter of the basement, checking the state of the windows. Most of them were either painted shut or stuck in the closed position, but one in the back corner near the security camera had a mechanical lock and no contact sensor. I tested it and found the wood screws stripped out. A visual deterrent, yes, but one good yank and the latch would lift with the window.

I recognized the security camera as one made by the same company as those installed in my warehouse. During my shopping, I learned that some cameras run at all times and the tapes get archived. Other cameras run only when the system is activated after hours, and the tapes are archived only if the system is set off. And the least expensive cameras only run once a system is activated after business hours and a disturbance triggers them and films the activity until manually turned off. The way to identify which of the three was by the small red light on top of the camera. Each camera has two small hemispherical objects on its top; one is the motion detector and the other is the camera light indicator. If the red camera light is on that means the camera's running. This one was not on, like the one in the other corner, thus I knew it was a less expensive system that filmed only when activated.

I made a mental note of this and returned to the boxes.

The next box held a collection of reference books and technical papers either written or dictated by Tesla, plus professional responses from his contemporaries. An old Bible contributed mightily to the box's excess weight.

The box next to it was marked *teatru. Theater.* My pulse racing, I hauled the container to the working table. Externally, it appeared different from the other archived boxes in that it had two crossing straps to keep the lid affixed. Inside I found the contracts for several London theater houses near The Strand, including the Lyceum's work orders, correspondence, and invoices for ancillary electrical supplies. It felt close, so close.

I inspected every invoice, every paper scrap, and everywhere George's handwriting appeared, as well as Stoker's initials and signatures as he signed for goods received. I turned everything over, everything upside down, until I found a handful of letters in envelopes addressed to George Anton from Abraham Stoker. Inspecting the paper as well as the contents, I could positively place them as authentic. But as I poured over each paragraph, each word, the only subject mentioned was the theater's renovation. As I read them in order, there was not a single reference to Stoker's manuscript, except some references in early 1896 to "the other issue."

I reached for the last file folder in the box, deeply disappointed that my senses had let me down. I had felt so sure that I'd find something in this batch. Indeed, that little voice inside, which had never betrayed me before, had told me to prepare to remove documents from the museum.

A voice from the stairwell sent an electrical shock through me: "We are closing now." It was the attendant keeping bureaucrat hours.

"Thank you," I said. "I'll put this box back."

Before leaving, I grabbed two pieces of paper and a pair of rubber bands and wrapped the security camera bodies and lenses.

Exiting, I found Luc waiting for me across the street. He asked if I was hungry.

"Very."

"I found a place with good *ciorba de burta*," he said.

The dish is the Eastern Euro version of menudo, something I had only once at a Serbian social gathering, my social life reduced to scraps from my brother's priestly invites. I agreed and we hustled to the restaurant under threatening skies.

We sat at a window seat and Luc ordered for both of us. He kept looking outside, seemingly preoccupied. I asked if he wanted a different seat. He declined. Only when a certain young lady walked toward the restaurant's front door did I realize the source of his distraction. Quickly Luc wished me good-bye and dashed off toward the young lady at the door, the familiarity of their embrace suggesting I would be alone for the meal.

I found myself staring across the street at the park, watching the employed hurry home to beat the rain. *So close to my treasure,* I thought. Wind gusts nudged the trees in the park and tossed papers, the rain burst, stopped, then restarted as if it were trying to allow the people intervals to get home.

With my soup and hard-crusted wheat bread before me, my thoughts were redirected back to the heavy box. *Why that box? Why was that box invading my head?* I asked for soup seconds and sipped weak tea while the rain laid sheets upon the busy street. Distant thunder warned of darker events to follow.

"Excuse me, sir." The waiter's voice startled me.

I looked up. "Yes?"

In a heavy accent he explained that the gentleman in the back wished to pay my tab. I declined and went to leave when the waiter said, "Mr. Bena."

I looked around to see if anyone was watching me before following the waiter to a booth in the back corner. It took a second before I recognized Alexandru Bena. He gestured toward the opposing seat, and I slid into the booth.

Mr. Bena instructed the waiter to bring my serving over to the table, then turned to me and said, "Looks like you found something."

It took me a moment to decide to answer. "How'd you know?"

"Your look," he said, "is different than the last two evenings."

"Good to know someone is watching over me."

He nodded. "Tell me what you've found."

"Why should I? You couldn't protect Mara."

That halted the conversation as his lower jaw clenched and his lips tightened. Tension mounted as the moments passed until he reached for his cloth napkin and dabbed his eyes. The waiter set my food in front of me and left.

"Allow me to start at the beginning, Mr. Joseph," he said.

I nodded.

"About a quarter century ago, my wife was watching television when she called me to come quickly. It was an American broadcast, and she repeated the names of the two boys being interviewed in a state-run orphanage in Romania."

He paused to let me guess. "Joseph and Bernhardt."

Mr. Bena nodded. "Petrescu Barkeley."

It took a moment. "So you are my benefactor," I said. A warm feeling enveloped me.

"Yes." A long pause separated his words. "I have long-standing connections with the Catholic Church, and I was able to send someone to get you and your brother the next day. I flew to Chicago and met with Mother Daniela and explained things as best I could. She understood, and took you in."

I pushed my food away and leaned on the table. "Why me? Why us?"

He pointed at me. "You need to know something." Then he reached into a small briefcase and produced a journal, much like the one Mara had given me, and opened to a certain page before handing it to me. "Go ahead, read. Start at the end."

It looked like a family tree, and my name, along with my brother's, was at the bottom of the lineage. Above it were my parents' family names, Petrescu and Barkeley, and the cities they grew up in. Dates of birth and death were listed. I recognized the left-handed writing. Then I noticed the tree only went up my mother's side.

"What am I looking for?" I asked.

"Keep going up your mother's side."

With each generation I noticed very long lives of the women, but not the men. My mother was the exception, a mere forty when she died. Then my eyes landed on her grandmother's grandmother, whose life spanned the years of 1688 until 1801. And her name was Contessa Gratz of Solingen. I knew the German city lay in the north Rhine region, and that I should know that name.

"I asked you about that name before," said Mr. Bena. "Do you recall?"

Yes, I did. "Countess Dolingen of Gratz, sought and found death in 1801." It was the name on the tomb in Stoker's prologue.

"And you are her direct descendent. That's how they know you."

"I thought it was just a name lifted off a tomb."

"Sort of," said Mr. Bena. "It is why that part was left off the manuscript. She was a human slave, and passed their Noble bloodlines down to you."

At that moment it made sense why I was being selected, for I had been followed since birth. It also would explain why my father chose to end the bloodline. I thought of Mara's words and asked, "How does Mara fit into this?"

Again his eyes watered and it took a moment for him to answer. "My wife and I rescued her in similar circumstances many years before you."

"You found her a safe place," I said.

"Not safe enough."

I felt infinitely sad for his loss, and said, "I'm sorry."

He nodded, then continued. "I must ask you this, Mr. Joseph: Do you happen to know where the original manuscript is now?"

"No," I said, "but my guide told me it is likely in the old wine cellar vaults in Castel Bran."

He nodded. "You realize . . . there will come a day when you need to escape."

I shook my head. "That's going to be tough, considering my legal mess. You know I'm the suspect in those murders."

"I know," he said, and slid a key toward me on the table. "Take this."

I looked it over. It appeared to be the key to a safety box with a number stamped—N279.

"That key opens a locker at the Bistriţa train station. There is only one bank of lockers, north wall. If you find the original manuscript and place it in the locker, my original offer still stands."

"It was four million dollars from the family, but I don't—"

"I know," he interrupted, and held up a hand to halt me.

"More importantly, whatever you find in this museum you will need to dispose of. Use that key. Inside the locker you will find a passport and some traveling money."

I did not need clarification to know he meant a fake passport.

"May God be with you," he said.

I nodded and held back several emotions. I had a lot to be grateful to him for. I whispered, "Thank you . . . for everything."

Parting ways with him, I returned to the Excelsior, where I showered and stood out on the balcony to watch the storm. I replayed my visit with Mr. Bena repeatedly. I realized that I must have appeared to be anything but grateful.

First, I should have hugged him, for it's not every day that you get to thank the person who saved your life. But I let him walk away into the night. True, I did not grow up in a home where people hugged each other, and certainly did not experience touch in my youth, so I grew up feeling something akin to static electricity jolts every time someone touched me. I keep distance. This time, however, I felt shame at allowing my benefactor to walk away.

As I replayed the conversation one last time, the connections became clear from my first meeting with him at Mara's and his words at dinner. When he said his family had been at war with the Dracul family for centuries, it meant he was a vampire hunter. Either he was given long life and turned on his master, or he came from a family who did. The answer did not matter; it's not like he carried around a business card spelling his vocation. What did matter was that he was there for me and my brother when we needed help the most, as well as for Mara, and for who knows how many other victims. Perhaps my upcoming conflict with the Noble family was enough repayment.

The storm progressed with the night. Trees bent, lightning crashed close by, rain splashed off the balcony, and the power flicked several times as midnight approached. Still I could not fall to sleep, thinking about the last box I'd handled, remembering the feeling that I had teetered on the verge of discovery.

I stood in the cool humid night air and smelled the aftereffects of a cleansing summer storm, while the horizon flashed a string of lightning strikes suggesting this was just a lull. Mist hovered over the trees in the park and the once busy street now echoed.

How differently people lived here. Oh, not just in language, but in mind-set. There is a sense of dark-horse fatalism whose roots are buried deep in Orthodox Christianity and its litany of superstitions, coupled with a sense of the small and rural and primitive that runs even through the big cities. Yet somehow the people hold dear their attachment to the land in some romantic way, proud regardless of who their conquerors are. One might remark that these people love their country dearly, while they wait to see who invades next.

And somehow I identified with their mind-set. I was trapped within borders, short on options, and resigned to the fact that my mortal fate rested in the hands of a superior enemy. Fatalism, indeed.

A chilling wind chased me inside, and I found an American cable newscast on television and felt a chill when I heard my name broadcast: "... Joseph Barkeley of Chicago is being sought as a person of interest ..."

I had checked in under my middle name, Winston, but at that point I knew it was only a matter of time before some official would seize me. An innocent man never imagines life as a fugitive nor considers his freedom as a moment-to-moment condition. I had to finish this search as soon as possible, and I realized that for the foreseeable future, it would be wise to plan as if I might have to flee at any moment. How does one live that way? I hoped Mr. Bena would come through with the fake passport.

I grabbed my coat and left the room as silently as I could, believing there was something in that box in the museum that held answers. I fled the hotel's back exit and turned up my coat collar. Outside was chilly and the wind saw to the constant stirring of things. Lightning crashed in the park across the street. The neighborhood lights went out, then on again. It was just past midnight, and no one braved the streets. Halfway to the museum it started to rain in earnest, hurling uneven torrents to the pavement. The sound of splashing echoed off the buildings. I pulled my jacket over my head and every half block stepped into recessed doorways to catch a break. During one such delay a police car slowly rolled down the street and I stepped back into the shadows.

After another block I found a doorway where I could wait and observe the museum. As I adjusted my eyes to the shadows, I saw movement on the other side of the museum. A man came into focus, a tall thin man in a long dark overcoat with the collar pulled up, hands in pockets. He held no umbrella, and just stood near the corner, back in the shadow of the building behind him. I saw a tiny red glow in front of his face, yet was not close enough to see if he had red eyes or if it was a lit cigarette. He looked quickly both ways before gazing back my direction. I retreated in the doorway.

I stepped on something.

A man grumbled.

I looked down to see a homeless man pressing against the doorway for shelter from the storm. When I looked back across the street, the man in the coat was gone.

It was time to move. Thinking it best to circle the blocks around the museum, I pulled my collar against my neck and clutched my travel bag tightly like a football. As I stepped into the rain, droplets pelted my face. No sign of life around the first concentric block, nor the museum block, so after my second trip around I ducked into the doorway closest to the unlocked basement window. I looked inside and saw no red lights on the security cameras.

Without the nerve to simply walk up to the window and break in I thought it prudent to take the example of the homeless man and crouch in the doorway until judging it clear. During that half hour several cars drove by, a couple holding hands strolled leisurely by under an umbrella, and the man with the collared coat failed to reappear.

I saw a policeman on foot shine a flashlight in the doorway where the homeless man lay, then continue on. I waited another fifteen minutes before making my move. The heavy wooden window stubbornly gave way and I slid through the opening and onto the floor before springing back up to close it. The building felt quiet. Stepping over to the stack where I'd left off, I flicked on my lighter and found the weighty box unmoved. Something drew me back to it, a question unanswered lingering in my mind. I knelt, opened it, and grabbed the heavy Bible in its presentation box. *A Bible in Tesla's archive?* I mused consciously for the first time. *Why?*

Suddenly a movement in my periphery froze me where I stood. Someone had just walked by the opposite-side window and stopped. Whoever it was wore a long coat with boots and bent to look in the basement. I continued kneeling and hoped he did not circle the building because I had not drawn the window completely closed. I heard my heart pounding in my ears and felt my pulse in my neck. Soon as the stranger passed, I stashed the boxed Bible in my bag, quickly returned the file box to its place, and hustled back to the window. There I looked both ways and, seeing no one, climbed out.

One block into my return trip I passed a darkened doorway and saw a man in a long coat standing back in the shadows. I could smell the tobacco when I passed and picked up the pace back to the hotel. By the time I got to the front door I looked back and saw him, or someone dressed just like him, standing at the corner watching me, a lit cigarette in his mouth. I entered the lobby and ignored looks from the desk clerk as I headed for the elevator. Upstairs in the room I washed away the chill and hung my clothes to dry before opening the Bible's presentation box. Making the sign of the cross and kissing my crucifix, I lifted the leather-bound volume out of its aging wooden box. The hinges predated Colonial times.

The Bible jacket turned out to be a rather obvious false cover, revealing dozens of handwritten pages both in Stoker's and George's handwriting. First I took inventory—it looked like at least two chapters penned by the author, a marked-up typed manuscript, a stack of letters from Sonia to George, and several pages of George's notes.

I looked at the clock. In seven hours, I'd make a punctual return to the museum. I brewed a cup of instant coffee and left it on the other side of the room for fear of spillage. What to read first? I started with what likely would go the fastest: George's notes. Skimming the pages I found that George kept the sketches Stoker drew and made comments about their accuracy, along with lists of vampire traits, one column for the accurate ones and the second column for the fabled ones. Another page had the family tree of Vlad Dracul and his four sons. It was the same as in the journal I had taken from Mara's place, except this one listed the sons' wives.

Mircea was the oldest, and although no wife was listed, the space had been filled with a question mark. Vlad Dracula was married to Elizabeth; Radu the Handsome wedded Luiza; and Dalca's bride was named Erika. Below the family tree were handwritten notes by both men. Stoker suggested that Vlad be reunited in the same crypt as his wife, and the assistant noted, *Must never breed again.*

Next Stoker wrote, *Wife dead.*

The assistant wrote, *Not dead—undead.* Below that a question mark in what appeared to be Stoker's handwriting remained un-answered. Recalling what Sonia had said about vampires surviving dormant if not dismembered, the word *undead* became clearer.

In the following pages George's notes mentioned an apparatus designed by Tesla intended to project a concentrated beam of light held so tightly together that it had properties sufficiently disruptive to disable electrical and mechanical devices. The idea was that light beam particles would hit a target with such force, it would disrupt any object at the atomic bonding level. I recalled seeing a similar description, though less specific, in his correspondence with President Wilson's War Department. Obviously Tesla had been developing either laser and/or microwave technology long before it was known to the greater world.

George drew a sketch of the device pointed at a box shaped like a coffin with heat lines rising, as if he thought he might be able to cook a vampire in its sanctuary box. I recognized the sketch as similar to one in the journal Mara had given me.

On the next page was the sketch of what looked like a lens. Not just an ordinary lens; it was shaped like an insect's eye, flanked by an exploded close-up view. They are not like mammals' single focal point lenses, but rather a series of shutters, hundreds of them, each with a focal point that relays images to the brain. Rather than seeing something still, the eyes detect motion as it moves from shutter to shutter. Like standing in one of those fun house rooms filled with mirrors where images come from all directions at once. When an object is still you cannot detect its location, but as it moves you can follow its path.

I looked at the sketch again, in which it appeared that George intended to use Tesla's laser beam to shine in the eyes of this creature to disable it. If a sudden bright light were to invade a dark mirrored room, it would appear to be coming from all directions, rendering the victim senseless until it looked away. That must have been what happened in the cemetery when my flashlight momentarily immobilized that creature while Dalca's warriors moved in. A laser beam would presumably intensify that effect.

Perhaps that illustration represented the vampires' eyes, and Tesla's beam a method of disabling them. I read on.

Another page had a crude hand-drawn map that resembled the shape of the Carpathian Mountain footprint. Along the left boundary the letters *MRC* were printed with an arrow pointing west and southwest. The top had *RtH* printed with an arrow pointing north. An arrow pointing east in the right side listed *Dlc*, and the bottom had *VIII* and an arrow pointing south. Linking those initials to the family tree I assumed that to be the territories each of the warring brothers was charged with guarding. Obviously Vlad III had the biggest job keeping the Ottoman Turks on the south side of the Danube and off the Wallachian Plain. Dalca's territory faced the Moldavian Plain and was assigned defense against Asian invaders, while Radu the Handsome guarded the North Carpathians from Hun descendents. Mircea lorded over the western front and seat of the Hungarian Empire at the time, plus the part of the Balkans that eventually became Yugoslavia. No wonder there was a clash in the Baia Mare cemetery—it lay in the north sector, Radu's territory. And Radu, if alive, would know that Dalca's purpose was to exhume his wife.

I moved to the written correspondence, most of which Sonia had penned to George expressing her love, along with details of her progress building their house in his absence. She wrote of her fear for his safety, understandable in a dangerous industry such as electricity. Her last letter referenced his previous communiqué, and although I could not read all the Romanian, she seemed relieved he had taken care of something and that perhaps "maybe that was enough of a message that he will not repeat his mistake." The date coincided with ashes smoldering at Constable & Co.

Another letter at the bottom of the stack lacked a postmark. As I unfolded the fragile paper, another page fell out. I picked it up and recognized Stoker's handwriting:

April, 1897
London

Mr. Anton,

When I enlisted your assistance in a certain capacity relating to my manuscript I did so with the expectation that your role would be subordinate and that the totality of your suggestions would be just that, mere suggestions. It is neither warranted nor appreciated that you "insist" on any changes to my work, for at all times you are to remember that it is, after all, my work.

Be warned of this—I am aware you attempted to make contact with my publisher at Constable with claims of copyright violations. He knows better, as my relationship with him precedes your introduction. Future contact will not be . . .

There the first page ended, and I found none subsequent. Here it was, proof of their falling-out. By its date, the disagreement appeared to have taken place just as the original first editions headed to print.

I looked at the clock—two hours had passed. This was in keeping with my normal schedule, but a day at the museum still lay ahead, as I thought it best to not vary my routine.

Next I thumbed through the typed manuscript. The pages were not in good shape, and I handled them nimbly. Although the story was similarly constructed as a series of journal entries, and the names were the same, the events opening the story were completely different, as were the concluding chapters.

The story began as a mysterious stranger lands on the shores near Whitby in England. Immediately the midnight bloodletting attacks began, but the character was more werewolf than vampire, blending in during daylight hours and attacking in the dark. No mention of Jonathan's visit to Dracula's Castle opened the story. The ending was similar to that of the the second editions, whereby the protagonists chase the villain back to Transylvania and slay him.

George's handwriting was all over the typed pages, pointing out violations of vampire conventions and suggesting he change the daytime habits and the entire opening scenes to make the villain more conniving. *Not charming* was noted repeatedly, and corrections dotted every page where the villain appeared. *Voivode* was written over the word *Count* referring to Dracula.

I looked up and three more hours had passed. I could see why the publishing houses had passed on the story as first presented, as it resembled Jack the Ripper events of that era mixed with garden-variety gothic yarns common at that time. Disposal of the villain was also anticlimactic, as they ambushed the count and swiftly killed him.

Not until the villain morphed from a maniacal human to that of an immortal legend did the protagonists' deeds rise to the level of heroism, thus the enduring nature of the story. I also realized why George wanted to keep this manuscript in his possession, for it might better argue his case of greater influence.

That left only the last chapters to read, handwritten by Stoker on Lyceum Theatre stationery with a note to the publisher to change the prologue and final two chapters to the attached. It began with a prologue, the story of a woman named Elizabeth who takes her own life in despair that her husband has been killed in battle. The time frame mentioned was 1476. Her chosen method was a jump from her top-floor window in a corner bedroom of the Grand Castle. I stopped. The description matched my room's dimension and its views at Castel Bran. A great cry went out over the valley when the Master returned from war to the news of his wife's death, and vowed revenge against those who had schemed against them.

The second to last chapter chronicled the Master's revenge. He, the Count Vlad Dracula, discovered that his two brothers, the Defender of the East and the Keeper of the North, had indeed sent messengers to deliver the false news of his demise to Elizabeth.

Thereafter months passed and Count Vlad called a summit to discuss a truce between the feuding brothers. They met in the middle, which would have been Dalca's residence, and Vlad's warriors grabbed both his brothers' wives and slew them. In part it read:

> . . . and with argint swords dipped in their blood, their bodies scattered equally about the waters of Acheron, in Demeter's hull, beneath the eyes of the Lord, and a loving foundation, the bloodlines ceased.

The final chapter tells of a great battle as Count Vlad Dracula is slain by his brothers, much like the published first editions I authenticated, except the killing was done not by the novel's human protagonists but instead by the brothers Radu and Dalca.

With only minutes before the museum opened, I quickly showered and prepared for a day of work and realized the gravity of these chapters.

Luc joined me in the lobby and we began walking. It was a quiet commute until Luc said, "You get what you were looking for last night?"

I meant to ask him the same, but instead responded, "What do you mean?"

"Doesn't look like you slept."

"Worried."

"You'll have to do better than that," Luc said.

Just then we reached the corner across from the museum. Two policemen spoke with the attendant outside the front door.

22

I approached the building as if all were normal, halting a respectful distance away from the discussion, allowing the curator to announce my arrival. He introduced me as an invited guest. My heart raced with the realization that if they looked at the basement security cameras it would be obvious who had covered them. Of course, I had also been named as a wanted fugitive, so this could have gone very badly indeed. I thought back to the time, only days ago, when I signed the declaration of citizenship, and hoped that Ms. Pope's words about reciprocity in neighboring countries were correct.

I pointed toward the door and spoke as innocently as I could in English. "Is it open? Okay to go in?"

"Of course," said the curator, following me in to unlock the basement door.

I sighed silently in relief. They must not have looked downstairs. Only as I swung open the door did I dare look across the street, to where Luc was standing, and make sure he saw me enter the building. Moving at my normal pace, though my heart urged me to hurry, I removed my jacket, laid my work pad and pens on the table, and walked over to pick up a box. Opening the top and lifting out a file, I sensed someone looking at me. Careful not to panic, I lifted the page out of the file as usual and held it to the light, while my peripheral vision detected an officer watching me through a basement window. Perhaps he knew. Not only about the break-in, but about my fugitive status. Or maybe he simply had a knack for smelling guilt in his presence.

The officer walked around the building looking in one basement window after another while I tried to look calm until they left. At that point, I pulled the makeshift covers off the cameras and tried to slow my pounding pulse. Clearly, I was not cut out for a life of crime.

I finished skimming over the remaining boxes, checking dates, and finally concluded that I had inspected all documents from the 1890s. As noon approached, I let the curator know I had completed my work and asked for an invite back if need be.

"Of course," he said.

I met up with Luc at the hotel and checked out. Together we walked to the train station for tickets through Bucharest to Bistriţa. Luc suggested I take the window seat. I took his advice and, as any wanted man would do, turned my head away from people and stared at the passing landscape.

I have always had a figurative blackboard in my mind. Whenever I want to remember something, I imagine that it is written upon the slate, and thus I see it. Even numbers, when I want to remember them, I see in chalk form on the board. As I gazed out the train window, the words *not dead—undead* would not erase from the board. Dalca's wife was not dead; he expected to find her in the cemetery—suspended, dormant, as Sonia said—and take her home. I shuddered at the thought of their reunion, then tried to imagine what Sonia had suggested, to take advantage of their animal coupling to kill the Master. Alas, my mental chalkboard had the capacity neither to capture such a scene nor to imagine its successful outcome.

I fell asleep watching the Danube River boat traffic and woke to a uniformed man saying to Luc, *"Paşaportul."*

Luc showed his, then pointed toward me. "He is with me, a guest of the Dracul family." Then Luc motioned for me to unzip my jacket, and as my crucifix came into sight the officer quickly stamped my passport and moved on.

Despite my best efforts, eventually fatigue won out. I exchanged vigilance for fatalism and resolved that they were either going to get me or they weren't. *Just don't do anything stupid, like call attention to yourself.*

I once again drifted back to sleep.

⊶⧆⊷

Our trip ended on Monday afternoon in Bistriţa. While Luc ducked into a washroom, I found the storage locker and stashed the Bible. Inside were the promised cash and passport, which I left, and an unsigned note that read, *You are the strongest among us. I am proud.* Even without a signature I recognized the paper used as a page torn from the journal Mr. Bena had shown me in the restaurant.

We caught up with the Gypsy carting his copper wares back to Dumitra. While he cast a knowing look my way, he eyed Luc with suspicion as I asked if Luc could join the ride. The Gypsy grudgingly cleared a spot on the cart, and the balance of the ride was—as in previous trips—silent.

I removed my jacket, for the season had taken hold, and the air filled with birds and things on their menu. Summer has its own song. Every spring the fans walk to Wrigley Field in the early afternoon with their light jackets and hands in pockets. Then one day, usually in early June, you walk there and the sunshine has warmed the jacket off your back. Entering the park, you notice the brick walls have overnight turned ivy-green, and it's like attending a grand picnic, with entertainment. What little breeze is the first promise of a sustained summer, the mosquitoes have not quite rallied, and you count it among your most beautiful of days. Such was that day, the grass swaying in the wind while the sun reflected late snow off the Carpathian peaks, the only sounds the horses' hooves and cart wheels over the ancient rutted path.

Again we traveled the entire two hours to Dumitra without the inconvenience of having to share the road with competing vehicles, and I dismounted the cart with a handshake while the Gypsy's children stayed safely in their yard, calling to their dad.

Luc told me he would be staying at the inn and pointed to the place on the hill where I had checked in during my first visit here. "You let me know when you're going somewhere."

"I will." I bade him farewell and walked hurriedly through the village, to the stares and retreats of the locals. The window dolls remained out of sight, a *No Vacancy* signal to suitors and scoundrels. Here and there dogs growled and cats slinked out of sight.

I walked straight to the little church, making no detour, and knelt there before the cross. What I was about to undertake required aid from forces much greater than human, and so I beseeched God for help, pledging that I would gladly give my life if it meant protection for others, *spasi i sokhrani*, and comfort for the fearful hearts of these villagers who did not deserve to live this way.

"Pass the cup to me, Father," I whispered.

Still praying as I left and crossed the bridge, I found Sonia's door open. Inside she was busy baking bread, many loaves more than she could consume. A knock produced a quick turn of her head and a smile. Three kisses on my cheeks, and we embraced without reserve. It finally felt normal.

"Alms?" I pointed to the oven. She looked puzzled. *"Oferte?"*

She smiled and gestured toward the village. "Some here, they not take even bread from me."

"I know better." I washed up.

"After I gone, much legend will grow of this place." She nodded toward a chair. "You look *obosit*." *Tired*.

"Up all night reading a Bible," I said in deliberately vague terms.

Sonia's expression signaled that she knew the item I spoke of, but she, too, spoke matter-of-factly. "Oh, yes? Where?" The rest of her response came into my head and not my ears.

On this subject we should not voice.

I nodded and conveyed my thoughts. *Bistriţa train station. I left the Bible in a locker there.* I handed her the bundle of letters. *I found these.*

Sonia gasped, then hugged the papers to her breast as she sat in her chair. A pained smile turned the corners of her mouth upward with a quivering lip as she opened each one, then dabbed her eyes as she read.

I thought you'd want them back.

Feels like . . . ieri. Yesterday.

I conceded with a nod. *I found what I think I was looking for.*

There was a profound sadness in the room before she spoke. "It is a long time to miss someone."

I gave her a moment to collect herself.

She nodded in return, turning each letter lovingly in her hands. "That is just the start of longing if you end up in the wrong place." A moment passed as she sniffled before looking back at me. *You were saying?*

Did you know of arguments between your husband and Mr. Stoker?

Yes. One of Gheorghe's letters to me was apology for saying too much to the man . . . over pints. Too close to facts.

"Over pints?" I said out loud.

"Over pints, yes."

"Why would he do that?"

She returned to her silent words: *When Gheorghe first meet him,*

Stoker was only writing plays then, gothic plays with unnatural creatures. Gheorghe attended the shows and went out with his host after.

And talked over pints.

Men do foolish things over pints. She was not happy. *Told Stoker his creatures all wrong.*

He wrote all over Stoker's notes, too. The same thing as you said. Correcting what Stoker had wrong, suggesting changes.

She nodded.

But then later he regretted it. Did George not know these papers were for a book? For international publication?

No. My husband thought he wrote only plays. Gheorghe described his office at the teatru *as being filled with piles of paper and notes with script names on top. Stoker did not tell him he was writing a manuscript; much artist thievery then.*

I showed her the harsh letter from Stoker accusing him of approaching the publisher. *Did your husband go to Constable?*

No answer returned. Sonia straightened in her chair.

The dates coincide with George being in London on the days of both fires.

"Let me ask you, Mr. Joseph," she said aloud. "Do you ever do something that others see as breaking law, but you do only to protect something from harm?"

"I just did," I said. *They're in your hands.*

My husband deeply regretted what he did, that he opened his mouth.

That your culture's secret would become so public?

Not only that, she thought. *He feared the author had said too much for his own safety. For our safety.*

A silent moment passed. *Along with the letters I found copies of the original chapters that went into the burned first edition of Dracula.*

You would be wise to burn them.

I thought they were a treasure that belonged to the ages.

You will not think so if that family breeds.

Are the wives suspended?

Suspend, yes, both like insectă, she thought.

Then why did Dracula not kill the wives?

All the Nobles know it would mean . . . sfârşitul. Extinction.

Sonia seemed to be describing some vampire version of mutually assured destruction, in which Noble wives were somehow considered off-limits, even to their enemies.

Did the two brothers really kill Vlad Dracula?

Yes. She gestured to indicate he was dismembered. *That is what happens when you scheme against a Noble wampyr.*

Revenge for kidnapping their wives?

Yes.

What happened to the other brother, Radu?

She did not answer, but instead stood from her chair and led me to the kitchen. "Come, let us eat."

Before me she placed a plate of sausages and half a loaf of hard-crusted bread with a side of flavored olive oil. I turned down the *ţuică,* the plum brandy, for coffee. Two bites and I could say without reservation it was the best bread I ever ate. It must have come through loudly enough that she responded, "*Mulţumesc.* You are most gracious guest."

"I do mean it."

Sonia smiled. "After a hundred years or so, a woman should get good at something, yes?"

We both laughed. Eating was not the time for hosting unpleasant talk, so we spoke of other matters during our dinner. I took wide-eyed pleasure listening to her soothsaying tales from her American trip; she recited an impressive client list that included presidents, authors, and business titans.

As Sonia cleaned the dishes at the sink, I looked at her. By that, I mean I really looked at her, not as a gracious host, but as a woman. Not that I knew women, not even in the Biblical sense, but to have such a wife at home while off pursuing a vocation must have presented George with real challenges, the red-blooded kind. To have someone love you so much that a century removed still brought tears, that is the type of love any sane man would protect.

Sonia turned her head in my direction, hurriedly finished her task, and returned to the table. She refilled my coffee before sitting down. She looked in my eyes and then covered my hands with hers. Unlike the protective pat on the hands, this was a touch that told me I belonged there, right there. Also, I did not feel the usual jolt, like static electricity, but rather warmth that traveled up my arms.

"Thank you," she said aloud.

I knew she had been listening, and blushed. Then I briefly considered that maybe George got away periodically to have some thoughts to himself.

She tilted her head up slightly and laughed. "Maybe."

"Perhaps men need more privacy than women," I said.

She recognized that I was rather troubled about the coming

events and returned to solemnity. *Remember, Joseph, that all great conquests are built on single step. Take each one and do your best.*

Mulţumesc.

You have been scheming.

I nodded.

All your thoughts move toward murder now, yes?

Not murder—self-preservation, I thought.

Tell me your plan.

The brothers are at war, aren't they?

Only over one thing—each would die before letting the other mate again.

So if I find one of the wives, I can set one brother against the other, set up an ambush.

You would make a deal with the undead? she thought.

I'm certainly dead if I don't find Dalca's wife.

And you would double-cross him over his brother?

I could not answer for sure, since I had not met Radu, nor had Sonia answered my earlier question about him.

It is possible, she thought. *But consider it the last double cross you will ever do.*

I know.

She looked at me for a long time, a companionable silence growing between us. *Do you really want to know?*

She wasn't simply talking about Dalca's brother Radu. No, I had a very clear idea now that Sonia knew the exact location where both wives were buried.

Do you really, really want to know, Joseph?

You would take this knowledge to your grave, wouldn't you?

"I would," she said.

At this point my blood surged with the realization that she had withheld knowledge that cost me a trip. I pushed away from the table, stood, and paced her small living room. This time I pressed her for an answer: "You knew that your husband was the assistant for both Stoker and Tesla and didn't tell me. You've known where the wives' bodies are buried all along. Why didn't you tell me these things before I went on that trip?"

Silence! she shouted at me, not with words but in thought.

I shut up and listened.

You needed to be tested—

"No," I interrupted, "I needed answers. And you have them."

Tell me, Joseph. Her thoughts calmed and words slowed. *What would be your plan if you were to come to this knowledge?* She pointed to the seat and I returned to the table. *Were you in danger there?*

I thought it over and concluded that the trip was immeasurably enlightening. I shook my head.

She reached across and stroked the side of my face once, clearly conveying that I needed to trust her. *Tell me your plan.*

Because if it's not a good plan you won't give me the answer, right?

She nodded. *I have more at stake than just my knowledge.*

Unless I could create some sort of Tesla-inspired microwave or laser transmitter and use it at just the right time against Dalca, killing him would have to be the old-fashioned way, a swift and silent attack.

As you suggested, it must be an ambush. I waited for her answer.

In response, she posited this question: *Remember the fight in the cemetery?*

I nodded.

How did Radu know his brother was coming to Baia Sprie?

I thought a second, and an image popped into my head of the merchant who sold me my brother's gift. *The merchant who tipped him off when he saw my crucifix.*

She acknowledged with a nod. *The merchant has been replaced. The new one belongs to Radu, the Keeper of the North.*

Geography—that is Radu's backyard.

An affirming smile told me I was right.

So Radu can't bring his army down here for an ambush.

He'd have to come alone, swiftly, or the winged creatures announce his arrival.

She had a point. *Sneak in and get it done or risk a full-scale fight to the death by mobilizing all his warriors and leaving the home front unguarded.*

That was how corruption and family wars started across Europe during the Crusades.

I shared with her my plan, such as it was: I would attempt to get an audience alone with Radu to tell him I might have located his brother's wife. Since that would spell the end of my usefulness to Dalca, I'd tell Radu that I would like to exchange my knowledge of this gravesite for safe passage out of Romania. Details of the ambush would not be set until finding the wives' exact locations.

Sonia nodded. *Repeat what you know of their location from the original epilogue.*

'And with argint swords—'

Whose words are those? She lifted an eyebrow.

I thought a moment. *Your husband's . . . Romanian word for* silver. *Multiple swords.*

Yes. She nodded for me to continue.

'. . . dipped in their blood—'

My husband chose his words, his written *words, carefully.*

Dipped, not drenched.

Show me—how does one dip? she asked.

I gestured. *In slightly, then pull back.*

But not remove all the way.

'. . . their bodies scattered . . .' I thought a second. *Cut up and strewn about?*

Did he write 'cut up'?

I shook my head.

Then keep to only what he writes.

Just scattered.

She waited to see if I understood before posing a question. *When you scatter grain, is it whole?*

No, it's in little pieces.

She lifted an index finger. *But is it whole?*

Well, each grain is whole. She smiled, that certain brief beam to let me know when I comprehended. *So the wives are buried apart?*

She nodded. *Go on.*

'. . . equally about the waters of Acheron.' Acheron is a river in the underworld, and on the other side of it is hell.

When did that place come into your head before?

I looked at her in surprise. I realized that the *Acheron* image had come to me the first time I crossed that little river from the church to Sonia's house. *You did that?*

She smiled. There it was again. *Yes, I placed that in your head. Why?*

To see if you were the one. Now go on . . .

'. . . *in Demeter's hull.*' This one I thought I knew, since *Demeter* was the name of the ghost ship that carried the count to Whitby.

Not a ship. Move ahead to next.

'. . . *beneath the eyes of the Lord, and a loving foundation* . . .'

She held up two fingers. *See comma. Those are two places.*

'Beneath the eyes of the Lord' is . . . *well, everywhere,* I thought. Then I recalled from my previous search that as you get to the end of the clues they get more literal. *Eyes of the Lord . . . eyes of the Lord. I had seen them . . . the cross, no . . . in the church . . . a* painting on the ceiling of Jesus looking down. *When was the church built?*

Go look.

Momentarily I was stumped until realizing the cornerstone should reveal the answer. We walked hurriedly across the bridge and bent to look at the cornerstone. The date read 1714, and above it read the name of the settlement, DEMETER.

She nodded and we returned to her table. I thought of the connection—that *Dumitra* is the Romanized form of *Demeter.* She confirmed it with the smile. That also meant that whoever supplied the ship's name had seen that cornerstone.

Yes, she acknowledged. *Have you wondered why there is no grave-yard about this church's grounds?*

I had not, but that would explain it—unholy ground. It also suggested that others knew it as well. *Which of them is there?*

Dalca's.

That would be Erika. '. . . *and a loving foundation.*' I paused, puzzled.

Use the first word again.

Beneath . . . beneath the eyes of the Lord, and beneath a loving foundation.

Think!

I did not get it. *Where is she?*

Sonia stared at my eyes but did not project any thoughts my way. A minute passed, then another and another until she took her right index finger and pointed straight down. My first thought was that Radu's bride, Luiza, resided in hell; then a streak of blistering heat traveled my spine as I realized that the "loving foundation" was literally the foundation of George and Sonia's house.

"Yes," she said out loud. *Jyezz.*

Sonia's house rested atop the grave of Radu's wife. I checked the distance by walking outside and casually stepping off paces from the river to the church, and they equaled the distance from the river to Sonia's house. *Scattered equally.* That is why she and George had built their home there, and that is why she, as she said, had more at stake.

At that moment I understood why I had certain tests I needed to pass in order to fulfill my mission, and one of them was that trip to the museum. Not only did Sonia have to learn to trust me, but she had the wisdom to know that if I learned things on my own, I would be more likely to believe them.

"I'm sorry to question you," I said.

Her smile said all I needed to know—that she trusted me.

23

Fresh knowledge of what lurks under the floor changes the way you sleep. The night spawned noises that triggered visions of a vengeful Noble vampire. When I asked Sonia how long it took for her to sleep soundly above that foundation, she said it was only about thirty years. What frightened her most were earthquakes, which the region felt every couple years.

I also learned that George's father had been a stonemason who rebuilt the Demeter church in 1811 after Napoleon's troops scorched the earth on their way to Russia. While working the previous year at Castel Bran, he had met one of Vlad Dracula's human slaves bound for a birthday party—a slave who'd decided against taking a particularly sensitive secret to the grave. George's father was hired on for work in Dumitra and later confirmed the man's tale, ultimately bequeathing the secret to his son while constructing stone foundations over both burial sites.

I went to the inn early that Tuesday morning to meet Luc for a daily briefing. "I found something," I said.

He paused and looked at me. "In that Bible?"

Another lie-detector spike surged through my body. "Yes."

"Well," he said, "you're lucky you went back and got it, then."

I nodded and told a critical lie. "There's a series of landmark descriptions."

Luc seemed to buy it. "Where are they?"

"Up north."

"You know I can't go up north."

Radu's territory, I thought, nodding, and then looked down. "I know."

A long silent period passed before he spoke again. "You know what is going to happen to me, and *you,* if you don't come back."

"I know."

More silence. "How long?"

"I'll be back Thursday in time for the ride back here." When he didn't respond, I asked, "You got somewhere in Bistrița you can spend the week?"

A brief smile told me yes. "I'll ride in with you."

The Gypsy waited for me at his driveway's end that morning. I handed him three loaves from Sonia and asked him to wait for Luc. We shared a quiet coffee in the interval. I felt sad for the Gypsy, as his inventory of large copper kettles and other cooking pots never seemed to shrink. In a rare moment of inquisition he asked me what brought me to Dumitra, and I told him in Romanian that I was an American here working in Braşov and looked up a relative, Sonia, a blood relative from my mother's side. Despite it being only a half-truth on multiple levels, that seemed to satisfy him, and was likely to become common knowledge across the village by nightfall. Spreading this information had not been my idea, but Sonia's.

Luc hustled down the hill with his bag and thanked the driver for waiting. In Bistriţa I checked the locker before departing north to Baia Mare. Only the cash and passport remained; the Bible was gone. The forged document showed I would be a Canadian citizen, Allen Petric, with an address on Hoover Street in Nelson, B.C. A Romanian Customs stamp showed I had recently entered the country, quite legally. I thought about the photo and recognized it as the one taken at UPS when I picked up my parcel from Ardelean.

I placed the passport back in the locker and boarded. Once the train left town and entered the countryside, I began recognizing landmarks and locating my position on a map, and the journey seemed to shorten. Either for reasons of repetition or perhaps because it felt like everything was closing in upon me, the place seemed to have shrunk. *What a small country.* It really was like being stuck in Oregon. Not that Oregon's a bad place, but you'd love it less if the borders had walls. One other thought haunted me: I did not want to leave without Sonia. That would have been abandonment.

Before reaching my stop, I noticed a man passing me in the aisle. It was not so much his looks, but his smell. It was the same brand of cigarettes I had smelled the night I extricated the

Bible from the museum in Belgrade. I should have noticed it before—the smell of American tobacco. European and East Asian tobacco smells much stronger, and the cigarettes are not rolled as tightly as American brands, giving each unique signatures. By the time I turned to look at him, he had left my train car for the one behind. I had not made out his face.

In Baia Mare I walked from the train station to the square and did not stop anywhere or display my crucifix until entering the merchant's shop, where I did not speak until I was the sole patron. I asked if the man was the new owner and if he spoke English.

"*Da,*" he said to both.

I lifted the crucifix from under my shirt, and he immediately locked the door and drew its shade.

"May I see that?" he asked.

I slid it off my neck and watched as he gave it a close examination, rotating and inspecting it before looking at it under the glass.

"This is extraordinary," he said. "Where did you get this?"

"It has been in the family," I said. Another half-truth, as I did not tell him which family.

"How may I help you?" he asked.

I held my hand out and he reluctantly returned it. "I wish to exchange it for one of equal value."

He asked me to repeat it, in case he did not get it right.

I said, "*Puteți vă rog schimba acest articol?*"

He nodded. "I will ask around." His complexion had since turned pale, and his hands shook as he lit a cigarette.

"*Cât timp va dura?*" *How long will it take?*

"I do not know."

"Because I must depart the morning after tomorrow."

I left him with the name of the hotel where I was reserved. There I waited the day and night, taking only light meals and watching international news, though I must admit straining to hear my name on CNN to no avail. It is tough trying to sleep when expecting a visit from a Noble vampire. I made the most of afternoon naps.

⊰⊱

On Wednesday afternoon I opted for a walk to the old town square to enjoy the open-air market. Vendors lined the perimeter while a band played traditional Romanian songs on a central stage. A small crowd, mostly young people, danced a mixture of both traditional and modern steps in front of the stage, ringed by a crowd of swaying observing adults. Several conflicting food smells wafted in my direction while I avoided direct contact with the crowd.

Still several hours before sundown and so close to my mother's grave, I felt the solemn need to visit once more, if for no other reason than the selfish notion of closure. I rented a bicycle and rode north to All Saints, and upon approach thought the place looked rather peaceful, albeit neglected, and walked the bike up the rutted path. No one else was around, and I pushed through the gate and walked into the Paddock of the Damned. Around my mother's tomb—now returned to its proper state—the impression made by the lid when I was there the last time was visible, along with the damage to the neighboring headstones.

"I'm sorry," I whispered to the neighbors. "I caused this."

I placed a hand on my mother's tomb and, as much to scold as to lament, said, "Why? Why did you do it?" I could barely make the words come out of my mouth, knowing her choices had ruined the lives of the ones she was supposed to love. "And why the hell did you have us?" This was the part that I found damnable, to bring children into the world knowing the blood she would infuse into our veins.

I knelt to pray when something caught my eye. There, at the bottom of the sarcophagus, chiseled into the stone, was the same insignia imprinted on the presentation box that contained my crucifix. I bent to brush it off and get a better look. Sure enough, it was the Dracul family stamp, the dragon's tail wrapping the bottom of a cross.

At that moment, my brother's reaction made sense. He must have seen it when he knelt to pray beside her grave. Before leaving, I inspected all the other graves in the Paddock, but found no others with the stamp. I left with a profound sadness, not so much for myself but for the choices she made. I begged God for mercy on her soul as I rode back into town.

I returned to the park bench in the square and passed a couple hours observing the festivities from afar, occasionally walking off energy, as I found myself checking the sun's position. Just after sunset, as I contemplated returning to my hotel room, a tall man approached me. He had Slavic features and wore tightly laced boots under pressed jeans. He sat without asking.

Immediately I smelled cigarettes. Not uncommon there, but again I recognized the American tobacco smell. I worried when he reached into his jacket, but he was only pulling out a pack of cigarettes, a hard pack of Camels, and offered me one. *"Doriți o țigare?" Would you like a cigarette?*

"No, thank you. I don't smoke."

He tapped one into his hand but did not put away the pack. "You know," he said, "the very first writing instruments were camel hairs."

I knew that trivia, which suggested this was no chance encounter.

Again he offered me the pack. "Go ahead, take the whole pack."

I just looked at him, and then looked at the pack.

"They're from Mr. Bena. He sends his regards."

I'm sure my eyes widened, and he thrust the pack in my direction. I took it, opened the lid, and saw a phone number.

The man came a bit closer and whispered quickly, "When you need to escape."

And just as quickly he was gone. I memorized the number before destroying and trashing the cigarette pack. Five minutes later, two tall men stepped in front of me, both middle-aged and looking out of place in trench coats with their collars up. "Joseph Winston?"

I nodded my head. Neither appeared to have the red eyes or jaw structure of Regulats.

"Come with us." The man spoke with a slight Eastern Euro accent.

Not sure if they were police or my intended contacts, I asked, "Who are you with?"

"You will soon know."

"Are you with the authorities?"

"We have only one authority."

"What is his name?"

"You will soon know."

They didn't try to muscle me away in front of a crowd. I took that as a good sign, but I wished that I had set up some sort of signal or phrase, a *qui vive* watchword with the merchant, so that Radu's representatives could identify themselves.

Reluctantly, I fell in line between them and followed them out of the square. A couple blocks down the busy street, they stopped at a large German-made SUV shaped like a squared-off safari coach. It only took a couple minutes to exit town, and I recognized we were bound in the direction of Baia Sprie. Five minutes later, the SUV pulled off the highway at a place that looked familiar, the same route I had walked before. The vehicle steered into the driveway in front of the old structure that resembled a haystack.

The men got out of the car and opened my door. "You know the way."

"The cemetery," I said.

"The Braithwaite residence."

I knew the way. Radu had picked the only place we both had visited. Across the road I found the small path that led over the old bridge and continued up the hill. At that point my senses registered that something was missing—the night was not filled with bats or birds or the sound of mosquitoes. Obviously he was not yet there. The path was dimly lit under a cloudless night and a sliver of moon. Stumbling over the stones, I turned east and entered the cemetery under its tree-lined entry, the summer having filled the limbs since my first trip there.

Recalling Braithwaite's tomb was located about halfway across and in the back, I set out that direction, carefully avoiding stepping on headstones. I stopped when I heard something, looked up at the sky, and wondered what the hell I was doing. The sound of several mosquito clouds circled the graveyard periphery. Overhead a hundred bats convened, and I knew I had company.

With eyes adjusted to the dark, I spotted the lone cross perched atop the tomb of the late Loreena Braithwaite and walked that way with my eyes down, guiding my feet. Once there, I took out my GPS and memorized the coordinates and shone a light. The site was as I recalled it, with a cross (since repaired) at the head of the tomb and another laid onto the stone, giving the appearance of a strap. More mosquito clouds buzzed in the distance as I looked around trying to see them.

When I faced the tomb again, someone was sitting on it within arm's reach. I jumped back so fast that I landed on the seat of my pants on the neighboring headstone.

"Why did you come here?" The man's voice owned the same deeply aged quality of Dalca's, but without the sneer.

I stood but kept my distance. From ten feet away I could see he had similar features to his brother's, but carved more carefully of Roman design. Of course he had the thin mustache and swept-back straight hair, but his eyes were not set like an insect's, and his nose was proportionately straight. Much like the photo of Tesla, he had the serious Slavic stare of answering a challenge.

Like his brother, he had the signature smell, though perhaps not quite as acrid.

"Why did you come here?" he repeated.

I did not know which visit he was referring to, this one or the first time, so I answered in chronological order: "I thought that tomb held the remains of your brother."

"To claim to know my brother is to suggest you know who I am."

"I beg your pardon." I looked down. "*Sărut mâna. Mă numesc* Joseph Barkeley."

"Joseph Winston Barkeley." He emphasized my middle name. "As you can see, this . . . young lady does not wish to be disturbed."

"Yes, sir." I bowed my head. "I made the mistake of disturbing her."

"Tell me of this mistake."

I looked up at him. It was difficult not to stare with his red eyes glowing like small lamps and his mouth open enough to reveal long teeth and a red tongue. "I was trying to do business with a foreigner, a stranger, and did not realize that I had interfered with his family's business."

"I see," he said. "And why do you come this time?"

"Well . . . Should I succeed in finding what this foreign businessman is looking for, my usefulness to him will end, and I fear that I will be eliminated."

"So you wish to make a deal for your safety."

"Yes, sir."

"Many a human have approached me to make deals over the

centuries. Some of them hunters." He spread his arms wide as if addressing a crowd. "They are scattered all about you."

Then he made a sound that vaguely resembled a laugh, but came out more like a hiss. A bat swooped down and bounced off his arm as he swatted it away. He had huge, cartoon-proportioned hands. Before I could see him move he was off the tomb and standing behind me, and I heard him take in a long deep breath through his teeth as he smelled me.

"I smell . . . fear, desperation, weakness." He breathed deeply again, his nostrils ranging from my right ear to my left. "I see you are one of us." He held the last *s* through a hiss. "At least a drop or two."

"My mother."

"Lucia . . . Petrescu . . . Barkeley," he said. "I knew of her, from a long line of Gratzes. Pity, that one. You carry your father's filthy name as a burden." I stood silently as he circled me, still sniffing. "Yes, Mr. Joseph, we know everyone in our little community."

"Your community is not growing," I said. "That is why I came here this time."

"To join?"

I shook my head.

"I did not think so." He was a tall creature, well over six feet. Now he was breathing directly in my face. "I smell . . . perfidy."

"I have pledged no fealties to your brother."

"Come now, human." He turned in dramatic fashion and paced before me, passing his arm through the air like a lecturer in search of a word. "Perfidy is like . . . a wandering atom, for soon it will attach itself to another."

"I come here to exchange, not to offer to be your slave."

"What could you possibly have that I want?"

"Information . . ." I could barely get out my response. "About what you want most."

His eyes started to glow a brighter red, and he leaned toward my face. "After your first visit here you should have discovered what I want most, or else I would consider you too stupid to deal with." He circled behind me. "Now, human, just so we are in full understanding, tell me what I want most. Tell me."

"What you want most is to know where your wife is."

"Hmm. Yet you also must know that if you simply tell me where she is, you fear your usefulness to me will end as well."

"I do not know where *she* is."

"Then why are you here?"

"I know what you want second most."

"Oh? Like a game . . . I see. You think you will set the rules and I am the contestant. Go on to the second round. Something like that?"

His eyes glowed bright red, and in a blink he grabbed me with one of his huge hands across my chest and lifted me in the air. He stepped toward the great stone sarcophagus, lifted its stone cover, and threw me in with the dead Miss Braithwaite, then lowered the top back over me.

I don't know how long I was entombed. As soon as I understood what was happening, I took a deep breath, held it as long as possible, then let it out. A couple quick breaths, and then I held another deep breath. I was almost petrified as I realized that my worst fears were suddenly becoming reality. To be buried alive is an unspeakably hideous fate. Too tightly pressed to move, I could not even bring my hands up to my face. The stone was cold and the sides cramped, as I shared the small space with bones and dust and decaying cloth. Each breath sent dust into my nostrils and exhausted the small amount of oxygen remaining. I felt nonexistent bugs on my face and my skin began to crawl. The cold of the stone began to warm, and sweat poured from my body. I felt too frightened even to pray.

Then the stone lifted. As I went to raise myself out he pushed me back down. "Not yet, human." He threw something in with me and lowered the stone again. I held my breath. Whatever he threw in began to panic and brush against my leg. I tried to kick it but my legs were too confined. When it squealed I realized it was a bat. I don't know how long he left the cover on, but it felt much longer than the first time. Our confinement afforded the bat the chance to bite my legs repeatedly.

When the stone moved again, the bat escaped and I called out, "*Vă rog.*" Please.

"You break easily, mortal." He lifted me out of the box with one hand and lowered the stone cover.

"Thank you," I said, brushing my face off and patting down my legs. I bent and gagged from the smell attached to my nostrils.

"Do not thank me, Christian. I only sought to show you what happens when you cross me. See, with my brother you will simply be tossed out of the tower and become a kabob. *Splat* . . . over quickly, and on to your . . . swift judgment." He pointed at the tomb. "But when you cross me, this little box becomes your home." He knocked on the top. "Oh, don't worry about suffocating—we'll drill a small airhole. And someone will come around every . . . twenty-eight days or so . . . to provide you with nourishment."

He gave a most convincing, cruel smile, displaying large sharp teeth.

"I know better than to cross you," I said.

"Save your blandishments, mortal. Only know this, that your fate will be the same as what my wife has been going through." He inhaled, and a long hiss carried past his bared teeth. "For a very long time."

"Înțeleg." I understand.

"And the bonus question is?" he asked.

"What you want . . ." I shivered as the chilled night air evaporated my sweat. ". . . second most is to know where your brother's wife is."

He studied me from a distance, swooping in for a couple sniffs. I assessed him to be less trustworthy, more mercurial than Dalca, for the Master had only one demeanor, contempt, which he doled out in varying measures.

"Hear me, mortal; I do not wish to repeat myself." He stroked his chin and narrowed his red eyes. "My dealings with your kind suggest that if you have located my brother's wife, then you have also found my wife. You would give me both, but first you wish for me to eliminate your most immediate obstacle. Then you have only one of us to scheme against, not two. And one who is doubly grateful for your help."

The sarcasm was unmistakable, but I nodded. Several bats took turns diving toward him. He swatted them away, took another long breath next to my head. "I do not smell confidence," he breathed into my ear. "You only think you know where she is. This I can tell."

"I think I'm close," I said, "but it's only one of them . . . unless they are together."

He stepped over to the sarcophagus and lifted the lid as if to invite me back in. I tried to speak but could find no words as I shook. Bats swooped about and he swatted another away.

"*Now* I smell the proper fear," he said, lowering the lid. "That's better."

In the instant it took me to look downward, he was behind me with his mouth against my ear. "I do believe that you have come closest of the mortals to finding her. In fact, you would not be here in person if I could just go get her myself. Behind enemy lines, to use a human term. No, you think you are safe because you think I need you to find her. Think again. I only need to have you followed, for you will show me. I don't need for you to tell me. Now, go back to your little house with the *babă*, and maybe someone will come calling on you."

My mind reeled. It chilled me that somehow Radu knew I'd been staying with Sonia. "How will I . . . ?"

He was gone, and with him followed the sound of a hundred mosquito swarms and thousands of bats.

24

I left the cemetery under my own power and stumbled my way back over the bridge. When I reached the old road I thought it would be easier for everyone if I just stepped out in front of the first truck that passed. But none did. While trying to decide if I should go into Baia Sprie and ask for sanctuary at the Catholic church or hoof it five-plus miles back to the hotel, I heard a voice from across the street. "Over here." It was one of Radu's two men who'd driven me to him. A quiet return ride to Baia Mare ensued. We exchanged no words at the hotel door.

When I awoke the next morning, I put on CNN News while preparing to leave. Just as I stepped from the bathroom, I heard my brother's name.

"... *here at the church where Father Bernhardt Barkeley is believed to have disappeared this morning before first services. The priest is the brother of Joseph Winston Barkeley, the man wanted for questioning in the brutal ritual killings last month of two people. Joseph Barkeley is believed to have fled to Europe, and authorities suspect that he may have been in contact with his brother ...*"

The fear of the previous night suddenly seemed trivial. Whoever orchestrated the murders in the States had obviously nabbed my brother. I struggled to shake my worst fears about his fate. Whatever it was, I prayed it would be swift. There is a passage in the Bible that speaks of the martyrs crying out to God from under an altar about justice for those murdered, and all I could think about was seeing his pleading face among the victims.

Again I thought: *None of this would have happened except for me.*

I learned that when you're in trouble, your mind fills with tension while you yearn for an abrupt ending to the suspense. When someone you love is in jeopardy, anxiety is equally strong, but you feel less prone to hope for a quick end. Not knowing seems marginally better than learning the worst news possible. Such was my state of mind riding the train back to Bistriţa. En route I rehearsed what I would say to Luc. When I arrived he was at the station, and we headed toward the edge of town.

"What did you find?" he asked.

"I found a few local spots." I bent the truth. "I'm going to have to do some excavating."

Luc acknowledged this tripe with a suitably suspicious nod.

We took a quiet ride to Dumitra. Certainly I could not have told a convincing tale to Luc. My body felt strange as well, legs all numb, much like they had been inside that tomb, and each rush of breeze across my face felt like the opening of the lid. I shuddered several times reliving the experience. Rain began falling as we reached the village limits, and I told Luc I'd meet up with him in the morning. I ran the remaining distance to Sonia's house. It was open, as she had told me to come and go as family, but when I stepped in she was not home.

I lay down to take a nap and awoke after dark to the sound of a thunderclap as lightning struck a nearby hill. I felt my way to the bathroom and turned on a light—Sonia was still not home. The house felt utterly empty without her, as would my life.

I washed up and looked around for what I might use as a raincoat when I heard the front door open. I ran into the front room just as Sonia walked in. I dispensed with the three kisses and went right to hugging her. I'm sure she could feel me shake as she held me tightly.

I helped her with her overcoat and took a seat at the kitchen table while she brewed coffee. Sonia looked at me, and her smile turned serious as she stared into my eyes. "I am sorry for what your heart goes through, *draga mea.*" *My dear.*

"Thank you. It's my brother. I . . ." Words failed me.

"I know. I know." After a moment, her thoughts reached mine. *Your trip? Radu?*

He was . . . how it feels to be confronted by Satan, I thought, trying to express in my thoughts how one's footing on earth feels altered when confronted by a being of such superior power and intellect who holds your life carelessly suspended.

He is a monstru, worse than Dalca.

I nodded. Dalca was at least predictable.

When you are around him, do not think of his demise. He will smell it on you.

Again I nodded. When I conveyed to her my memory of being thrown in the tomb, she covered my hands and looked down; her eyes watered when she looked up. Then a feeling came through, as if she had projected to me what she felt, and it was not like a guardian, but something *she* had felt long ago.

I waited for her to straighten up before continuing. *He did not respond to my offer.*

That makes sense. She paused with a thoughtful brow and downward look. *He has human spies that can observe you, see if you give away your position.*

She was right, of course, because if he thought that was his only opportunity to extract information from me, I would still be there. And if he believed that I knew where his wife, Luiza, lay, he would likewise have kept me.

I continued, *He said someone would let me know. And he knows I have been staying with you.* I did not relay that he referred to her as *babă*. Old woman.

It means you'll be forced to trust a stranger.

Like Luc?

Your guide?

I nodded.

Well, Luc is human, she thought. *So far you have been able to trust him, but like any human, he will let you down.*

I sipped the strong coffee. *I don't know if Radu will call me to a meeting or if I'll have to tell his messenger where she is.*

Oh, he will not entrust such a thing to another. On this matter he will deal directly with you.

I closed my eyes and considered the risk. Then, rubbing my hand over my forehead, I thought, *Whatever I choose holds risk for you.*

The risk was mine when I tell where they are.

Can you leave and be safe?

"No place is safe," she said aloud.

Several minutes passed. *Have you considered the possibility that he will not show? That he will choose to make treaty with his brother instead of war?*

Yes. I will still ambush Dalca, but I hope that Radu will not be standing by and allowing Dalca to get to his wife first.

You cannot plan for all contingencies.

I nodded.

Who do you think might be able to help you set up this ambush? Someone who might know of the tomb?

An image of the priest popped into my head, since he lived next to the church.

Correct.

How old is he?

A little older than the babă. She smiled weakly.

I've been thinking of a weapon.

Yes?

I was thinking of a crossbow. I've talked to the Gypsy about his. It might be adapted to our purposes.

Arbaletă. Is good.

I'll also need a laser pointer . . . maybe two laser pointers.

The device that make narrow red light?

Yes.

There are superstitions against such things here. You may have difficulty finding such a thing.

I nodded, but I remembered seeing one in the street shops in Bistriţa that sold cheap electronics and stolen cell phones.

"The best-made plans are born of a sound sleep," she said aloud.

We closed our conversation and I went to bed. Despite my intentions of rest, the face of my brother kept invading. From the day he dressed to go to America until seminary graduation day, his smiles never quite reached his eyes, as if he did not deserve a moment's happiness. Or perhaps he felt greedy for taking what was meant for someone else. I tried not to think of his fate.

It was long after midnight when I was jolted awake by the sound of pounding on the front door. Quickly I jumped into my clothes and ran to the door, Sonia a hurried step behind, pulling a robe about her nightclothes. She nodded for me to open it, and I saw a man standing back away from the porch in front of a black horse-drawn landau. He had a long coat pulled up at the collar, a tall hat, and his eyes matched the glow of the red lantern running light. Night breezes stirred the two obsidian horses as they stood impatiently pointed into the forest.

He looked at me and spoke: *"Vino cu mine."* Come with me.

I looked at Sonia, and without speaking she said, *Make the right decisions and God will protect your soul.* Then she reached up to caress my cheek.

Just before taking my seat in the carriage, I saw the figure of a man walking back over the bridge, away from me and toward the village. By his stride I could tell it was Luc. He was not looking back.

A last glance at Sonia and the carriage door closed behind me. It was ornately appointed inside, with heavy fabrics of burgundy and black. Two soft bench seats faced each other, and I chose the one looking forward. When the door closed it locked with authority, becoming a cell. I had no windows to view the outside and no door handles to grant escape. The ceiling was made of polished wooden slats, and a single dim bulb glowed with the conviction of a six-volt idiot light. Four leather looped straps attached to the pillars in case the ride turned bumpy. The interior had that smell I'd come to recognize—vampire.

The stallions propelled the vehicle forward, and it bounced and jostled deep into the forest. Branches scraped the sides and top of the coach with several sharp turns, and I gripped the straps. The trip took only a few minutes, and the horses slowed to a walk before halting. I heard the sound of wooden gates opening; the coach inched forward, and the gates closed behind us.

When the stagecoach stopped again the door opened. Stepping out, I was inside Dreptu's monastery walls facing the large center tower. I dismounted by stepping down onto a gravestone. The driver told me to follow. I trailed him down the winding steps to the floor of the structure and past the spike pit toward the tower's main door. No other activity stirred, but I smelled vampires. He held the door and I stepped inside.

The entrance led to a large room, an assembly hall, with stone walls and a substantial wooden staircase at the far end ascending to the second floor. When I reached the far end of the room I saw a door behind the staircase entrance. Much like the basement door in Castel Bran, it was heavy oak with a locking mechanism. Except this door was unlocked and sprung. I stopped and awaited instruction, and the driver pointed me toward the door.

Once inside, an earthen smell assaulted my nose. Stairs, much like the stone steps of the castle, curved down into the darkness, with red lanterns mounted on the walls. At about forty steps I arrived at another locked door. Again, the driver opened it. Just as my eyes adjusted to yet a darker room, a shove from behind knocked me to the ground. And ground it was—no floor.

The heavy scent of burnt blood told me I had an audience with Dalca. While my eyesight adjusted to the low lighting, I saw several pairs of red eyes surrounding me and assumed my audience also included dozens of his Commons.

From beyond the row of eyes came Dalca's voice: "This way, human."

His guards parted, and I was allowed to approach his great throne of oak wood, with trimmings of gold and a crown of iron spikes with dragons wrapping the poles. His scent was heavier than his subjects'.

Dalca pointed to a small layer of straw in front of me. "I had them lay out new rushes . . . just for you."

The driver pressed my shoulders down till I knelt on the straw. "Yes . . . Master," I said.

"Tell me of your progress, human."

I had rehearsed this during several train trips. "The museum in Belgrade is in disarray, but—"

Dalca interrupted. "That is how humans begin their excuses, by telling of others' misdeeds."

"I only meant to say the research has taken longer than I hoped, Master. But I was able to inspect about twenty percent of the archives."

"Tell me what you found."

"The material is not labeled or filed by year," I lied, "but I found several files containing original correspondence from the decade the manuscript was written. There were many vague descriptions in his notes, with crude maps and references to landmarks."

He drew a long breath through his teeth. "I smell . . . anxiety."

"Because I have no answer yet, Master. I have only a list of landmarks that the maps indicate where I should try excavating."

"Look at me," he said. "Do you think you are the first human to try to buy time?"

"No, Master, but I just don't have the answer yet."

Dalca slid down from his throne. "Come." I followed him out of the room and up the stone stairs to the first level. When we reached the grand staircase, two Regulats grabbed my arms and lifted me, and we ascended the tower quickly. Like an express elevator ride, everything moved past me in a blur. When they finally put me down, I felt unsure of my footing.

I was ushered through a pair of tall wooden doors into a large ballroom, its walls decorated with colorful fabrics and torches, a floor of wide plank oak, and tall cathedral ceilings. I figured it must be the top story. At one end was a small curtained stage elevated about three feet, and at the other a large fireplace. The room was not well lit, with only a couple wall sconces glowing amber.

My heart skipped several beats when I saw the double doors open to the balcony and the night sky beyond. This was the high-dive platform to the shallow end. I followed Dalca toward the stage with two escorting Regulats, and we climbed the three steps to where a stage curtain draped from the ceiling. From behind the curtain I heard a noise—it sounded like a grunt.

The Master turned to me, and the two escorts grabbed my arms and held me in place. Dalca leaned into my face, his teeth only inches from my eyes. "So you decided to take up arms with my brother." He breathed on me, eyes glowing lethal red.

In a blur he turned and ripped open the curtain. I froze when I saw a guillotine, its blade poised to drop. It took a moment to see in the dim light before I realized there was someone strapped in. Dalca lit a lantern and lifted it to the face of the prone prisoner. It was Bernhardt! Gagged with a cloth wrapped around his mouth, again Bernhardt grunted and struggled to move.

I panicked and began shaking. "No!"

"Well," Dalca said, "since you have decided to bring my brother in on this, I thought I would respond in kind."

"I'm sorry, Berns," I said, scarcely stifling a sob.

Dalca put down the lantern and walked around me, pressing his mouth toward my ears as he spoke. "Unlike you, who wishes to have my brother annihilate me, I am going to give you a choice." He lifted the lantern and illuminated my brother's face. "Tell me." He lifted the lantern in my face. "Who gets to live? You? Or your brother?"

I thought of Sonia's parting message—*make the right decision.* But I did not need to ponder the question, for of course I would give myself up for my brother.

"Take me," I said.

Dalca reached down and removed Bernhardt's gag.

"No!" Bernhardt shouted. "Don't do it, Joseph."

Dalca circled and hissed in my ear again, "Tell me who will live. *Tell* me."

"Let *him* live," I said. "Take me."

Again Bernhardt shouted, "No!"

Dalca looked at me one more time for the answer.

"Let him live," I said.

"Then forever hold your peace, human." And with that Dalca walked over and reapplied the gag in Bernhardt's mouth. He unfastened the guillotine yoke and said, "Now he will live . . . forever." Then Dalca bent and sank his teeth into Bernhardt's neck as my brother's body convulsed and he began to scream.

The two Regulats held me back, one of them holding my head

in the direction of the guillotine, forcing me to watch. It was only seconds before Dalca finished and stood. He offered no emotion as he stood over my brother with blood dripping down his chin onto his victim. The muffled sound of Bernhardt's sobbing echoed across the large room.

Dalca walked over to me and with a shove to my chest knocked me to the floor. In an instant he was on me, dragging me by my feet toward the balcony. I clawed at the floor, looking back at my brother still strapped into the machine. Once on the balcony, Dalca held me out over the ledge by my feet.

"Look down, human," he said. "Behold your destiny."

I was not ready to go, but I did not want to face the future, either. I tried not to struggle. He dangled me for a tortured minute, perhaps longer.

Then he turned and threw me back inside on the floor. I slid several feet across the wooden planks and felt my skin burn. A second later Dalca leaned over in my face and said, "I just wanted to remind you what's at stake here, human." He lifted me by the neck and held me closer to his face. "Now go find my wife."

25

Released to walk back through the forest that night, I saw no sign of my brother, while the wolves howled in the hills and the half-moon blinked through fast-moving clouds. The Regulats were furious when they evicted me from the monastery, spitting on me and shoving me to the ground. If not for Dalca's orders, I would have been skewered and posted as a warning to potential traitors.

In the woods every buzz sounded like a mosquito squad and every broken branch seemed to portend an ambush. I kept one foot in front of the other, never looking back, in the hopes I'd make it out alive. Even that did not seem to matter as much as before, as fresh visions of my brother brought the shame of knowing that I had sealed his fate in extended torture. Gone were the memories of studying together by flashlight in the convent basement, of watching Bernhardt take his vows and say his first Mass, all replaced by the surety that I was en route to a violent end, just another in the long line of disposable humans placed in the way of that family. Oh, how I wished Dalca would have thrown me out the window and sent my brother home intact.

When Bernhardt and I were kids tossing on cots in the convent, I used to worry at night, not so much fearing the dark but distressed that the next day might bring a new set of parents or, worse yet, parents for only one of us. I felt responsible for Berns; I always sought to answer his questions as comfortingly as possible, to assure him that the next day would be like the previous, to set an example of stable behavior. It led to my lifelong dedication to order, never wanting to give the nuns any reason to search for adoptive parents. Despite our admittedly unusual living situation, I did not wish to roll the dice on possibly worse conditions. It's not that we felt loved, or even happy, but we lived in a safe holding pattern. Yes, we knew even then that things could always get worse, as they'd been in the Romanian orphanage. What would become of him, and the nuns, now?

Sonia and Father Andrew had kept a vigil that night and were still praying when I came through the door. Their first response was to thank God for my deliverance, and their second was a hearty welcome home. Sitting across the table from Sonia, I mentally conveyed images of what had happened, including my suspension over the ledge. She swallowed hard and told me, *Dalca will send your brother back to America and keep an eye on him.*

And if they go after him again?

Like anyone who knows too much, they will just kill him there.

As they did George, I thought.

Yes, as they did my husband.

"Is there no limit to their evil?" I asked aloud, rhetorically.

Father Andrew responded, "They pay no price before God."

"So all their misery is here," I said. "Might as well spread it around."

Sonia pointed to the priest. "I told him what you have planned."

"When do we start?" Father Andrew asked without hesitation.

"Right now," I said.

"It would be wise," Sonia said, "to wait until sunlight."

We all retired, but I failed to chase away violent images featuring my brother, and with every wind gust and creak of the old house I jerked awake. Then, just as I fell into sleep, I dreamed I was falling, falling. I looked up and saw my brother had thrown me out the tower balcony, and my eyes snapped open. But the dream kept returning.

In the morning, the three of us met at the church and locked the doors behind us. Kneeling before the altar, the priest led a prayer: "Forgive us, Lord, for what we are about to do. We vow to rebuild this blessed house once the evil beneath it is destroyed. Please send us your strength and wisdom to defeat this evil, in the name of Your Son, Jesus Christ."

"Amen."

I made the sign of the cross, stood, and looked up at the ceiling, and studied the face of Jesus. The artist had successfully married sorrow and judgment into His expression, and the Lord's eyes followed the observer about the room. The innocent might find comfort, but for the guilty, such as me, the urge rose to flee His omnipresent gaze.

"I was not here for this church's christening," the priest said, "but look at this."

He pointed to a spot on the floor directly in line with the front door, centering the altar. Embossed into the wooden floor was the image of a Western-style cross with its singular crossbar, as if burned in and stained over. It measured exactly six feet by three feet wide, the length pointing toward the altar. If one were to draw a rectangle defined by those dimensions, it would roughly equal the size of a casket. I looked up; it lay centered beneath the fixed stare of Jesus.

Without saying a word, the priest pointed to a square peg in the wooden floor. It looked like a large dowel pin. He pointed to a second on the other side of the cross, seven feet apart. Stepping to the bottom of the cross, he pointed to two more floor pegs, and if you drew connecting straight lines to all four they formed a rectangle around the casket, allowing two feet to spare on all sides. It was almost instructing where to dig to allow two feet of buffer space.

The priest looked at me and asked, "What is your plan?"

"Well," I said, "the first thing is to excavate. We'll dig down till we find the tomb. Then we'll find out what's in it. When . . . if we establish that it is his wife, then we convince Dalca to come here. Lure him down in the hole. Ambush him while he's . . . distracted. Then treat the body in such a way that he cannot come back."

Both nodded gravely, and Sonia spoke first. "It can be done. The key is to convince him there is no danger."

"Go on," I said.

"He will be looking for ambush from the time you tell him until the moment he sees his wife. There is only one moment when he is vulnerable enough for your attack."

"So when he fully turns his attention to his wife is when we attack."

Father Andrew spoke. "He cannot be allowed to take her and get out of the hole."

Sonia pointed at me. "And you cannot be in the church—he will smell you."

"Or see my body heat." I thought a moment, trying to picture his movements in the church. "Will he look up?"

Sonia answered, "Perhaps quickly, and then down."

Then the attack should come from above, as I had envisioned, since he would spend his time in the hole looking down. But it would have to be precise and swift, because vampires move quickly enough to dodge shots and evade bomb blasts.

"First things first," the priest said, interrupting my thoughts. "First to dig hole."

"You're right," I said. "Do you have any ideas on how to excavate down to that tomb?"

Father Andrew produced a piece of paper from his pocket and spread it on the floor. "I draw last night." We all knelt to look. It was a rectangle with four square pegs in the corner, just like the wooden floor. "I was in Iaşi in 1941—"

"The pogroms," I interrupted.

"Yes. When roundups begin, several families hide neighbors under wooden floors." He pointed to the drawing. He used a pencil to indicate sawing along the rectangle's lines. "They dig deep enough space for storage and brace up at pegs." He drew a picture of four bedposts supporting the pegs under the floor.

I said, "That's how they reinforce tunnels when they build them."

"Yes," the priest said. "If we can break through foundation, we haul out material."

Sonia added, "Carve out the wood rectangle and re-cover each day."

Father Andrew nodded. "No interrupting service."

"Why not just tell the congregation you have a plumbing leak or something and close it down for a couple weeks?"

The priest gave a weak smile. "My son, over half this town is unemployed. They would show up every day with shovels. Try to help."

Sonia asked, "What about your *gardă?*" *Guard.*

"I'll tell him something . . . maybe that we'll be excavating a reliquary or some such thing."

Father Andrew asked, "Do you trust him?"

I gave a look and shrug that suggested I had my doubts. After all, that was Luc coming out of the woods when my carriage driver arrived. Up to this point, Luc's actions suggested he both wanted me to succeed and him to stay alive long enough to see it. Still, he was the one charged with feeding Dalca information, or disinformation, as it was.

"Trust him or not, you need him."

"I don't know how long it will take to excavate," I said. "Do we have a pick and shovel?"

"No," said Father Andrew. "I will have to borrow tools for digging, but I can do wood work."

That was good, I thought, because I had never worked with wood and feared I would butcher it.

He said, "The Gypsy digs the graves." He was referring to the cemetery just outside the village.

He would also be, I hoped, the source of my weapon. "Can he be trusted?"

The silence suggested he would be a gamble, and considering the stature the Roma held in that part of Europe, odds favored the house of Dreptu. But when I looked at Sonia, she appeared disappointed.

"What?" I asked.

"It is not *he* we should question," she said. "It is *us* he will have to trust."

"She is right," Father Andrew said. "He risk everything for no return."

"What would we have to offer him?" I asked.

Another stretch of silence followed before the priest said, "I speak with him this morning."

"I'll compile a supplies list," I said.

I wrote the list, plus a second in Romanian and placed the items in order of need, then handed it to Father Andrew as he went to enlist the Gypsy's help. While he was gone, I measured the floor and looked at the chalk marks, trying to picture the space below. If the outer measurements of the tomb were six by three, then that two-foot buffer looked snug at best. "It looks tight," I said to Sonia. "What do you think?"

"I think you trust person who put in pegs."

Just then the side door opened and the priest returned, followed by the Gypsy in his driving clothes. He removed his hat and crossed himself before entering. We thanked him for coming. The Gypsy looked at the three of us and saw the floor. The priest told him we needed to excavate under the foundation to get to a reliquary, and the Gypsy eyed each of us before looking at the supplies list.

"*Cât de mult?*" he asked. *How much?*

"*Doi metri,*" I said. *Two meters.*

The Gypsy took measure of us before looking around the church at the crucifixes and paintings. He looked up at the ceiling, crossed himself again, and said, *"Te vei lupta cu satana."* *You will fight Satan.* Then he left.

As we stood around looking at one another, a voice sounded from the back of the church. "What are you going to do now?"

It was Luc, and the three of us jerked our heads toward him.

"How long have you been there?" I asked.

"Since the prayer." So he'd heard everything. He must have arrived early for my daily briefings and hidden in the back row. I should have looked for him. Luc left as abruptly as he'd spoken without saying anything else.

For the rest of the day, we looked through the priest's woodworking tools and garden supplies and tried not to tally the odds against us or all potential dangers, including the possibility that Luc was already recounting our discussion to Dalca. We volleyed different ideas, including hiring an outsider to excavate through the foundation and I would dig the rest, but each new thought fell victim to the obstacles of reality, some financial and some practical. By the day's end we sat at Sonia's kitchen table, eating soup and bread while sipping strong coffee in silence. No one dared say we could not do it, but it was obvious we needed help from the great invisible hand.

"We sleep on it," said Father Andrew.

My night worries returned. First, thoughts of Berns, then concerns over failure, until any gust of wind, any broken branch or noise outside took me to wit's end. I gave up sleep and sat at Sonia's table after midnight. All my thoughts followed the path to defeatism.

As my head nodded wearily, I suddenly recalled the telephone number on the cigarette pack and the envoy's message—*When you need to escape.* I had plenty of information to unload on Mr. Bena, from the whereabouts and numbers of Dalca's forces to Radu's existence and something of his location and methods. Plus I knew almost for certain the most important things of all— where the two wives lay buried. If I could get to a telephone and the locker in Bistriţa, I could seek this escape.

Your father was not a coward.

I looked up and saw Sonia in her bedroom doorway. "He could have taken the two of you and run back to England."

"He chose to fight and destroy evil," I said.

"Yes," she said. "What will you do?"

I knew that my decision to bail would spell the fatal end to Sonia and two priests, one of them my brother. It seemed obvious what I had to do. Sometimes cowards have no choice but to fight.

We continued to plan through the weekend, leaving the church untouched for weekend services. On Monday morning, Father Andrew arrived early at Sonia's door and urged us to hustle to the church to witness a prayer answered. Opening the church door we found the Gypsy kneeling on the floor carefully sawing the planks. He told us not to wash the wood or it would look different from the rest of the floor, and warned us not to set the planks outside in the sunlight or get them wet because they would swell. Two hours later he had cut the perimeter and begun loosening the boards. By the end of the day he had removed the planks and placed them upside down on a cloth tarp. As we held them in place, he braced the back with a Z-bracket so we could maneuver the planks as one slab. They did not fit snugly back into place, and the Gypsy filed the adjoining planks to size. By the end of the first day, we had the slab back in place, except it did not quite lie flush in the floor.

The second day the Gypsy left us with instructions to chip away at the subfloor until we reached the stone foundation. It took the entire day to accomplish, and the Gypsy chuckled at my day's production, then laid layers of tarps on my work to shim the slab flush to the rest of the floor.

After Tuesday's work I stood on the church front steps and looked up to the inn on the hillside. Even at that distance I recognized Luc sitting on the second-story porch, lifting what appeared to be binoculars to his eyes. I waved and he lowered his spyglasses.

On Wednesday the Gypsy arrived just before sunrise, his cart filled with supplies, including picks, mason's tools, shovels, buckets, and several burlap sacks. He instructed the priest to mark off an area in his fenced garden next to his residence equal to the size of the wooden rectangle. He took his pick to the edges of a stone in the foundation and worked on it for the greater part of an hour, and rather than pulverize it into something unusable, left it intact and started in on another stone.

After a day of our taking turns on the pick, the first stone was ready to be lifted out of the foundation. The following morning the Gypsy brought three of his teenage sons to help lift stones out of the foundation and into a sling. Carrying them to the garden, the man instructed his sons to place the stones in the exact placement they were in the foundation. They accepted the challenge as if assembling a puzzle. The work was dirty and dusty, and every evening after finishing the priest and I swept, dusted, and picked up tarps while Sonia prepared dinner.

It took another day to remove the stones and place them in the garden before taking a pick to the compacted dirt. On Monday morning, the Gypsy pulled up before sunrise with his horse cart filled with burlap bags. His sons unloaded them in the fenced garden, and he said they were for carrying the dirt. After removing the wooden slab he demonstrated the first one—lay it out, fill it with as much dirt as you can lift, then cinch it up like a purse net and carry the bag to the garden and place them in rows.

"Only shovel dirt once," he said.

Made sense, but it was a lot of bags. It also kept curious villagers from looking over a garden fence at a growing dirt mound and asking questions. The bags suggested something harmless, like root-balls or potatoes.

Each day we picked and dug and shoveled, the ground the density of compacted clay. Some days we measured progress only by inches in our confined space. Each foot we dug deeper without pay dirt brought more anxiety, as I knew there was a limit to the Master's patience, as well as Radu's. Luc's demeanor seemed to reinforce my worries, as he paced, acting like a boss standing over us, tapping his fingers on a timepiece.

Father Andrew took meals with me and Sonia, but it was quiet. Over Thursday dinner Sonia sent a thought across the table that our guest could not hear: *You are avoiding eye contact with our guest. That is not good leadership.*

He's being—

He has as much of his neck at stake as you. So does Luc.

I nodded, then asked, "How's your soup?"

Father Andrew lifted his chin and grunted.

Sonia smiled. *That's better.*

It was a time of high anxiety for all involved, since the project had not yet yielded results, and expectations measured in extremes. No one ventured to guess the consequences of an empty hole. After dinner Father Andrew returned to his residence before the sun expired.

Sonia cleaned the table and I offered to dry the dishes. She responded, "Whatever makes you worry less."

I smiled and remained seated. Over the weeks I had come to appreciate her, to value her companionship. She shared her wisdom, as opposed to dispensing it. She pushed without shoving. She understood the motivations of man, and while infusing me with knowledge and ideas, she somehow managed to make me believe that somehow I had conjured them on my own. I thought that if I was to ever settle with a woman, I would be searching for one just like her. And certainly someone as attractive—

Suddenly she turned her head my direction, halted her drying, and said, "And if I were only a hundred and fifty years younger . . ."

I flushed with embarrassment and excused myself to the porch.

Friday morning Sonia sent me off with a smile that I had not seen before, and I kept replaying it as I worked in the hole. It was distracting. So much so that when I raised my pick and Father Andrew shouted, *"Oprește!"* (*Stop*), I thought I did something wrong.

He pointed to a spot and jumped into the hole. While I rested he brushed away at the spot until a hard surface became visible. It looked to be smooth stone. He crossed himself and asked God's forgiveness and guidance in the coming days. We began brushing off the top of the hard slab. There were no markings on the stone to suggest who or what we might have found.

"What do you think?" I asked Father Andrew.

A voice answered from above the hole: "I think you should

leave that thing sealed until you're ready to fight." It was Luc. I jumped.

The priest answered, "I think he is right."

Luc reached to help me out of the hole. "If she is intact and you open that tomb, her lungs will fill and she will just get up and leave."

"Thank you," I said.

"The Master has inquired about your progress," Luc said. "I told him you have several excavation sites that look promising."

"Thank you, again." I brushed myself off and offered him my hand. "When do you think would be the best time?"

"The only time he is vulnerable—the hours after his next feeding."

Sonia dropped in to tell us dinner was ready and looked into the hole. "Join us," she said to Luc. Then she knelt and pressed her hand against the cold stone. She looked at me and shook her head, and before leaving, we placed the wooden slab over the hole and locked the church. During dinner no one said a thing; we all ate quickly so the priest could return to his residence prior to sundown.

Once alone with Sonia, I asked, "What did you sense from Luc?"

"He is sympathetic, but still unsure."

"What's keeping him from going to Dalca and telling everything?"

"Have you seen his neck?" she asked. "Unmarked. He has not yet been offered the long life."

"He keeps it covered. Why would they not enslave him?"

She said, "He has either not proven himself yet or they do not see a talent in him they can use."

I thought it over. This must be his first big test. "And what did you sense in the hole?"

"Maybe it was just fear, but I sensed . . . something."

"Trying to communicate?"

"No. Not enough strength, like a signal. But something there."

That night as I lay in bed exhausted, I felt the encroachment of the deadline, emphasis on *dead*, and wondered how professional soldiers coped with impending battles and the random chance of slaughter. With just more than a week left before the full moon, the hourglass seemed to drain with greater speed. The attack would have to be on the full moon night, as Luc suggested. George's notes confirmed that the hours just after feeding were when vampires were vulnerable to attack—the gorging blood caused their bodies to halt adrenaline flow and instead draw water content from their undigested nourishment. More precisely, that meant sometime between midnight and dawn of the full moon night.

I needed to somehow contact Radu and tell him of our attack date, and at the last minute lure Dalca to the hole. When I met Radu in the cemetery, he said someone would contact me. Correct that—*might* contact me. Since that evening, I had figured that he must have a human slave somewhere in the village observing events. But I was not going to wait for a contact; I vowed to find a way to alert him.

On Sunday night I tossed about and visualized how to mount the weapon in the rafters. I had mentioned my needs to the Gypsy, and he seemed to both listen to my ideas and simultaneously dismiss them in his usual taciturn manner. Oh well, I thought, that part of the endeavor was no more ill-fated than any other.

I found myself falling into a coffee-buzz sleep when suddenly a great rumble approached from every direction. It sounded like a pack of motorcycles. The house began to shake, one violent shove as the rumble turned into a roar. I heard Sonia scream from the other room. The house shook and shook for several seconds until it settled into a rocking motion. A photo fell off the wall, and everything on my dresser scattered. After what seemed like a minute, the house settled like an elevator reaching its floor. Dogs barked in the distance.

I had never lived outside of Illinois and was unfamiliar with earthquakes, so I was terrified when it started, believing the creature was breaking out of her tomb, either under the house or the church, and continued to sweat with fear long after the house settled.

I ran into Sonia's room where she was bent and reaching to pick things off the floor. We sat on the edge of the bed and hugged each other. She was breathing hard and sobbing. An aftershock gently shook the house, and she grabbed tighter. Several minutes passed before we moved. She reached for a robe to put over her nightclothes, and I went to open the front door. She stopped me. "No. It's okay. It is just a quake."

Of all the nights to get hit with a random earthquake. We waited out the rest of the night at the kitchen table, enduring several small aftershocks. I had lived through Chicago weather all my life, from winter blizzards to hearing the spring tornado sirens and seeing funnel clouds in the green bumpy skies, but at least a tornado chooses its victims with random precision, whereas an earthquake spares no one.

The event, strangely, was not discussed in the village, another superstitious belief. But the Gypsy was shaking when he visited the excavation site and begged off work that day. I was too nervous not to work, as was the priest, and we filled dozens of bags with dirt and lowered the hole to the bottom of the sarcophagus. We encountered an unexpected obstacle when we found two handles attached to the sides of the tomb. Placed two-thirds of the way to the top, and another two-thirds of the way toward the end of the tomb that I took to be the head, I guessed they must be pallbearers' handles. Strange, though, since there were only the two of them, and their grips looked more like sword hilts than anything else.

At day's end Father Andrew showed me the mounting frame he had made, a reinforced wooden rectangle that resembled a window frame. "Let us measure," he said.

Walking through the village, I saw Luc up at the inn with his binoculars raised, and waved. He did not wave back. Reaching the end of the village, we found the Gypsy in his grass-roofed shed in his back pasture. He pulled back a burlap cover on his bench to reveal a crossbow.

I smiled and said, *"O arbaletă."*

"O arbaletă." He placed the crossbow in the frame and it fit like a benchrest with a little adjustment space on the sides. Then he

showed me how the weapon worked. The wooden bow, called the tiller, bent as the string cocked back into a slot on the stock. He said he had restrung the frayed wire and replaced the nut, the rolling pawl that retained the string.

He placed a short arrow, a bolt, in the stock's slot and opened the window to his shed. Demonstrating how to shoulder the weapon, he took aim at a hay bale and pulled the trigger. Instantly the arrow stuck its target. He did not smile, but rather handed me the bow and pointed to a second bolt on the bench. I cocked the string, lifted it as he said, checked the firing range, and pulled the trigger. My bolt stuck about two feet above the first one. Then he told me to measure the height from the church ceiling to the intended target; we would then set the hay bale to that distance.

I looked at the bolt and asked him about the metal tip.

"Cupru," he said. *Copper.*

"Argint," I said. It must be silver. George's notes on conductivity and reaction to blood were explicit.

He looked puzzled, but finally nodded. *"Argint. Da."*

Back at the church I used the ladder to crawl up into the rafters above the excavation. The old wooden churches often had two ceilings, one just above the congregation to help retain heat in the winter months, and another at roof level. Between the two ceilings a set of rafters helped support the roof structure. The face of Jesus was painted on the lower ceiling.

In the rafters I looked for a place to mount the crossbow frame. It was several feet up to the roof, and that, too, presented a challenge of how to fire the weapon remotely. After climbing down, I shifted the ladder and attached a piece of string from the face of Jesus and let it down to the top of the tombstone, where I snipped it. I rolled the string up and returned to the Gypsy's shed, where he marked off the distance and placed a hay bale target. The crossbow had a set of iron sights, and at the ten-meter distance there was a little drop in the bolt's trajectory. Considering this would be fired straight down from the ceiling, I held confidence in the fixed sights.

Having marked the ceiling spot directly over the tomb, Father Andrew drilled a small hole to see if we could mount the crossbow above that point in the rafters. Although there was uneven space between the studs, the gaps measured wide enough to bolt the crossbow into place with the aid of spacers and shims.

"Were you planning to be up here?" asked the priest.

"No," I said, "he would smell me."

The priest nodded. "Then how you fire?"

"I'm working on it."

My best idea, at present, was to run a string and pull it from a remote position, with a lead weight applying the needed pressure to set up a hair trigger.

Just then Luc entered the church, walked straight to Father Andrew, and presented him an envelope. Luc was not smiling. The priest opened it and read the single page. He handed me the note and said, "You work fast, no?"

I recognized the handwriting and the stationery, the same personalized stock I had received before. It read:

To Father Andrew,

The honor of your presence is requested at a birthday party to be held at the Monastery on the evening of the Rose Moon. Dress is casual, meals will be served . . .

That was only five days away.

When I looked at him I saw guilt in the form of eyes averted, for the invitation could only mean that the priest was either one of their slaves or perhaps one of their spies.

26

In the church the Gypsy mounted the crossbow in the benchrest, leaving enough play to adjust its aim with a hand crank.
I helped lift the weapon to the rafters and bolt it solidly in
place. Father Andrew drilled a hole in the painted lower ceiling with just enough clearance to allow the bolt to pass
through to its target. I placed a hay bale over the tomb to protect it, then climbed up into the rafters to take the first shot. The
arrow grazed the bale and shattered on the slab. After adjusting
the aim with the hand crank, the next round found the bale, but
not its target. Eight tries, plus three more confirming shots later,
all worked with precision, and the bolt tip sunk into the midpoint
of the bale each time.

Next we rigged the remote firing device by running a thin

wire from the rafters and outside, through a small hole, alongside a gutter spout. However, when we pulled the wire, the motion over the pivot point jostled the crossbow's aim and the shot missed its target by more than a foot. Father Andrew looked at me with panic in his eyes.

I said, "Don't worry, I'm working on it."

As for my own qualms, I envisioned the possibility of repeating my Loreena Braithwaite mistake, not getting a shot at Dalca, and having him lose his patience and attack me. I also considered the possibility that his bride's remains were there but unusable.

Sonia touched me on the shoulder and said, "You worry about things you have no control over."

I nodded.

"Work on what you can."

"*Mulţumesc,*" I thanked her, and looked around at the others. "Any ideas when you think we might open this up and see what's inside?"

No one responded for a moment until the Gypsy posed a question. I did not catch its meaning, so Father Andrew translated: "How far dog smells another in heat?"

I nodded and gave it careful consideration. If her scent was strong enough, Dalca might be able to smell her the scant distance to Dreptu. But if the smell was modest, I could prove her existence by obtaining her scent on a piece of cloth.

Sonia warned, *You must wait until very last moment to take her scent.*

She was right, but that left no time to notify Radu.

When he wasn't praying, Father Andrew fretted nervously,

as would anyone with only four days until execution. In the middle of our conversation he interrupted. "I must go make my last confession."

It seemed strange at first, but it made sense, for even priests go to confession.

"I shall go see Father Ionescu in Bistriţa." And looking my way, he said, "Come with me."

Before leaving, I took Sonia aside and said, "You should really come with us and leave the area."

"Why?" she asked.

"If this all goes down wrong, Dalca is going to go after you first."

"Do you really think there is a place where he cannot find me?"

"At least you'd have a chance," I said. Then I reached for my wallet and retrieved the locker key. I pressed it into her hand. "Here's the locker key, N279 in the Bistriţa train station. There's some traveling money in there."

"I have faith that you will take me there," she said.

Then I thought of Alexandru Bena. I had written the telephone number on a piece of paper. "In the pocket of the coat you gave me, there is a phone number. Call it and ask for Alexandru Bena."

Again, she reached up to touch my face. "My days will end here. With you."

I nodded.

"Besides," she said, "Dalca will be looking for me to be home at that hour, as he will pass my house only." She tapped her nose, indicating that Dalca would be able to smell her presence. "Nothing should appear out of ordinary."

"Înțeleg." *I understand.*

"Don't forget your red pointer," she said as I was leaving.

"Thank you." We hugged.

After washing up for our ride into town, we climbed in the priest's truck, a 1967 International Travelall, green with bench seats that smelled of wet horses. Stopping at the inn, I asked Luc if he wanted to ride into Bistrița for an errand, and he eagerly washed up, grabbed a jacket, and piled in with us. The ancient SUV protested going to work, but it bounced nobly along the dirt road while the sun set. Up and over the hill the lights of Bistrița came into sight, and Father Andrew paused to take a nostalgic look at the view.

After dropping Luc off at an apartment of some acquaintance near the Bistrița train station, we drove to the part of town where shops sold cell phones and electronic gadgets. After six inquiries I found only one laser pointer, a used one at that, and paid the superstition premium price of fifty dollars US.

As we drove to the west side of town and out onto a rural road, the priest slowed the truck and said, "Many things I regret in this life, and all involve disobedience to God."

Knowing secondhand the loneliness of priesthood, I offered my honest assessment: "You have given much so others will not have such regrets."

He looked straight ahead. "My first hundred years I spent breaking His stone tablets. My second hundred I try putting them back together."

"That's confession enough," I told him, my best attempt to comfort the man.

He shook his head no and said that the Regulat that had visited him with the moons died in the same war as Sonia's Regulat. Afterward they both dedicated themselves to keeping secret what lay beneath their houses.

"I knew this day would come," he said. "It seems like a long time to get here, but now that it arrives . . . it seems as though it came all too quickly."

"Înțeleg."

"Over the decades Sonia and I talked about who would come to defeat the evil." He looked over at me. "I knew it would be a man of great courage and character."

"Instead, I showed up," I said. "Well, wish me luck anyway."

He tried to smile, but it only turned the corners of his mouth down. "Remember Jeremiah, Isaiah, David?"

"Old Testament, yes."

"Ordinary men God gave great strength when needed," he said, "and He will do same for you."

"I will pray for you, Father."

"I shall need it."

"Why? From what I see you've been a good priest. Trust me, I know the difference."

A stretch of silence passed when he seemed to want to say something else. Finally he spoke: "I'm not a priest." He looked straight ahead and not at me. "I just showed up when they needed one. I came to this abandoned church and rebuilt it."

"How did you . . . ?"

"I went to seminary as a young man."

"Did you quit?"

"No . . . expelled."

"Oh." I did not want to ask him how long he had lived his lie.

"Right after the first Great War—your president was Coolidge—I violated my celibacy vows. Repeatedly."

"You did the *job* of a priest. That makes you a priest." I hoped.

He shook his head and looked away. "Please pray for me."

We arrived at an old wooden church, another high-steepled, three-centuries-old structure with a single light burning dimly in the rectory window. The grounds were fenced and hosted a large cemetery.

"I shall be a while," Father Andrew said. "At least an hour."

I nodded and said I would be on the grounds. The night was cool and windy, and as the trees rustled overhead a sense of resolution settled over me, for I knew we were going to confront unbridled evil and hope God guided our arrows, or bolts, as may be. Make that singular—we had but one shot.

I found another *troiţă* near the cemetery entrance and knelt to pray. I prayed for the priests, both my brother and Father Andrew, and gave thanks for sending Sonia and the Gypsy into my life. I asked forgiveness for breaking promises and destroying the lives of others. Like a man who invents a great explosive device and then is stunned when it's employed to kill people, I was unworthy to petition for favors, but still I begged for mercy anyway.

Overhead the trees rustled. I stopped and looked up just as the moon rose over the Carpathians. It was almost full.

"It will do you no good." Radu's low voice startled me, and I jerked my head in his direction. "Over here." I looked and saw him sitting on a tomb in the cemetery. "I was told you were here." His eyes glowed red like lanterns. "Come closer."

I entered through a creaky wooden gate and stepped within twenty feet. He wore no coat or hat, just dark traveling clothes.

"Closer."

I closed half the distance and heard him sniff heavily through clenched teeth.

"So you have found something."

"Yes."

"I smell . . . apprehension . . . but more confidence than our last meeting."

"I found a tomb."

"Just one?"

"Just one. No markings."

"But you have not unsealed it," he said. "Not yet."

I nodded.

"Speak, mortal."

"Correct, not yet."

"And it's not the tomb of my wife, is it?"

"I don't know."

"Clearly you fear you have only one chance, and you want me there to keep you off the sharp end of the stick."

"Yes, sir."

"Tell me where the tomb is."

As I hesitated, a huge cloud of flying things arrived, an assortment of birds and bats.

"As you can see," he said, "I cannot travel anywhere without drawing the paparazzi. I must go now, but if you want me there you will have to tell me where it is."

When I failed to answer immediately his face moved suddenly to one inch from mine.

"Now!" He showed his teeth. "Tell me."

"The church in Dumitra." Before I could say anything else he was gone, so I yelled, "This Rose Moon." The birds and bats all departed with him, traveling north.

Father Andrew concluded his business, and we picked up Luc at his friend's apartment. It was a quiet ride back to Dumitra, and I could tell the sight of the moon unnerved the priest, so I offered to drive. He shook his head and drove on. It was bumpy.

The next morning I walked to the Gypsy's and found him working in his smithing shop. He directed me to a seat to wait while he finished a delicate task, that of weighing the crossbow ammunition, as each bolt must weigh the same to achieve consistent trajectory, given a set string tension. He lifted the last arrow and handed it to me for inspection. It was not copper-tipped like the others.

With a proud but grim smile, he said, *"Argint."*

"I can never repay you," I said.

He gripped my shoulder and shook me. *"Hai să mergem."* *Let's go.*

We walked toward his driveway with the bolt wrapped in cloth under my arm, and as he lifted the horseshoe magnet to open the gate, it seemed as if we simultaneously discovered the solution to our remote firing issue.

"How does this work?" I asked, indicating the magnetic device.

He explained mostly with hand signals, but basically the gate operated like a garage door at the end of an electromechanical event chain. His magnetized horseshoe passed over the fence post and briefly broke the electrical connection, causing a hook to fall at the gate latch. An opposing spring tension pulled the gate open until it reached the end, then ratcheted to reverse, and the spring tension pulled the gate closed. By the time it swung closed the electrical connection was reestablished and the hook was in the up position to receive the latch and close the gate. Same principles as modern garage door openers, except his was operated with copper wires, a couple connections, and a dry-cell battery mounted in the center post. He said he had to adjust the spring tensions with the various seasons of the year, and intermittently recharged the dry-cell with a coil mounted on a stationary bicycle.

For our crossbow application, the most important issue was that the string tension not pull around the pivot, but rather lift the hook straight up like a finger would, and thus not jostle the weapon. It was roughly the same design that keeps a garage door opener from derailing.

The Gypsy retrieved materials from his work shed to make a garage door opener—a set of springs, a small hook, wire, connectors, string, and the dry-cell battery. By the end of the day the mechanism was in place, the springs attached to the rafters just above the crossbow with a string looped through the hook, gripping the trigger like a finger. We dry fired the bow to test the mechanism, and although there was a delay from activation to firing, the weapon remained on target after the trigger pull.

Our next issue was one of distance and how far remote we could be with flimsy hard wire strung from the rafters, out a side window, down the side of a drainpipe, and lying in plain sight on the ground. We ran the wire toward the rectory and over the short stone fence, but with that much length the wire failed to conduct enough charge to make connection and initiate firing.

Where the wire traveled into the wall we then placed a tiny red lightbulb to indicate the charge had reached its destination. Next we shortened the wire to just the over the fence, but it still would not fire. Again we shortened, and again and again, until the wire was just at the bottom of the drainpipe. Only then did the red light glow.

Because Dalca's vision would detect my body heat, I had to stay on the other side of something he could not see through, like the stone fence, meaning that when it was time to fire I would have to jump over the fence and run to the drainpipe to make the connection, a forty-yard dash or so.

We were short on weapons, ammo, and time, and as the day of the Rose Moon arrived we found Father Andrew praying in the church and sprinkling holy water in the hole.

"Someone will come to escort me this evening after sunset," the priest said. "Until that time this should be covered."

We moved the wooden slab back into place on the floor and spent most of the day listening to Father Andrew sob and give instructions on what to do in his absence. We were to announce to the village that he had died during the night and the church was to be closed until a replacement priest arrived. The day passed as quickly as any I had lived, and as he ate his last meal of bread and water, he passed it around and asked us to remember him in our prayers. It was like comforting a death row inmate.

He waited outside the front door in his black raiment with its prominent white collar. Luc walked up to the church steps and informed us that a bus was approaching. Father Andrew addressed each of us, offering a last blessing and the sign of the cross and asked that we pray for his soul's safe delivery. He quietly took a seat on the bus and did not look back.

After the bus disappeared into the woods, Sonia slowly walked to her house. I could see by how her shoulders shook that she was crying.

Luc looked at us and said, "You don't have much time."

We went to work while Luc watched the door. First the Gypsy and I removed the flooring and climbed into the hole, where we had four automobile jacks stationed at the four corners of the tombstone. With the help of two of the Gypsy's teenage sons, we pumped the jacks until they secured the overhanging corners of the sarcophagus stone cover. In unison we pumped the jacks once, then again, then again. All we accomplished, however, was to press the jacks deeper into the dirt.

We burned candles in the darkened church hole to keep the village curious from inquiring why the building might be lit up. I worked on the upper right side, leaning on one of the tomb's strange, hilt-like handles. The jacks' bottoms were now underlain with flat stones to provide a firmer base, and we resumed our pumping efforts, but this only worked for a moment, the resistance quickly becoming too great to continue. I looked at the Gypsy, and his candlelit face told me not to show concern. We continued trying to pump the levers.

Suddenly the tomb made a sound—like stone cracking.

"One more," I said.

We all leaned on our jack handles at once, fearing one or more of them would snap off. Nothing.

"One more, as hard as you can. Now!"

When we put all our weight on the handles, the tomb literally rumbled. We froze. Nothing happened.

"One more time, at once. Now."

That time the stone sarcophagus cover sounded like it had cracked, and then a rush of air jettisoned from the inside, or perhaps it was an exchange of air, and a short hissing noise followed. Our candles blew out.

I lit the backup lantern and the hole glowed. I saw terror on the faces of the others.

"Go up top," I said, pointing for the boys to leave the hole just as a compound of smells insulted our noses, the stink so wretched that my eyes watered. It smelled like burnt hair, decaying flesh, and a neglected Dumpster.

The Gypsy and I pumped each jack in turn, again and again, the levers all working freely now, until the stone top lifted completely off its mooring. I bent to see if I could see anything. Nothing. I needed to open it further. Carefully we jacked the slab until it rose a foot off the tomb. I picked up the lantern and moved it toward the opening. The Gypsy would not look inside, but I did.

I saw her. And she looked intact.

She had a long thin face sunken to show her bone structure, with her jaw open and two canine teeth prominently displayed. Every feature was long, bony, and pointed. It was hard to tell in the lantern light, but she looked as ashen as one could be and still be described as having human-looking skin. Her straight black hair fell to her sides and extended all the way to her feet. Her eyes appeared to be closed and sunken. I moved the lantern closer to her body and noticed her long spindly fingers, the joints bulging and nails at least a foot long. She wore a wedding ring on her ring finger.

Something else glinted at her breast. Two things, in fact, extending from the sides of the tomb to her narrow chest. When I cast the light more directly, I saw two sword blades on the inside of the tomb sticking straight into her upper torso, one from each side, lancing her chest through and through.

"... *and with argint swords dipped in their blood* ..."

Of course, I thought. Her captors drove the swords into both sides of her chest, pointed at her heart. She could not move in any direction without them piercing her heart. She was still undead, suspended ... and not at peace.

When I moved the lantern again, one eyelid was partially open. I recoiled in terror and heaved myself back against the side of the hole.

"We gotta close this!" I said.

"*Batista!*" the Gypsy shouted. *The handkerchief.*

I had almost forgotten why we opened it. I grabbed a cotton handkerchief from my shirt, reached it into the tomb, and rubbed it on her hands. Then, as shakily as I've ever done anything, I forced myself to ever so gingerly remove her wedding ring. I feared she would grab me, but the woman never moved. Before withdrawing, I reached up to her face, emboldened, and wiped it with the handkerchief, from the top of one cheek, down along her neck. I folded the cloth, wrapped it in wax paper with the ring, and wrapped that in a leather swatch. Then I banded it with a string of garlic.

We eased the lid back down by releasing the car jacks and climbed out. I was shocked to see it was already approaching midnight. The Gypsy walked his boys home, and I cleaned up and prepared to walk to Dreptu.

Sonia was silent until it was time for me to leave. I could see by her eyes that she had given up many tears.

"*Te iubesc,*" she said. *I love you.*

I nodded and turned to walk into the woods when I saw Luc on the path, waiting for me.

"You will need an escort," he said. "Give me the package." When I hesitated, he snatched it out of my hand. "Let's go."

We walked into the woods at a hurried pace. The temperature had dropped during the previous hours, and a steady wind beat the tops of the trees. By the time the full moon stepped above the Carpathians, several clouds threatened the clear night. *Another mistake,* I thought as we walked deeper toward Dreptu into the surround sound of wolves waiting for their meal. Thousands of birds lifted from branches in the trees as I passed, followed by hordes of bats, all headed toward the monastery. Luc remained silent, and I followed suit.

We came upon the bus parked at its stopping point and called inside, just in case someone had managed escape. When I turned around there were four Regulats staring at me, their lips quivering in anticipation. By their complexions and movements I could tell they had not yet eaten that evening.

One of them spoke: "You are not invited to this one."

Luc responded, "I am taking him to the Master."

"You presume to tell—"

"He found something," Luc interrupted. "It cannot wait."

The Regulat's expression changed from shock at Luc's impudence to a wary eagerness. His nose twitched as he tested the air. "Give it to me."

"I don't believe you can touch it," he said, showing the small package wrapped in garlic.

The Regulats parted, but spat upon me as I passed. Across the open space and into the woods we met another pair of Regulats, who also questioned our intentions. They, too, looked unfed. One of them shoved me to the ground as I passed and promised to be my disposer. Luc passed unmolested, though all peered at the object he carried, trying to get a glimpse or whiff of what the package might contain. Once at the front door, we were again questioned and led through to the courtyard. The party was already fully engaged, music blaring out of the tower, and walking down the steps to the lower level I saw a woman get tossed out the window to the spike pit below. Only at the last second did a scream escape her mouth before her body split on a stake. Several others had met gruesome ends before her: At least a half dozen impaled bodies hung limply, some of them still twitching or moving their jaws.

A crowd of Regulats jumped from their tables when we approached and stood in blockade formation before Dalca. Several hissed and grumbled; the others, who remained silent, looked to have been fed. From my vantage point I saw the balcony doors open and a man walk off the edge with a blindfold over his eyes. He did not have a chance to scream as he dropped headfirst onto a spiked pole.

"I have come to see the Master," Luc said.

From behind the crowd Dalca's voice boomed: "Let the humans approach."

A couple was tossed out the window and landed together on a spike. A splatter of something hit my hair.

Dalca leaned forward on his throne and pointed at Luc's hands. "What have you brought that you deem worthy of interrupting this gathering?"

I was close enough to the spike pit to see the victims' faces. One of the men's legs was twitching as if still alive, and his head bobbed. Blood leaked from his mouth.

Luc slipped subtly behind me, grabbed my jacket at the shoulder, and roughly pushed me ahead of him as a jailer might.

Dalca leaned forward on his throne. "Speak!"

Another person came flying down and landed with a splat.

"I caught him raiding a tomb," said Luc, "and found him with this." He held up the leather wrap.

"You dare to offer me *usturoi*?" Garlic.

Luc unwound the garlic string from the leather and handed the parcel forward.

I answered, "It is what I promised."

With a motion of his hand, Dalca halted the celebration entirely. I looked up and saw a figure on the balcony with his hands together, praying. It looked like Father Andrew, with Regulats on either side of him.

"Master, I beg of you a favor," I said as he unwrapped the leather from around the cloth. "Please."

He looked at me with one raised eyebrow. "What? You are in no position to bargain, human."

I pointed up at Andrew. "Please release the priest."

Dalca waved me off dismissively, returning his attention to the package, unfolding it once, then again until finding the ring. His eyes glowed crimson as his body froze. Then his head moved quickly as he scanned the ring from all sides.

His voice sounded low and thick: "Tell me where this grave is."

I said, *"Miroase." Smell.* I motioned for him to smell the cloth.

Dalca sniffed first, then his eyes glowed again as he brought the cloth to his mouth and took in a long deep breath over his teeth. He let out a growl so loud and distinct, the wolves went silent and the birds scattered. The Regulats moved away from him.

In less than a second he was in my face, lifting me off the ground with one hand.

"Where is she?" he cried.

I shook with fear. "Will you release the priest?" I barely got it out.

"Yes. Where is she?"

Luc answered, "I'll take you there."

He shook me, and I thought my neck would break.

"Where?"

"Under the church foundation."

He released his grip and eyed me with mistrust.

"The priest?" I asked.

Dalca looked up, pointed toward the balcony, and said, "Release him."

With that the Regulats grabbed Father Andrew by the shoulders and tossed him. I heard him scream all the way down. He landed on two spikes right in front of me; one stuck a leg and the other passed through his neck. I swallowed hard, realizing I should have expected no more. I looked at Dalca.

"You asked me to release him." He shrugged. "They released him."

I looked away. "I'm sorry," I whispered to the priest.

"We leave now," Dalca shouted.

Luc asked, "What shall I do with him, Master?"

"Bring him."

Luc grabbed me by the shoulder and hustled me away. Dalca shouted back to the others to continue their party.

The music resumed and Dalca called for his carriage, which arrived at the front door as we did. Luc shoved me inside the coach and jumped in with me while Dalca took his station as the driver. The carriage burst forward and we clung to the leather handles. Sonia was right—he would keep me alive until he was certain he had found his wife. Between the bouncing and yawing of the vehicle, I was shaken nearly senseless. In what seemed like an impossibly short time, the carriage slowed, then stopped.

Dalca snapped open the coach door, reached in, and yanked me outside. He had parked on the near side of the bridge, not crossing into the village. The night had lost its full moon behind dense clouds, and a spray of rain hit me as I stepped out.

I had not factored rain into my electrical plans.

Dalca grabbed me by the chest and carried me toward the bridge. In his other hand he carried a rat. I heard him breathe deeply as we passed Sonia's house, and I smelled the blood on his breath. He moved his eyes quickly about. Luc followed behind.

"If I see anyone, I will snap your necks—both of you." In a blur we arrived at the front of the church. "Where?"

Luc said, "Through the side entrance, in the middle of the floor, under the eyes of Jesus."

He squinted in distrust and shoved me forward. "Show me."

I ran to the door and opened it. Dalca looked side to side before entering, then only briefly looked up at the face of Jesus on the ceiling. His head kept moving as he slowly approached the excavation site, and as he looked into the hole he took a deep breath through his teeth and exhaled. When he looked back at me his eyes glowed a shade of red I had never seen.

"Leave," he said in a voice that sounded like a growl.

Dalca leapt into the hole with the rat as I closed the side door and ran to my spot over the stone fence.

Luc was not to be seen, nor was the Gypsy. I wondered what had become of our plan. Perhaps they had either run for home or taken different positions.

Listening for sounds to come out of the darkened church, I heard a whisper to my right.

"Joseph."

I looked but saw nothing.

"Joseph."

When I saw a hand reach up out of the ground I sprang back with fright, clearing the stone wall in a vault.

"Joseph," the voice called a third time.

Peeking back over the wall, I saw a small light shine on the face of the Gypsy as he lifted a sod-covered board. He must have built a foxhole in my absence and topped it with material the vampire could not see through. I jumped back over the stone wall and into the foxhole with him and waited, shamed that I would think him a deserter.

It did not take long. Moments later I heard a howl that exploded through the night and shook the very air around us like thunder. Anyone within a couple miles was sure to have heard his voice. Afterward, there was a moaning sound that must have meant he'd discovered what position she lay in.

"Erika," I thought I heard him moan, though I would have believed myself too far away to hear his low voice. "My beautiful, beautiful Erika. I'm here, I'm here. Take this." I heard the rat squeal one last time.

The rain picked up and began splashing off the ground into our faces, creating mud. *Of all nights to rain,* I thought. Lightning cracked in the woods, followed by a roll of thunder.

From the church, Dalca emitted several loud grunts, as if he were trying to lift something, or pull something.

The Gypsy pushed me. *"Hai să mergem!"* he said, pointing to the church. *Let's go.*

Up and over the stone wall, I ran across the slick ground to the church wall, the Gypsy a step behind me. We knelt at the drain spout and removed the plastic cover from the dry-cell battery, and the Gypsy quickly attached the wires to the terminals. He pulled out his magnetic horseshoe and touched the terminals. Nothing. The red bulb above failed to light; the rain had foiled our plans.

The noise inside grew as Dalca sustained a loud, long howl.

I recalled how Sonia described the act of vampires coupling, that they would be joined for several minutes until he finished, and only after he finished could they physically separate.

The Gypsy stood up and ran. I thought he was retreating until I saw him stop at the front of the priest's truck and fumble with the hood latch. He threw the hood open and quickly yanked the cables off the battery. He heaved the heavy auto battery out of the truck, then carried it back to our position.

Dalca's howl began to dissolve.

The Gypsy unhooked the wires from the dry cell and held them to the truck's battery terminals.

"Do it," he ordered.

I picked up the horseshoe and hesitated.

"Do it!"

I waved the horseshoe over the terminal and a spark spit from the battery, throwing the Gypsy onto his back. I heard the red light pop overhead. Nothing happened for a second.

Then a loud shriek came from inside the church, another

thunderous cry that resonated for miles, but this time a cry of immense pain. And despair, even.

Another lightning bolt struck the area, nearer the outskirts of the village, and the ground shook from thunder.

I looked down and saw the Gypsy motionless, his burnt hands smoking. I couldn't pick him up, so I dragged him over to the wall. As I eased him to the wet ground, Luc appeared at my side, a large hunting knife in each hand. I stared at him a moment, expecting the worst, but he set down the knives and helped me lift the Gypsy over the wall and into the foxhole, where we covered him. Luc handed me one of the knives. I nodded, and we both knelt against the stone wall, peering over it toward the church.

The noise from the church had ceased entirely.

Luc said, "At the dawn, we also wish to be just ashes, ourselves."

Luc's words finished the poet's verse I had started in the carriage ride leaving Castel Bran. And as I turned my head toward him, I knew that we would be finishing this mission together.

"I had to scare you to make it look real," he said.

I nodded, keeping my eye on the church. At that moment, the church's front door exploded off its hinges and tumbled down the porch steps. Red eyes glowed in my direction. Dalca growled and stepped outside. He wore no clothes, but an arrow stuck out of his torso and blood ran out of the wound. The bolt had missed its target and the silver tip protruded from the left side of his chest near his shoulder, not the center shot I had intended.

In his current state, Dalca did not move in a vampirelike blur, but rather at mere human speed. Stepping my direction, he breathed like a man out of wind. He reached his right hand up to the arrow and yanked. It withdrew with a snap and pop. As I backpedaled behind the truck, Luc charged the Master and tried to thrust a knife into Dalca's heart, but Dalca sidestepped his attacker and redirected the knife into Luc's chest. From where I stood, I saw the blade emerge from Luc's back, his body lifting off his feet from the impact. Dalca released him, letting Luc fall to the mud with a wet thump.

Dalca moved slowly to the truck, knelt, heaved mightily, and flipped it in my direction. It rolled once before landing near my legs.

I turned to run and felt his huge hand grab my shoulder and spin me to face him. I lifted the laser pointer and pressed the button. The red beam found his pupil. Instantly his face froze, and Dalca swung his head aside to avoid the light. I raised Luc's other knife, knowing I would fail to find his heart before he found mine. But as I did so, suddenly Dalca's back arched and his torso thrust forward, his mouth opening wide but speechless. His blood covered me. I stepped back.

It took a second to register, and then I saw the silver arrow sticking out from the middle of his chest. Dalca dropped to his knees and let out a shriek as loud as a train whistle. It hurt my ears, and I covered them.

Behind Dalca stood Radu, holding the long crossbow bolt. He withdrew it almost faster than I could see, then thrust it through Dalca's heart once more.

With Dalca kneeling, Radu produced two daggers of his own, raised them to shoulder height, and drove them into Dalca's sides, inward toward the heart. As Dalca cried in pain, Radu pulled another long knife from a sheath, raised it like a headsman's axe, and swiped it across Dalca's neck. Dalca's head fell into the mire before his body flopped over.

Radu reached down and lifted his brother's head to his own face, and after staring into his eyes for several seconds, spoke calmly: "Look upon the face of your killer."

Dalca's mouth tried to speak something, but nothing came out except blood. The last red glow of Dalca's eyes faded to darkness just as a third lightning strike lit the area. Radu looked at me but said nothing. He pulled the silver arrow from the body and walked into the church. I stood at the door while he went into the hole. I heard a thump, followed by the sound of the stone slab sliding back into place.

The last I saw of Radu, he was walking over the bridge toward Dreptu carrying his brother's head by the hair. The carriage followed him into the forest, the horses trailing their master. A distant thunder rolled.

I looked in the hole. Radu had placed the stone cover back over the tomb. The sword hilts were still in place. I could only guess at Erika's disposition.

I raced to Luc, but found only his lifeless body, a fallen hero. I said a quick prayer: "Please, God, receive this soul. He died that others might live."

Then I ran to the foxhole and shook the Gypsy. After a moment he stirred, smelling of singed hair and burnt skin. His hands had second- or third-degree burns, and I think he had soiled himself, but he was alive and regaining consciousness. Eventually I walked him back to his house before returning home to Sonia. When I walked in, she was praying. She gave one last offering of thanks before embracing me in a long hug.

"Is it done, *dragostea mea?*" she asked. *My love.*

I nodded. But in truth, it wasn't. I had a hole to fill.

EPILOGUE

The Hunter's Moon is October's full moon, in some places referred to as the Blood Moon. Normally the biggest of the birthday parties, it passed without any revelry in the woods. Despite the Master's death and the northward migration of his Regulats, the locals still boarded their windows nightly, avoiding full moons altogether. I suppose they always will.

As I write this it is the dead of winter, a season much like the other winters I lived through in Chicago, though with slightly drier air here, and without lake-effect snow entirely. Still, it is a time for hot soup and fresh bread in the kitchen and logs for warmth in cast-iron woodstoves.

I warm my hands and feet and think of my brother, as I always do on full moons, hoping he is not some Regulat's monthly diet. He had safely returned to Chicago and his parish, performing his normal ordained duties. I heard from him when a moving truck pulled into Dumitra with my inventory of books from Chicago— most of them, at least—and a brief letter. I stored the books in the church rectory until a suitable warehouse could be constructed on church grounds. Dumitra has no Internet service, so I set up shop by renting a private space in an Internet café in Bistrița. I commute there regularly with the Gypsy and take orders under an assumed name. I see Luc's grave in the village cemetery every time we pass, and just like the locals, I make the sign of the cross with each passing.

One exceptional autumn afternoon, the Gypsy halted at the most scenic overlook and directed me off the cart. He peeled back the tarp that covered his inventory and proceeded to tap the largest container. He offered me a cup, and I realized that what he sold in town was not the copper pots but the plum brandy, țuică, which he brewed in his copper still.

The Gypsy swept his arm toward the valley and said, "It is beautiful day . . . American."

It was my first drink on native soil.

My brother's letter spoke of frustration with my choice that night in Dalca's monastery tower. Bernhardt had been completely ready to die then, he wrote, though he offered me his forgiveness. I was not ready to accept the latter, for my mistakes did not result from a single decision, but many. I miss Berns badly, and if I could change places with him, I would do so without hesitation. I know that he understands that, but it makes my enduring guilt no easier.

Berns mentioned that one of the nuns had passed, not the Don, and it reminded me that I owed them a debt I could never repay.

My life continues quite separately, day to day, from the vampire world. At least for the most part. One morning, while I was working in the café, Arthur Ardelean arrived with news that he had a new employer; same family, just a different address farther north. Before leaving, he offered to let me know—for a price, of course—where I might be able to find something that would add to my rare books inventory, an item of great value. I thought of all the tragedy that manuscript had inflicted and passed on his offer. For now. I wished him luck but did not offer to keep in touch.

From Sonia I have had to get used to hearing *te iubesc—I love you*. See, I never heard it, or at least don't remember hearing it in my life, until she said it. I have found my emotions sprinting toward her, but my nerve has not yet caught up to my heart. She understands. She always understands.

From time to time I hear shrieks in the woods at night, and while the villagers still cower, the original source of their fears is gone. I know, because I walked out to Dreptu in the days that followed and found it deserted. Not even the caretaker remained. What drew me out there? I don't know. Maybe it was more than just one thing.

First, I did not want simply to sit in Sonia's house and quake with each full moon and sunset. It's bad enough visualizing what lies below the house's foundation. Second, someone had to go check on the place and report back to the villagers, for they were more frightened than ever, the fear of change being immeasurably greater than the fear of the known. When I walked into the woods, Sonia reminded me that I was going there for the entire village, not just for myself. That gave me strength, even if I was never to return. In that case, at least, the villagers would know not to retrace my steps.

The monastery gate was open, and I walked into the courtyard, where amidst the medieval headstones a huge new mausoleum stood. An iron gate keeps out the curious, but I could see the stonework was fresh. Inscribed is his name, *Master Dalca Drakula*, spelled the original family way, and the year of his birth, 1438, but no date of death. Above the inscription was the family insignia, the dragon wrapped around a cross.

When I emerged from the woods, I walked to the church and rang its bells, and the entire village turned out to hear the news. Great skepticism preceded their relief as they waited for the next full moon to see if the nights would prove safe. By harvest time the village put on a great feast and I was welcomed as a citizen, a hero, though I felt as extrinsic as I had that first stroll through town. I really have little choice but to stay, though, as my legal troubles in the United States have made me a fugitive. And I hope the Field Museum is not still waiting for its fifty large.

It is said in the Bible that a wise man looks back after encountering a stumbling block. But what of the man who tumbles over them all? Is his foolhardiness not twined unto his fears? Such a man sheds all his friends, and in his aged years hears only the echo of his own thoughts. If only I had obeyed my brother's warning and never come here. And still I cannot shake the images.

Many a time have I been tempted to call the number on the cigarette pack from Mr. Bena, but as of yet I have not. Like the convent basement in which I spent my youth, this may not be the best place, but fear of losing it keeps me from seeking other places. And Sonia would not leave.

Sometimes I look at Sonia and judge all my efforts worth it.

Do I miss America? Of course. I miss my brother most, and some of the conveniences of my adopted country, but mostly I miss my freedom. It is freedom that gives weight to dreams, and whether you lose that freedom by your own behavior or the usurpations of an authoritarian government, you find yourself living day to day without the adrenaline born of fantasy, of belief. And so with your freedoms depart your best efforts. At one time in my life, at the end of each day I petitioned God's forgiveness when I had not given the day my best effort; I then asked for another day to prove myself. Now, without the freedom to dream of tomorrow, I simply pray to God to give me the chance to give my best effort.

I have not heard from Radu. Not yet, at least. Certainly I must have convinced him that I did not know his wife's whereabouts or I would not be able to pen this. I know he broods up there in the northernmost Carpathians, ruling over his flock as Noble vampires do. I trust there will be a day . . . no, make that a night, when a knock will come at my door and I will be summoned to his presence. Or else the knock will come from the *poliţie*, armed with extradition papers. But that day is not today, and with God's grace it will also not be tomorrow.

As for the fake passport, I retrieved it and an envelope of traveling cash with another unsigned note that simply stated, *Never more proud.* I recognized the paper. I won't use them unless Sonia goes with me. We shall see . . .

For now, I will close this account . . . and hope that no one knocks on my door.

the end